Strike Two, You're Out

TIM HASSETT-SALLEY

To Alli –
My fellow BSU Bear.
Enjoy!
Tim Hassett-Salley

for
Cecily

i

PROLOGUE

"I thought it was the beginning; I didn't know it was the end."

~Bobby Whitlock, Keyboardist for Derek and the Dominos

1978

Joe and Georgie returned to their blanket, dripping from their dunking in the Atlantic. No one actually swims here in Rhode Island; the water is freezing even in August. They towel dried, then sat down facing the water. Joe tried not to stare at her nipples, still erect inside her cold, wet bathing suit. He clicked on the portable AM-FM radio Eric had given him the night before they shipped off to Vietnam. The telescoping antenna was a wartime casualty. In its place was a wire coat hanger. Amazingly the radio was able to pick up WDRC from Hartford. Chris Rea's new song, *Fool If You Think It's Over*, was playing, having been requested by some heartbroken teenager somewhere in Connecticut.

"Would you mind turning that off?" Georgie asked, sweetly. "I like to just listen to the surf and the seagulls." She resumed combing out the tangles in her waist-length, dirty-blond hair.

This was their first official "date." Four days earlier they had gone on a double non-date with Joe's friend, Eddie, and his girlfriend, Tammy, to a state park. Joe had been pressed into service by their mutual friend, Hope, to show Georgie a good time after a traumatic breakup with her longtime boyfriend. Joe dropped her back home afterward and asked if she might like to go to the beach sometime, just the two of them.

Joe wasn't the kind of person who could just lie around on the beach all day, especially if the only music was to be provided by waves and birds. But his cutoff jeans took forever to dry so he lay down on his stomach in the direct sun to start the drying process. Georgie followed suit, reclining at a safe distance about a foot away.

Glancing over at Georgie as she pretended to sleep, Joe found himself getting aroused at the sight of this lovely teenager in her modest one-piece, turquoise/green swimsuit. After several minutes of, "should I; shouldn't I, should I; shouldn't I" Joe breached the invisible bunting board with his right hand and clasped her left hand. Georgie returned the squeeze and opened her eyes and smiled.

"Wanna go for a walk?" asked Joe.

"Sure."

He followed her down to the water's edge, wondering how it was possible that she looked just as good from behind!

They walked westward along East Beach. The sun was still high; otherwise this scenic walk would have been too romantic to have been believable. They strolled without speaking as Georgie was listening to the crashing waves and Joe had no idea what to talk about. They stopped when they encountered a middle aged man with an off-leash black, Labrador retriever. They played with the dog for a minute or so then Georgie turned to resume their walk. Joe took a step toward Georgie and, placing a hand on her shoulder, leaned in and kissed her softly on the lips. She returned the kiss and they paused there for a second, as if to preserve this moment for posterity.

This kiss, as unremarkable and insignificant as any first kiss, would seal their fate and start these two lovers down a path from which there could be no return.

1

1975

"I still can't believe we're going to Nam," Eric whined.

"I know, man," Joe added. "My life isn't exactly going as planned either. I bet your recruiter told you you'd be safe now that the war is "over."

"Yeah, he told my mom 'the Marines aren't sending anybody over there anymore. And even if they do send anyone, they need Marines with experience. Nam's no place for the uninitiated.'"

"Looks like we're about to get initiated," Joe added. "The judge told me I had to go into the Corps to 'learn some respect for other people.'" He laughed, "We just spent the last fourteen weeks learning how to kill other people."

They sat there for a few minutes without talking; the only noise coming from Joe's lime green Panasonic transistor radio his mom bought him a couple years ago when he had his impacted wisdom teeth extracted. They continued to pack their duffels with all the government issued clothes and supplies they could stuff in a bag. There was also room for a few personal items: an instamatic camera, gum, Bible, pencils, writing paper, envelopes, Playboy, Slim Jims, transistor radio. Anything else they needed would be provided by Uncle Sam.

"What about toilet paper?" asked Eric, remembering stories his cousin told him about surviving in the jungles of Southeast Asia.

"We're MSGs! We're not going to be in the bush," Joe shot back. "We'll be living in the Embassy."

Looking back over the last three and a half months of his life, Joe was starting to piece together the logic that had him now shipping off to Vietnam, to a war that was supposedly over. He should have known something was up when, on the first day of basic training, the recruits were told they would be receiving "ECT" or "Expedited Condensed Training" meaning, instead of the usual twelve weeks of Marine Corps boot camp, they would only be there for nine. *Why would they be rushing us out of here? Surely not to make room for new recruits coming up behind us….recruiting is at the lowest point since Korea. Why then did they need us in such a hurry?*

These questions were compounded when Joe and Eric were plucked from their squad and recommended for Marine Security Guard training; a job not usually offered to green recruits who had been Marines less than ninety days. Then, four weeks into their abbreviated six week MSG training at Quantico they were abruptly mustered for inspection, graduated, and given orders and ten day leaves.

Speculation abounded in the group of newbie MSGs. *Are we being sent in to enforce a DMZ like they have in Korea? Are we starting the fighting back up (and ignoring the Paris Peace Accords)? Are we going in to get the last few Americans out? But there are already Marines there. Can't they get the civilians out? Can't they get themselves out? Do we need marines to get other marines out?*

The hardest part for Joe to accept about life in the military was that there was no "democracy" in the military branch of a democratic country. And for as little free will as there is, there is even less communication. They knew where they were going, but not why they were going there, nor what they would be doing once they got there.

"What is that shit you're listening to?" Eric snarled.

"I dunno, just some song."

"That song sucks. Get a new station!"

"That's the only station I can pick up inside this armory."

Eric grabbed the transistor radio. "Let me see that." He threw it to the floor and stood up so he could finish it off with the heel of his combat boot, extinguishing Karen Carpenter's melodious voice.

"What the fuck? You asshole, my mother gave me that! We're leaving in the morning. Where am I gonna get a new radio?"

"That's what you get for listening to shitty music." Eric sported a sly grin as he backed up a couple steps to avoid the clenched fist he knew was coming. He reached down into his duffel. "Here…" He handed Joe a new AM-FM radio, still in the box.

"Where'd you get that?"

"My dad runs an electronics store. I grabbed twenty of these when we were on leave."

Joe noticed Eric's bag was jammed with so much stuff he could hardly gather the top rings to clip it. And his helmet liner was still on the floor (*priorities,* Joe thought).

"What'r you gonna do, smash everyone's radios and give us all a new one?" Joe asked sarcastically.

"Man, you've led a sheltered life," Eric responded condescendingly. "These gook women over there will do anything for American junk. I mean, they'll give you a blow job for a pack of gum! Just think what I'll get for a radio!"

Joe thought about the two packs of gum he had just put in his duffel, wishing he had packed more. By now he had unpacked the new radio and was extracting the nine-volt battery from the wreckage of his transistor radio. The AM-FM crackled to life. Joe extended the telescoping antenna and fiddled with the tuning dial. John Fogerty's voice belted out…..*better run through the jungle*…..

"Cool! CCR! Now that's more like it. No more of that Carpenters shit you listen to. This is some real music." The symbolism was lost on these Vietnam-bound marines.

The other newly minted MSGs were starting to file past, their backs hunched under the weight of their virgin gear and their anxiety over their uncertain futures. The eight selected for Vietnam deployment seemed especially hunched, in spite of the assurances of the brass that they would not be in a fighting role over there. None older than twenty, these green fighting men collectively trusted no one higher than a sergeant. They had all been lied to before.

The guys formed a line at the phone. Not a phone booth; just a black desk phone on a short table with no chair. There you could make your one 3-minute call home to Mom and Dad. If there was no answer, you went to the back of the line. If you had a girlfriend, you had to choose who to call. If you were smart you would have arranged to have your girlfriend at your parent's house.

Joe thought this whole "last call" business was contrived bullshit. He was just home on leave two days before and said his goodbyes as his mom and dad watched him board the greyhound from Hartford to this armory 900 miles away. The greyhound station goodbye was the worst. Much worse than the boot camp goodbye. Joe had dreaded boot camp more than his parents did. They knew no one dies in basic training. Joe's dad always sang the praises of boot camp: "best shape of my life. Plenty of food, fresh air, indoor plumbing." For guys in the WWII generation living on the verge of poverty, the service was a step up. For the first time in his life his dad had a bunk he didn't have to share, new clothes that had never been worn by anyone else, three meals a day….guaranteed, indoor toilets, and hot showers!

But for Joe, with all the trappings of middle class life (except for having to wear his brother's hand-me-down clothes), the idea of getting killed in Indo-China was not a step up and was an extreme measure to take just to get new clothes.

Saying goodbye in person at the station gave him a sickening feeling. This might be the last time he would see his parents. If he hadn't taught that Puerto Rican a lesson, he would be headed off to St. Domenic's College right now as a freshman in the class of 1978. He had been accepted to the school before the verdict came in. The college had granted him an open-ended military deferment so he could "serve his country." The deferment letter had been written by the ROTC director assigned to the admissions office. In it, the captain cited Joe's "courage when so many of your peers had requested academic deferments to avoid serving."

"We would be honored," it went on, "to have you join our campus community when your service ends. Godspeed." Attorney Goldberg was successful in keeping the college in the dark as to the real source of Joe's "courage."

Lance Corporal Joseph Davis (and the rest of the guys within earshot of the little brown telephone table) waited stoically for their turn on the phone as each poor teenager endured his three minutes of personal-public hell. Some called grandparents instead of parents (there were all different reasons for joining the Marine Corps). Some deliberately called wrong numbers. All prayed there would be no one home. There was a seasoned Marine Security Guard stationed next to the telephone table. Joe wondered sarcastically if there had ever been a riot when someone refused to hang up at the end of their allotted three minutes. Joe wondered which congressman that MSG knew to get an assignment like that.

Some of the guys said their goodbyes through tears, some through clenched teeth. Others just responded "yes ma'am" or "OK" to whatever was being asked on the other end. Everyone promised "I'll write."

Joe's sister Sue answered the phone. Immediately she cried in a panic, "Mom and Dad aren't home!"

"That's OK Q." He had given her the nickname Suzie Q, then shortened it to just Q. "I said my goodbyes to them the other day. I really wanted to say goodbye to you one more time. You take care of yourself and be careful. Stay away from Andy Reynolds. You tell him if he touches you I'll kick his ass. And if you need something before I get back, you give my buddy Brian a call. He's looking out for you."

Joe's time wasn't up. He still had two minutes left but his voice was getting husky. "I'll write. Gotta go now, Q. Bye."

That night all the guys were turned in well before the lights-out call, all with their freshly shorn buzz cuts bristling against their woolen makeshift pillows. Absent was all the nervous chatter of the night before. They were comrades now destined for an uncertain future, a future so grave and beyond their control, individually or collectively, that the usual macho ball-busting reverie would seem out of place. It took Joe a long time to fall asleep knowing he would be a man the next time he returned stateside, and trying to come to terms with the events of the last three years that resulted in the unimaginable: shipping off to Vietnam.

2

1972

First day of tobacco picking. He was wearing jeans and a tank top. Some people call them muscle shirts but most kids his age don't really have muscles yet. When you're fifteen in 1972 and you want a job in north central Connecticut, just about the only place you'll find one is on a tobacco farm. A stitcher if you're a girl, a picker if you're a boy, like Joe.

He had finished his morning paper route by six. He liked to go early anyway so he could bring his dog around with him. Buddy goes off leash because no one is up that early to complain. After three years Buddy knows the whole route. He usually keeps a one or two house lead on Joe. That's fine because Joe doesn't want him right with him as he puts the paper between the screen door and the wooden door. All the inside dogs start barking when Joe closes their doors and he doesn't need Buddy to be jumping into that chorus. Joe needed to hold on to his paper route as it provided year round income. Tobacco picking was just here for the summer.

Joe made himself a couple ham and cheese sandwiches; one for breakfast and the other he put in a paper bag for lunch, along with an orange and a Slim Jim. He filled up his Thermos with water and kissed his mom goodbye as he headed down to the garage to put on his work boots. The big brown bus picked them up down the street where the school bus normally picks them up during the school year. Only now, there are only two getting on at his stop. Any older kids from the neighborhood were able to find decent jobs when they turned 16. Younger kids were stuck for the summer doing nothing. It seemed strange to be getting on a brown painted school bus in the heat of the summer.

Even at 7 AM some of his other friends (the ones whose fathers could afford to play golf) were already off to work, riding their bikes to the country club to caddy for some doctor or lawyer their father knew from the club. They'd come home after a (half) day of work, sweaty in their plaid pants, but with a pocket full of tip money and a couple of new dirty jokes that one of their rich benefactors told them. A far cry from the tobacco picking kids who returned home mid-afternoon encrusted in sweat, dirt, and tobacco resin.

There were three kinds of people who picked tobacco: PRs, PAs, and "regular" kids like Joe. PRs were Puerto Ricans. Puerto Ricans, or "migrant workers," as his father called them, had been coming to Connecticut for picking season for decades. They stayed in long, open walled dormitories (Joe and his friends call it the Barrio) for several weeks each summer until all the tobacco was harvested. They started their year in Puerto Rico or the Dominican Republic picking and chopping sugar cane and tobacco, and moved their way up through Florida and Georgia picking fruit, and then on to and through the Carolinas and Virginia picking the early tobacco harvests. They stayed for about a month in each locale, then migrated north. At the end of tobacco season in Connecticut, they headed still further north to dig for potatoes in Maine's rocky fields. Not a bad life if you don't mind going ten months without seeing your family while you live in a dusty barracks with dozens of other men in towns where residents would call the police if they saw you out walking the streets.

To kids like Joe, the life of a migrant worker was irrelevant; as if they lived in a different world, or worse, they didn't even exist.

The other class of people picking tobacco were the PAs. PAs were kids from Pennsylvania reform schools who had earned the "opportunity" to come to Connecticut for the summer to work on a tobacco farm as a reward for good behavior. *How bad must reform school be,* thought Joe, *that picking tobacco in 95 degree heat would be a reward!*

On the girls' side, there were just two classes of people working in the tobacco sheds: local high school girls, aged fourteen and fifteen, and YWCA women. These "women" were sixteen and seventeen year old married girls from Florida who came to Connecticut every summer (a fresh batch of newlywed underage girls every year) who boarded at the YWCA in the city and were bussed in every morning. Spending the summers away from their husbands increased their chances of putting off motherhood, at least for a few months. The girls and the boys had no contact all day; the girls working in the drying sheds, and the boys picking outside under the netting.

Joe had wanted to get started on the farm as soon as school let out but he couldn't apply until he got his Social Security card. After applying at the post office it had taken nearly four weeks for it to arrive. At last he could start. His friends assured him that he was lucky for the delays because "all the really hard work" was done. Some of the kids actually skipped the last two weeks of school to start at the farm. Joe thought that was a fine idea for losers who wanted to make a career out of picking tobacco.

The "really hard work" entailed working on your knees for a few weeks. Tobacco plants, like tomato plants, grow suckers as they leaf out. The low suckers need to be "pinched" to promote the growth of what will become the real leaves. Then, as the leaves become ripe, they are picked from the bottom of the plant. So, for the first few weeks, you are on your knees, or worse, bending over to pick the leaves near the ground. By July, the remaining leaves are conveniently growing at or above waist level.

This whole primer on tobacco picking, including the summary of the migrant and penitentiary farmers' experience, Joe was able to learn from more experienced kids during his twenty minute bus ride out to the farm on his first day.

After handing his work papers to the bus driver upon arrival, he followed his peers out to the gauze covered tobacco fields. Wide thin sheets of gauze were suspended by posts and wires about eight feet high creating a hot house effect for the plants. The sun's rays could get in, but the heat could not escape. So, while the ambient outside temperature might be in the 70s and 80s, under the gauze it stayed in the humid 90s, or worse.

Immediately dispensing with the pleasantries, the foreman, Mike, started showing Joe the ropes. Mike was only a few years older than Joe. Joe figured he was one of those kids who skipped the last couple weeks of school each year to get a jump on their future seasonal career working on a tobacco farm. "This here is Connecticut broadleaf cigar tobacco. You know what that means?" (not waiting for an answer) "It means these leaves are the wrappers for the cigars. They can't be cut, torn, ripped, bent, or bruised. If they are, they're no good. This isn't the cigarette tobacco they grow down south that can be all chewed up and spit out and still put in a cigarette. You with me? They gotta be in one piece. Now, you're getting $1.30 an hour. If you can pick faster you can get an extra five or ten cents, depending on how fast you pick."

"What if I pick slower? Do you give me less than $1.30?" Joe asked, not intending to be a smart ass.

"You don't want to pick slower than everyone else. You wanna stay up with your group. You fall behind, there's some PRs here who'll mess with you if they can get you away from the group. Don't be a wounded zebra. You with me?

Now I'll show you how to pick. What's that….your lunch? You gotta leave it here at the end of the bent 'cause you need both hands to pick. Here's some string. Tie your Thermos to your belt. Now take your left hand and hold it out like this." Mike extended his left arm with the palm of his hand facing up. "You're gonna pick the bottom three leaves from each plant as you move down the bent. You put the three leaves all in the same direction on your palm. Then the next three from the next plant cross over so you make a "V." See that? OK, you keep alternating until you have five sets in your "V" pad. Then you place the pad of fifteen gently in the bin. I'm not kidding. You can't throw'em, drop'em, or stuff'em in there 'cause they'll get squished and all the juice will come out and they'll rot before we can dry 'em.

When the bin is full, take your hook here and drag the bin down to the end of the bent and one of the PRs will put it on the trailer. Then get another bin and start all over where you left off. If you can't remember where you stopped picking, just check the plants. If it's bleeding where the leaves used to be, you already picked it. You with me? You got any problems, come find me or talk to the other kids. Don't talk to the PRs; they *dohn speak no eeenglish*."

By this time, Paul, who started in the next bent over, was already finishing up two rows over from that. "Forget that row," Paul urged. "Come over here and pick with me."

"It's hot as hell under here!" Joe complained.

"You better get used to it. It's not even eight o'clock yet. If you're gonna take your shirt off just tuck it into your belt. You leave something behind, don't bother going back to look for it. Oh, and don't pick the way Mike just showed you. You'll never keep up that way. You can pick twice as fast if you use two hands and press the leaves against your chest. See? Hold each one in place as you pick the next one with the other hand and pin it to your chest. Watch.
One…two….three…four…..five…"

"But he said to put them in groups of three and then five groups of three make a pad," Joe insisted.

"Listen," Paul instructed, "Just pick as many as you can hold and stuff 'em in the bin. The more you can stuff in a bin the better, 'cause dragging the bin takes most of the time. If you're draggin', you're not pickin'."

"But what about all the juices coming out of the leaves?"

Paul shook his head, exasperated. "Look, a guy buys a cigar and lights it on fire. You think he can tell that the juices got squished out and seeped into the dirt on some farm in Connecticut? Now let's go. Try to keep up!"

After about fifteen minutes, having crammed as many bruised and sweaty leaves as he could fit in his bin, Joe grabbed his hook and dragged the load the length of the bent, all the while thinking about that Slim Jim waiting in his lunch bag at the end of the row.

Sitting on his tractor wearing a large straw hat and overalls was José. Somehow all the PRs on the farm were named José! And José was enjoying a nice juicy orange that he was peeling with a large knife. When he saw his lunch bag sitting next to José on the tractor, Joe knew it was going to be a long day. At that moment he also realized what he hadn't noticed earlier as everyone was walking to the fields: he was the only kid carrying a lunch bag.

"Hey amigo, that's my lunch asshole."

"José" returned the salutation with a wide grin and a little flick of his knife to show his gratitude.

Ever since Joe was a little boy, he would pack himself a lunch on summer days and go off to find his friends or just make his own adventure in the woods. When his friends would go home for lunch, Joe would find a tree to sit under and eat his sandwich. Then he would find the nearest garden hose for a drink of water (or drink from the brook if he happened to be eating in the woods). Being the next to youngest child in his family, he learned not to hang around his house lest his mother find some chore for him to do. He always seemed to stay within earshot of the neighborhood because when his father's creaky old Chevy made its final assent up the hill to his house, Joe seemed to materialize in time to greet Dad as the wheels came to a stop in the driveway.

Now, after fifteen years of never missing a meal, Joe was fuming over the loss of his lunch.

Tuesday started out much like Monday. His dog, Buddy, was his alarm clock. Five o'clock, time to rock! He slept pretty good last night, considering he was still pissed off about the lost lunch and how his mind was racing to plan some revenge. After he counted out his newspapers and put them in his bag, he turned out the light over the workbench in the garage, and it came to him. He chuckled to himself, "How many times do you really get a *lightbulb moment!*" After he finished his paper route he ate breakfast and made his lunch. Today it was a ham sandwich with crumbled Fritos mixed in. He put a couple Slim Jims in his pocket. No orange today. He went down to the garage and put on his work boots.

"What was that? Are you OK?" his mom called down the stairs.

"I was just replacing a lightbulb and I dropped it. I'll clean it up."

At the bus stop Paul said, "So you're bringing a lunch again?"

"Yeah, I'll keep an eye on it today."

Along the stops a few new faces got on the bus. "Fresh meat" Joe thought. "Someone gets to tell the newcomers about the PRs and PAs, and how to pick with two hands." Joe smiled to himself.

After the completion of two bents, ready to move to a new area, the locals encountered José on his tractor about to enjoy a sandwich.

"Hey Frito Bandito!" Joe shouted, "No come este sándwich! Si usted come este sándwich, va a llegar en una ambulancia! No come este sándwich!" Joe warned.

José laughed, "Si yo tomo este sándwich voy a llegar en una ambulancia? Ha ha!" José flashed his wide grin as he dubiously considered Joe's threat. Then he took a big bite. He clutched his throat and screamed as he spit out bits of ham, bread, Fritos, and broken lightbulb. No one ran to his aid. The local boys and the PAs broke out into a chorus of "Ay Ay Ay Ay, I am the Frito Bandito, Ah HA!" as they moved past the tractor to the next picking area.

There were no more encounters with this "José" during picking season and the subsequent "Josés" didn't seem to have much of a mid-day appetite in the coming days.

When Joe returned home from the tobacco farm one day the following week, he was surprised to see the familiar blue Ford LTD in his driveway. In a town as small as Valley Park there was only one cruiser and one fulltime cop. All the kids knew, or at least could identify, Bob the cop. Bob also owned a brown (shit-colored, the kids called it) Dodge panel van with a shag-carpeted dash. When he was working as a NARC, he wore a wig and a denim vest and parked his van outside the 7-

11. But today, driving the cruiser, he was Bob the cop. Joe had never seen the cruiser at his house before. He was filled with dread. He walked with leaden boots up the blue slate walkway to the front door.

"Joe, do you know Officer Mitchell?" his father asked.

"Hello Officer."

"Son, do you know why I'm here?"

A dozen reasons flashed in Joe's head. "No, I have no idea."

"Do you know Manuel Ortiz?"

"Never heard of him. Wait, didn't he play shortstop for the Mets?" Joe cracked.

Joe's father stiffened up. Any kid, especially a boy like Joe, should pay the officer some respect or this might not go well.

"Son, this is not a joke. Mr. Ortiz is the migrant worker you assaulted at the tobacco farm," Officer Mitchell shot back.

"I didn't assault anyone. The only migrant I know of is that PR José who steals people's lunches."

"His name is Manuel Ortiz. He spent three days in the hospital bleeding from his throat. He hasn't been able to speak or eat solid foods. That's what swallowing glass will do."

"Well, I hope he learned his lesson! There have been no more stolen lunches since that happened to him."

"Did you lace your sandwich with broken glass?"

"Why do you think it was me?" Joe asked, maybe a little too defensively.

"There were a dozen witnesses. You were the only one who brought a lunch. You were heard speaking Spanish to him just before he choked."

"Well, somebody had to teach the thief a lesson."

"Son, I have to…"

Joe interrupted Officer Mitchell. "Would you stop calling me son? You're not even ten years older than me."

"OK *Joe*, I have to arrest you for assault and battery."

"He only got hurt becuth he thtole my lunch.   He threatened me with hith knife. I warned him not to eat my lunch the thecond day. I hope you're going to arretht him too!" Joe was starting to get agitated.

"Well, your family can file charges against him if you want, and I can't really advise you, but if you do want him charged for stealing a sandwich, you're pretty much admitting that it was your sandwich that cut him."

"Wouldn't the two thingth canthel each other out?" Joe offered.

"It's not up to you to assign penalties for sandwich theft. Mr. Ortiz is going to have to go back to Puerto Rico because he can no longer work."

"Well, he brought thith on himthelf. Not my fault he'th a criminal."

"He may never speak again. Permanent disability is not fair punishment for stealing a sandwich."

"What's going to happen to me now?" asked Joe, for the first time sounding worried, but getting control over his lisp.

"I've talked to your mom and dad and they're going to bring you to the police office in town hall where you'll turn yourself in. That way you can avoid handcuffs and a ride in the cruiser. You'll get fingerprinted, get your mug shots, fill out some papers, and go home. Your parents should call Mr. Goldberg. Oh, and the farm doesn't want you back."

Officer Mitchell continued: "Stay away from the barrio, stay out of trouble, and hopefully Mr. Goldberg can keep you out of reform school."

3

In the days and weeks after the booking and the initial consultation with Attorney Goldberg, his mom was very quiet around the house. His dad started spending more time with Joe, to the point of being annoying. Joe didn't know if the extra time was because his father was feeling guilty for not spending time with him, leading Joe to a life of crime, or if he was worried they were going to send his youngest son away to the juvenile penitentiary and he wanted to spend some time together while he could. Joe even thought he might be getting the extra attention just to fill his time to keep him out of other trouble.

With the start of junior year, most of the routine returned. Classwork, homework, marching band, and running. His new notoriety as a vigilante seemed to move him up a couple notches in the social order, both with the boys and with the girls.

After school, Joe fell in with the pack of runners on the first day of cross country practice. Some of the better runners had graduated last year so Joe hoped he would be more competitive this year. Of course, hope is no substitute for putting in the miles over the summer, so Joe just had to go with hope. There were some new faces too. A few freshmen and another junior who had moved into town over the summer also showed up for practice.

Some of the kids had new running shoes, but the superstitious kids, and the poorer kids, like Joe, just picked shoes out of the big box in the equipment closet. They tried to get the same shoes they wore the previous season. Nobody is bothered by their own smelly sneakers. Joe was able to grab the pair he had from last year. It was easy to spot them with the large "ED" straddling the stitching on the heels of the white running shoes. The shoes had been worn by Joe's older brother, Eldon Davis, when they were out-of-the-box new. These shoes had carried Eldon to the medals stand at regionals. Joe wondered if the shoes were slowing down in their old age. Although much of the life had been run out of the shoes, two years later Joe would have given all he had to be running in them.

It was great to see Coach Johnson out there too in his t-shirt, shorts, and Adidas Antelopes. For an older, stocky guy, Coach Johnson was a pretty good runner, keeping up with the kids on their early season runs. He kept up his running regimen that had been drilled into him twenty-five years earlier as the army tried to prepare a pudgy kid for the rigors of combat. He was a year round runner so he was in better running shape than most of the guys on the cross country team who thought they could just pick up where they left off two months after the end of the previous track season. Coach Johnson caught up to Joe as the pack spread out.

"Welcome back Ed. How was your summer?" Coach Johnson

and some of the other runners called Joe "Ed" on account of his shoes, but the nickname never really took because there was already an Eddie on the team.

"It was interesting. I'm just glad to be back at school," replied Joe.

"Yeah, I heard you got yourself into some trouble…"

"It doesn't seem fair."

"Well, sometimes things that don't seem fair at the time find a way of working themselves out in the end." Coach Johnson spoke from experience.

They ran on for a couple minutes without speaking, trancelike, with only the rhythmic sounds of feet striking pavement and labored breath marking the time.

Coach Johnson broke the spell, "You know, when I was in Korea, I had gone a long time without a break. My CO promised me a weekend pass and as the day got closer and closer I couldn't concentrate on anything else. Two of my buddies and I were going to go into the little town near our base and let off some steam, you know what I mean? We had this one punk in our unit. Name was Spencer. He was always causing trouble. It's a wonder no one on our side ever shot him. Well, he picked a fight with me and we went at it. I wasn't much of a fighter, but when you're in the army and someone starts something, you can't back down or you'll get labeled a pussy. So I fought him and a couple MPs came and broke it up with some whacks of their Billy clubs. They threw both of us in the clink for three days and I missed my leave. I was out of my mind about it and it wasn't fair, and there was nothing I could do."

He continued, "My buddies got their weekend pass and I spent the weekend in lockup in the cell next to Spencer. On Sunday the chaplain came by with an MP and they let me out. They let Spencer out too, and made us shake hands. Then the chaplain told me that Spencer had saved my life by getting me thrown in lockup. My two buddies were in a bar the night before when a commie bomb went off. Five GIs were killed, including my buddies. I would have been there too."

"Wow! That really happen?"

"Yeah, it happened. You see, you never know how things are going to work out."

"Did you and Spencer become friends?"

"Naw," he grinned, "he was still an asshole."

They both laughed and continued on their run.

4

"Hey Coach, that was a good run yesterday. Thanks. I talked to my parents last night. You know, they got me this lawyer to try to get me out of my situation, but it's gonna cost a lot of money. I just turned sixteen so I gotta get an afterschool job. I've been talking to the manager down at the drug store and he said I could work there a couple nights during the week and then on weekends. He said I wouldn't have to work on Tuesday and Fridays when we have our meets. I really want to be part of the team but I won't be able to come to practice."

"If you don't get your miles in you won't be much use to the team. You can't just show up on race day and expect to run fast."

"I know that. I'll run on my own after work. Let me try it. If I can't keep up you can cut me from the team."

Joe figured he could run after work and on weekends. He planned just to run three miles a night rather than the seven or eight miles his teammates were logging on their non-meet days. On the day after a meet, Coach Johnson let the guys have a "light" workout of three miles. They were to do a ten miler on their own over the weekend. Joe didn't see the need for 50 mile weeks. If he could do his three mile practice runs at almost race pace, "Isn't that as good as running six miles at 9-minute pace?"

Although he was dubious as to whether any kid would go out for a run at night after work, Coach knew Joe was dealing with a lot of issues right now. Running might be the only thing keeping his head straight. And besides, it's cross country. It's not like Joe would be taking the place of someone else who wanted to run. Any kid who wanted to run could be on the team. There's even a girl running with the boys this fall!

5

Joe's dad would talk to him sometimes; or at least try to, while they were driving somewhere. Joe's dad, in the driver's seat, would naturally look straight ahead while they talked. This also had the intended effect of melting the awkwardness. Joe suspected his father contrived an errand as an excuse to talk. Joe sensed a "rap session" coming on any time his father said they should go for a ride.

Joe's dad hated that car ever since the day he bought it, and would never drive it just for the pleasure of driving. He had gone to pick up his brand-new 1973 Dodge Colt and the dealer handed him the keys. Mr. Davis looked at the strangely shaped oblong keys and read the inscription: *Mitsubishi*. He handed the keys back to the dealer and said, "These are the wrong keys; I bought a Dodge."

"No sir, these are the right keys. The Dodge Colt is actually made by Mitsubishi."

"I'm not buying no Japanese car. We fought those Nips in the war. They bombed our ships. I'm not buying this car."

"I'm sorry sir but you already bought it. You signed the contract and the financing came through. It's yours now."

If Joe had to talk with his father, it might as well be in the car where they wouldn't have to make eye contact. He hadn't been able to look his dad in the eye ever since the lightbulb incident.

His after school runs with Coach Johnson were taking on the same dynamic. Running side-by-side, and facing straight ahead, Joe was the son Coach never had. Coach was the non-judgmental-adult-male-sounding board every kid needs.

"You ever been married?" Joe asked.

"Nah, (huff, puff). Wanted to once. Even got engaged."

Joe searched his minimal life experience for anyone he had ever known who had been engaged but remained unmarried, but came up empty. He ran through the possible scenarios in his head: she died, or she cheated on him.

"So, what happened?" he asked, as if Coach were a friend.

"I was eighteen. I gave her a ring the night before I shipped out to Korea. We said we'd get married when I got back in eighteen months. I got a letter from her one day telling me to plead hardship and come home. She was five months pregnant."

"But you didn't come home and marry her?" Joe asked incredulously.

27

"I had been gone eight months!"

It took a few seconds for this to sink in. Math is tough when you're running. "She cheated on you?!"

"I always knew you were an ace at math."

They ran silently for a while except for the rhythmic breathing and footfalls.

"Did you ever go home to her anyway?" Joe asked, knowing it was a stupid question, but feeling it would have sounded too accusatory to ask if Coach had dumped his pregnant fiancé.

"No, of course not!" came Coach's indignant response. "She was supposed to wait eighteen months and she only lasted three months, at most, before getting herself knocked up!"

"Did you love her?" Joe asked softly.

"Let me tell you something about love." All of a sudden, Coach was sounding a lot more like a parent than a friend.

Joe wished he hadn't asked. He knew he was about to get a lecture on "love" from someone who had been carrying around an angry heart for twenty-five years.

"Someday you're gonna fall in love, and you're gonna fall hard. You'll forget about your friends. You'll want to be with her all the time, and your heart will ache and your head will ache when you can't be together. You'll do things and say things you never thought you would. Everything else that mattered in your life, it won't matter anymore. She'll become your whole world….and it's great and it's awful all at the same time. She'll become the center of your universe and you won't even know who you are anymore, and you won't even care."

They were walking now, slowly.

"Sometimes things work out and you can spend your life with someone. And sometimes all your dreams get shot down and crash and burn on the ground. Now, I'm not saying you should avoid falling in love, if that was even possible. There's no one could even talk you out of it. I'm just saying be careful. Be careful who you trust. The deeper you go in the worse it's gonna be gettin' back out. As good as love feels when you're in it, the worse it is when you lose it. Just keep your eyes open. That's all I'm saying."

"Wanna turn back?" Joe asked, not realizing how profound his question was. He vowed to himself to heed this advice; a vow no one has ever been able to keep.

They jogged back towards Valley Park High as the early autumn sun nudged westward along its southerly route, never to regain the brilliance it had just a few miles ago.

6

Getting home from work at 10:10 PM, he was changed and out the door for his run by 10:15. Joe loved these three-mile runs through the darkened streets of this little town. He was truly invisible. Some of the houses were dark; some had a kitchen light on. Some had the blue glow of a television in the front room. As he ran he imagined the conversations that were taking place in the houses with the lights on, and the activities in the unlit houses. He knew who most of the people were in these houses since they had been his newspaper customers until he ditched his route for a "real" job at the drug store. He knew the girls' houses too, but they always seemed to have the shades down even if he could tell their bedroom lights were still on.

Outside, alone on these dark streets was his only chance to think. Sure, he had the whole school day to daydream, but he always was on guard not to drift too far in case he got called on. After all, he needed to keep his grades up to get into college, just in case Mr. Goldberg could keep him out of *juvey pen*.

After his arraignment on assault and battery charges, his case kept getting continued and delayed, and postponed, moved along, put off, bumped, and rescheduled, or any number of other euphemisms Mr. Goldberg used to explain what was taking so long. "The longer we can put this off, without you getting into more trouble, the better off we'll be," explained Goldberg. "You were charged as a juvenile, so the only place they could put you, if we lose your case, you know, worst case scenario, would be juvenile detention. So the longer this takes, the less time you'd be in there. They would have to let you out when you turn eighteen."

Joe didn't want to (or didn't think he should have to!) spend any time in detention (reform school, his mother called it). So the longer this took, the better. By winter of junior year he spent very little time even thinking about it. But when he did think about it, he hated having it hanging over his head. It's hard to make life plans when anything of real consequence is being decided by others. And this notion of "taking one day at a time" was just some nonsense espoused by people with no motivation to set goals.

By March of '73 changes were going on all around. The same girls he knew at school who never paid him any attention before were suddenly taking an interest in him. Was it his new "bad boy" reputation, or because he had a driver's license now? Or was it just springtime? The reason didn't matter to Joe; only the attention. He noticed his buddies were getting more attention too so it probably wasn't the bad boy thing at work, unless they were now perceived as bad through association with Joe.

The cynical part of him suspected that the girls who had set their sights on senior boys but were passed over for the prom, had to now recalibrate their goals and shoot for junior boys. Probably not a good idea anyway to get hooked up with a guy who in a few months was either headed off to college or off to Vietnam.

Joe's buddies had their own theory as to their newfound popularity with the girls: as the boys got their licenses, they were branching out beyond the confines of their small town into neighboring areas. This did not go unnoticed by the local girls. Joe loved the multi-school track meets that spring which brought together new contacts, both boys and girls, from throughout their athletic conference. Meeting girls for the first time, wearing just tank tops, running shorts, and shoes, was really a great ice breaker.

Greater change was happening outside the little world inside Joe's head. Nixon just announced that he was "working to end the conflict in Southeast Asia," and to that end, was scaling back the war effort. Then the real news: he was discontinuing the draft! Everyone knew that Nixon was full of shit, but this was something he couldn't go back on or there would be (more) widespread riots. Joe's older brother, Eldon, and countless other older brothers, were safely ensconced at their colleges on academic deferments. Now they could finish college (or not) without the draft cloud over their heads.

7

Joe's high school friend Eddie was a convenient friend. Eddie didn't have a lot of other friends, and usually no girlfriend *(I like you as a friend)*, so he was generally available to hang out with. He was also a last-born child so his parents didn't expect much of him. Eddie would mangle common expressions, like: "Catch 23," or "You need to nip that in the butt," or Joe's favorite: "It didn't pass mustard." Joe didn't know if Eddie was intentionally annoying, or maybe just a little slow.

Eddie's family had a round, above ground pool, and a pop-up tent trailer. His dad had a subscription to Playboy. Many hot summer nights were spent sleeping out in the camper, studying internal magazine spreads, and cooling off their overheated adolescent imaginations in the pool. Some nights the magazines were replaced with real live girls, as one of the neighborhood girls also had a backyard tent.

Overtly, Eddie's best friend was Eddie. But in reality, he

would latch onto anyone who was willing to be his friend. He was the kind of boy who could be friends with a girl because they knew he was all talk. *"All yak and no shack"* they called him. During the back yard, middle of the night pair-ups, Eddie and his partner just waited outside the tent until Joe and his strip-poker prize were finished inside the tent. A couple times, Joe even looked up to see Eddie peeking through the tent flaps.

One fall Saturday night in junior year of high school, Eddie called Joe to see if he wanted to go for a "run" with some other guys. Always up for a run, Joe put on his Adidas Antelopes and trotted down the hill to Eddie's house. He thought it was a little strange for Eddie to be going out at this hour for a run, but it was a beautiful crisp night and the streets were quiet. When he reached the house, Joe could see Eddie's older friend Dale (the one with the license and car) was there. Dale said, "Hey Joe, get in. We're going to meet up with some other dudes and do the "run" down by West School."

So they headed off in Dale's Buick (at a faster speed than seemed necessary) toward West School. They met up with five other guys by the playground behind the school. Dale, the apparent leader, explained that this was no ordinary run; rather, it was a game….a competition. Each team of three would be driven by their driver out to a preselected location exactly three miles from West School. Whichever team got all three of their runners back to the school first would be the winner.

Seems pretty straight forward. Sizing up the competition, Joe thought his team would have a decent chance. He knew he could run. And Eddie was a steady, reliable runner, albeit slow. Eddie would have been a member of the high school's football team, had there been one. Instead, he was the Clydesdale division of the cross country team.

Brian (all 130 pounds of him) rounded out Joe's team. Joe was relieved that portly Dale was the driver, and not a runner. Dale, having participated in the run before, explained during the ride to the designated drop off point that, although the course was three miles by the road, it was "legal" to run through the woods and people's yards if it was a more direct route.

Joe speculated his team had a tactical advantage, especially if Joe were to lead the way. Joe had developed an uncanny sense of direction during his dog walks in the woods near his home. And he developed superior night vision (real or imagined) from doing his paper route in the early morning darkness, and from his after work runs. At exactly nine o'clock, Joe's team (for it was Joe's now) set out in what Joe knew, and his teammates hoped, was the direction of West School. The three ran in line, step for step, which was difficult for little Brian trying to match Eddie's long strides. They ran their mission stealthily through the back yards and patches of woods so characteristic of that part of New England. They imagined they were special ops rangers racing to rescue some captive army grunt who strayed too far into the Cambodian jungle.

They ran with the thrill and excitement that comes with trespassing, undetected as they traversed the neighborhoods. But somehow (a coincidence?) there began a chain reaction of barking dogs and porch lightings. About 100 feet into the woods behind a home, they stopped to catch their breath. Without knowing how far they'd gone, and how far they had left to go, it was hard to set a pace. One thing for sure: they were going too fast. Joe used the break to check his internal compass. He didn't know these woods and there was no moon tonight. All he had to go on was instinct and ego. He knew they just needed to go forward. But which way forward?

As they crouched there, panting and gulping the cool night air, a flood light brightened the back yard behind them with yellow-grey slivers of light penetrating into the woods. A man's voice yelled out, "Who's there? What do you want?" The Special Ops team froze. Joe was just about to turn around and go back to the house to explain the finer points of the "run" to the man when they felt, a split second before they heard it, two quick shotgun blasts and what sounded like freezing rain as the rock salt tore through the brown leaves.

They were off and running at the first shot, sprinters trained to react to the starter's gun. They ran all-out and fell into line with Joe leading the others deeper into the woods. This time Brian was behind Joe as his small wiry frame sprung from the shot like a coiled spring before the lumbering Eddie's frame registered the gun shot. Joe deftly dodged tree after tree while Brian and Eddie matched him stride for stride, each watching only the feet of the guy in front of him. Joe dodged a nine inch oak at the last second, but Brian couldn't adjust in time.

"Ugh!" Joe heard the collision between boy and tree. Immediately he heard the second sound of two lungs worth of breath being forcefully expelled from a human body as Eddie, matching footfalls with Brian, slammed into him, pinning the little harrier to the oak. Joe kept running without breaking stride, abandoning "team spirit" and, momentarily at least, forgetting about the requirement of getting all team members to the finish. Before long he could hear Eddie and Brian crashing through the trees and brush trying to catch up. Soon they were out of the woods and onto a road with a solid double yellow line. As a small town, there were only a few of these "main" roads. Very few out here in the west end of town. Joe knew where they were, but it wasn't quite where he expected they'd be.

As they caught their breath for a second time, bent over and clutching their knees, Eddie and Brian started laughing. They laughed out of relief. They laughed out of the sheer slapstick of it. And now they laughed because Brian's laugh was so funny sounding with his nostrils clogged with dried blood from the Eddie-Oak sandwich.

Joe was not laughing. He worried that, any minute, the town's only police officer, Bob Mitchell, would be coming down the road responding to reports of shots fired in a residential neighborhood. Joe's attorney, Mr. Goldberg, had warned Joe to stay as far away as he could from trouble while his "light bulb" case was pending, and to especially watch out for "Bob the cop" who "had a target" on Joe's back.

Joe wanted to get back to West School as fast as he could and get a ride back home. But he felt uneasy and exposed to be out in clear view (police cruiser spotlight assisted) on a main road. Being in a group made them even easier to spot. *And what if someone happens to drive by the school and see the two cars out behind by the playground waiting for the runners to come back at 9:30 on a Saturday night?* Even honest answers coming from teenagers on a Saturday night are seldom believed.

On the other side of the road was a cornfield. This time of year the corn was already harvested. But the field isn't bare. The lowest ten inches of the golden stalks, now grey, were left behind, still standing more or less upright, to provide some protection from erosion until the fields are plowed and planted again in the spring. Joe thought, if he lay down between the rows when a car passed by, these stumpy stalks might give him enough cover.

But should I take off and abandon my friends? What kind of friend would that make me? Are they really my friends? Am I their friend? What if they get caught? Would they rat on me (even if I haven't done anything?) Joe didn't really know Brian well, and what he knew of his friend Eddie made him pretty sure Eddie would throw him under the bus if it helped his own cause. Joe's dad always warned him that if it came down to a white kid's word against a black kid's word, the white kid would always win.

They all had started breathing normally again. Having no idea of what Joe was mentally wrestling with, the other two wanted to know which way to go. "I can't believe you guys don't know where we are! We all grew up in this town and went by here every day for six years on the school bus. Follow me!" commanded Joe.

Joe took off in a near sprint into the cornfield. Fueled by anger and fear, he set a grueling pace. There was no more laughter coming up from behind, only heavy breathing and the stamping of uneven foot strikes as they hurtled through the rutted tire tracks left behind by the harvester in the dried mud. Had Joe known how much more running was ahead of him tonight, he might have eased the pace. They reached the end of the corn stalks having attacked the field diagonally. They splashed through the small brook that was the boundary of both the cornfield and the playground. There on the playground were the two cars.

"Do you smell something?" asked Eddie.

"I don't smell anything," replied Brian.

"You can't smell anything 'cause you got a broken nose. They're smoking pot," added Joe.

"I can't believe they beat us back here," complained Eddie.

The smoking group suddenly went still and quiet when they heard Joe's special ops team approaching. Recognizing the stragglers, their pot induced paranoia dipped a bit.

"Hey, what took you so long?" Steve chided.

Over the next couple minutes Steve explained how, after hearing the gunshots, he went back to find Joe's team, but not finding them, he returned to the school parking lot. Dale had stayed back at the school in case anyone showed up. They'd been passing around joints ever since.

Dale hadn't said a word and Joe sensed he was pretty high already. He guessed he had been smoking from the start and wouldn't have been much good rescuing friends running away from a crazy man with a shot gun.

Joe didn't listen to much his mother told him, but right now it made a lot of sense not to get into a car driven by someone who was drunk or high. Aside from the obvious safety concern, Joe was still spooked by the idea that Officer Bob might still be out patrolling, searching for the source and reason for the gun shots. Joe couldn't afford "guilt by association" even if he survived a ride home with an impaired driver. Joe told the others he was going to run the seven miles home and suggested the others might do the same. The others had all had enough running for one day, but evidently had not yet had enough grass.

Starting back on the road, alone this time, Joe thought about his mom and how she would be worried as it was getting late and she knew he had gone out for a nighttime run. He hoped that she had already gone to bed with the mistaken notion that he must be sleeping out in Eddie's pop-up camper tonight. Joe thought about his friend Eddie and Eddie's wider circle of "friends." He thought, *Maybe I need to be a little more selective about who I call a friend.*

8

From time to time, Joe would bump into his tobacco picking neighbor and mentor, Paul. They weren't in any of the same classes (Paul was not heading to college after high school) but they did take the same school bus. Paul was a quiet, damaged soul, but he lit up (or flickered at least) when he saw Joe. He would hum the Frito Bandito song and the two would share a laugh. Joe never understood why Paul would seek out, or even be open to a friendship with him. Back in junior high school, Paul was on the wrong end of a bullying incident (was there a right end?) There was a gym-class rule written in black marker on a piece of corrugated cardboard and posted on the wall inside the boys' locker room. "NO SOCKS, NO JOCKS, NO PLAY." There was another sign taped to the tile wall near the gang shower: "ALL BOYS MUST SHOWER." This second sign seemed obvious to most of the sweaty thirteen year olds; but apparently not all. Paul would show up for gym class with the requisite white socks and athletic supporter, and would participate in whatever activity was assigned that day (basketball, gym hockey, dodgeball, softball, etc.) but afterward, while his classmates would pile into the group shower, Paul went over to his locker in the corner and dressed himself, putting on his button down shirt right over his sweaty gym shirt. One day, the others, including Joe, had had enough and confronted Paul, demanding he either take a shower voluntarily, or he would get a team scrub down.

Paul resisted and the group of four or five naked boys restrained Paul and carried him, kicking but not screaming, into the shower. They pulled off his filthy gym shirt revealing bruises along his spine from his upper back to his waist. The raucous scene immediately turned silent as each boy realized why Paul refused to undress in front of others. A couple kids said, "sorry Paul," and they left him alone in the warm shower. Joe sensed Paul was crying softly. Joe was crying on the inside. None of the boys ever mentioned it again. From that day on Paul started "forgetting" his white socks so he would be excluded from gym class.

Joe now wondered how or why Paul had forgiven him because he had never apologized. But that was a few years ago. Maybe bullying victims are just grateful they are no longer being traumatized and that is enough to warrant forgiveness. Joe hoped his willingness to interact with Paul was apology enough and decided he should put it behind him, since Paul apparently already had. Next summer Paul would be headed back to the tobacco farm to teach a new crop of novice pickers, while Joe was headed off to an uncertain future. Joe carried the regret with him for the rest of his life. It is one thing when you find out something unflattering about an ancestor and you wear the shame for them. It is worse when you admit that a malignant behavior was perpetrated by yourself.

9

1975

No one had warned Joe of the stupefying boredom that was ninety per cent of military life. The other ten per cent, terror and excitement, he had been trained for. His father told him stories of the terrifying long days and longer blacked out nights working at a west coast munitions depot during the waning days of WWII. That was when a "colored" man's options were limited in the segregated armed services. His dad could only have dreamed about guarding an embassy in a mixed race unit of MSGs.

But scanning the quiet skies from the Embassy roof in Saigon was nothing like the briny smell of the mist coming off the blue green Pacific. The smell of cinnamon and butane, sewer gas and jet exhaust, filled the humid evening air, while South Vietnamese families huddled for their evening meal, observing the curfew and anxiously dreading the reputed southward advance of the North Vietnamese troops.

The MSGs invented a game, a play on counting sheep. But instead of counting wooly farm animals to induce sleep, they were counting cockroaches to stay awake. Joe and Eric had never seen, or even imagined, roaches the size they encountered in Nam. But Leroy, hailing from Houston, bragged that "these pussy gook roaches got nothing on our roaches back home." Joe made a mental note to cross off Houston as a vacation destination.

To Joe, the service felt a lot like the one year of baseball he played in high school. Good enough to make the team, but not good enough to actually play, Joe loved to go to practice but hated the games. Boot camp was like practice; the Embassy assignment was like sitting on the bench while the good players were out "playing" in the jungle. But, in a very real way, he was happy to be 'ridin' the pine.' And anyway, the "playing in the jungle" part was over for American GIs. Now the mission was to hold the embassy long enough to get everyone evacuated.

With the airfield still in operation only a mile away, there really was no way to tell whether planes entering the Embassy airspace were friend or enemy. That was up to the air traffic controllers to determine. Joe wished the airport would be shut down at night so they could consider any aircraft as enemy. But then what. The embassy had limited anti-aircraft defenses. No surface to air missiles, no RPGs, no heavy artillery. Only machine guns. They might be able to take out a low flying chopper with a lucky shot to the fuel tank, but not much else. Still, even in war, the fortified Embassy was the safest place to be during a war. The locals seemed to know that too, as they increasingly converged around the compound walls as rumors spread that the fall of Saigon was imminent.

Joe never thought he would hear himself saying it, but he really did miss high school. He'd had a couple good teachers and a good coach who, through exposing students to interesting books, had kindled an interest in reading. Here in Nam, everyone had the same book: the Bible. Some of the southern boys actually read it, and knew how to navigate the book. As a Catholic, Joe had never actually opened the Bible. He had never even seen anyone at home reading one. And no Catholic ever brought a Bible to church! Finally, out of extreme boredom, he took a look. Joe was sure there were guys pinned down in the bush on covert ops who were reading their GI Bibles with a sense of urgency and renewed focus. He genuinely hoped they would find the comfort and salvation they desperately needed in their precarious position. But in this "tit" assignment, Joe was reading the Bible more for its historical perspective than its spiritual reassurance. Joe enjoyed the Old Testament stories the most. Wars, feasts, famines, floods, polygamy, betrayal, antiquated notions of science and gender roles, slavery, and all those laws in Leviticus! This was entertaining reading!

Jeff was the most homesick of the group of MSGs assigned to defend the Embassy. He was a first-born son from Birmingham, Alabama. Joe wondered if he, himself, had been from a nicer place than Valley Park, Connecticut, might he be more homesick? But then Jeff proved that one can be homesick regardless where one's home is. Joe wondered if it had more to do with being a first born. Maybe Jeff missed most the non-stop adulation that all first-born (sons) received from their parents. Maybe it was the ordinal supremacy over younger siblings. An enlisted Marine certainly wouldn't be feeling anything close to that.

Maybe Jeff missed the unquestioned authority of any utterance emanating from his mouth. Joe and Eric automatically discounted by fifty per cent everything Jeff said just because he was from Alabama and no one could decipher his mumblings. The other fifty per cent, Joe said, was just pure bullshit. Joe wondered if Jeff missed home, because back in Alabama, Jeff wouldn't have to deal with people like Joe, and even if he did, he wouldn't have to treat Joe as an equal. Now they were Marine "brothers."

But Jeff went on and on about his family and all the quaint, genteel aspects of life in shithole Alabama. "I think I know his whole fuckin' life story," Joe would complain to Eric when the two were finally rid of Jeff. "Now I can cross off Houston and Birmingham from my must-see cities."

Joe and Eric hatched plans to see the country (minus Houston and Birmingham!) when they got discharged. They knew they would have to travel in civvies rather than their dress blues, given the reception previous waves of Vietnam vets had received stateside. They knew there would be no ticker tape parades with random young women running up to steal a kiss from the victorious returning troops. More likely: they'd be met with people carrying "baby killer" signs.

Joe didn't have any special girl he left behind in Connecticut to feel homesick for. For two years, with his court case hanging over his head, he feared he might end up, on short notice, in juvenile detention. He didn't want to get into a boyfriend/girlfriend relationship (at least that's what he said when the opportunity never seemed to materialize). "It wouldn't be fair to the girl."

He briefly had a girlfriend who fancied herself as a deep,

worldly thinker, and maybe this was true. She broke up with Joe because he said he wasn't against abortion. He wasn't in favor of it either; he just hadn't considered it. She said she was also against masturbation because Pope Paul declared it a sin and she wanted to know where Joe stood on the issue. Joe said he was opposed to girls asking boys questions like that.

There were a few other flings and also the awkward senior prom. After the prom, on the way to the after-party Joe took a short detour to a new, poorly lit cul-de-sac where homes were being built. Ringo Starr was on the radio singing "You're sixteen, you're beautiful, and you're mine."

"Hey!" Joe said, "That's just like you! You're sixteen, you're beautiful, and you're mine." Carol responded, "Well, I'm sixteen." At the (literally) eleventh hour, when push was coming to shove, Carol struck the defensive Heisman posture of a "friend….not a girlfriend."

Most girls were upfront with Joe, telling him they could be friends but couldn't date. Joe knew the reason. The fear of teenage pregnancy was always pervasive in the air, but a white girl getting knocked up by a black kid was especially scandalous. And there were no black girls in town, save Joe's sisters.

Joe's first and only sustained relationship with a girl was with Kim-Ly, here in Saigon. She was quiet, sweet, not demanding, and remarkably clean. Joe especially appreciated her cleanliness in this otherwise filthy, sticky city. When his buddies returned from their forays into the red light district, they washed down their private parts with a bleach and water solution and popped penicillin tablets like breath mints. Kim-Ly, as far as Joe knew, was not one of those "district ladies."

Joe felt he knew Kim-Ly, but he couldn't be sure. She spoke Vietnamese and serviceable French. Joe spoke neither, and the small amount of Puerto Rican slang he picked up on the tobacco farm was not much use in Saigon. Kim-Ly seldom spoke in English but Joe suspected she understood more than she let on. They communicated mostly in a primitive sign language they worked out. Their communication barrier seemed to disappear completely when they were alone together between the sheets in the corner of Kim-Ly's family apartment on Dien Ben Phu Street.

Kim-Ly had a cheap, plastic Japanese record player on the floor with a single mono speaker. Her record collection, if you could call it that, consisted of three albums of Vietnamese folk songs and a four-album box set of Chicago, "Live at Carnegie Hall." Joe recognized that her possessing the Chicago box set meant that he was not the first American to have visited Kim-Ly's home. He just didn't know if they were visiting Kim-Ly or her mother. Kim-Ly's father was among the missing somewhere in Vietnam; North or South, no one knew. Joe liked to have sex with Kim-Ly while listening to Chicago's "Make Me Smile," the long album version.

"Is this love? Or do I just love the sex? Can I actually be in love with someone I can't talk to and have nothing in common with? Does it even matter? Can't we just enjoy being with each other as a diversion to the calamity we are both stuck in?"

Kim-Ly was also discreet. Any of the men, boys really, in her community who were not dead, maimed, enlisted, deserting, or missing, would not have approved of their relationship. The women were more understanding, having lived through decades of foreign occupation and colonial rule, and themselves experiencing how the economic realities of wartime and the scarcity of eligible native men can conspire to alter one's moral attitudes regarding inter-cultural coupling.

Joe felt he was back in Valley Park, Connecticut playing cat and mouse with Officer Bob Mitchell. When he first got his driver's license, if Joe passed the town's only police cruiser on the road going the opposite direction, he was free to drive as fast as he wanted once the cruiser cleared his rear view mirror. Kim-Ly's mother arriving at the Embassy for her shift as a housekeeper was Joe's cue to head out the side gate and past the French embassy to spend his days at Kim-Ly's apartment without fear of detection.

On duty again up on the embassy roof that night, Joe and Eric were quiet for a while.

"Hey man, did you cut one?" Joe started to move away from Eric.

"I said 'safety,'" Eric replied in defense.

"Sayin' safety doesn't take away the shitty smell. What'd you eat last night?"

"Does it matter?"

"What?"

"What I ate?"

"It smells like shit!"

"All food smells like shit after you eat it."

"Yeah, but that fart was so bad I can't believe it ever smelled good when it was still food."

Joe was quiet again for a minute.

"Did you ever wish you were a Christian?"

"Where did that come from?" Eric fired back, defensively.

"I'm sorry, did you want to talk about intestinal gas all night?"

"Well, I did say safety."

"Do you ever think your life would be easier if you were Christian?" Joe asked, tuning serious again.

"You mean 'cause people hate the Jews? Ever wish you were white?"

"That's not really what I meant. I mean, Jews were waiting for thousands of years for a messiah, and then when one showed up, they didn't accept him and had him killed. Now you have to keep waiting for someone who already came and went, and there's no one else coming back besides the original one."

"That's what you believe…that Jews are just waiting in vain?"

"Yeah, that's what we believe. You missed your chance as a chosen people. You can't have salvation until you accept the Savior."

"Salvation? You mean, like heaven?"

Joe nodded.

"Jews were going to heaven long before anyone named Jesus came on the scene."

"You sure about that?" Joe challenged.

"Sure. I guess so. I dunno. I guess I never really thought about it before. I'm just a Jew; I'm not into the whole religion thing. You really into being Catholic?"

"No, not really." Joe's canned answer sounded disingenuous, even to himself. "I guess I've just been thinking."

"There's no atheists in foxholes." Eric offered.

"We're on a roof in a compound surrounded by a concrete and iron wall."

"Same thing."

There was no argument from Joe.

Sometimes on the roof of the embassy, Joe would get a little homesick looking at the American flag; the same flag flying in the courtyard of his high school. In one such weak moment of homesickness, Joe wrote a letter to Eddie back home, painting a picture of occasional exciting adventures dotting the landscape in a tapestry of stupefying boredom. In his reply back, Eddie told Joe, based on his description of life as an MFG in Saigon, it wasn't like being in a real war. Joe had a comfortable bed to sleep in every night while his marine brothers before him had to sleep out in the jungle making hootches out of their ponchos. He had plenty of good, hot meals prepared by a cook, and he was able to send and receive mail on a regular basis. This would be the last exchange of mail between the two boyhood friends.

In later years Joe would feel a mild strain of survivor's guilt for having "survived" a relatively stable and secure wartime

51

existence. Although he volunteered for the Corps under duress, and he had been dismayed to learn he would be shipped to Vietnam, Joe was willing to do what he was trained for, whatever he was ordered to do. He knew of guys who, facing the prospect of the draft, gambled with the National Guard, ignorant of the fact that some Guard troops get called to active duty in every war theater. Many ended up sacrificing far more than Joe had. A few years later, when it was finally a source of pride to be a Vietnam Vet, Joe was always a little sheepish about his own veteran status. He shied away from parades and avoided the VFW. He once attended a VA support group session to deal with his nightmares, but he shared so little in common with the marines and infantrymen who were eight or ten years older and who had all earned their PTSD by seeing combat in the "real" Vietnam war, that he felt invalidated. Still, he would not have traded places with them.

10

When Joe arrived to pick up Georgie for their date to the amusement park, she wasn't quite ready. Joe wondered what there really was to get ready? The ways and ministrations of females were a mystery to him. As (bad) luck would have it, Joe found himself alone in the family room with Georgie's father, George. They had met briefly before, prior to their first movie date, as was the custom at the time, but the meeting was rushed as the new couple was headed to the early show. Joe preferred to take girls to the early show so they would have some time left in the evening in case any other activities might present themselves.

Tonight it felt like an ambush, like the delay in being date-ready was all contrived to trap Joe alone with George. Joe was expecting the usual routine: a girl's father clumsily stumbling to find the words that could only be translated to mean "My daughter can go out with you as a friend but she is not going to have a black kid as a boyfriend. You keep your hands off her!" Most fathers delivered the warning shot in such a way that the meaning was clear, but they felt the message was delivered without sounding racist. Joe tensed up waiting for the "talk."

A big man of few words, George launched right into it. "Georgie tells me you're four years older than her."

"That's right, Sir."

Big George liked hearing "sir." Joe hadn't necessarily said it for George's benefit; it was just something drilled into him. That's the way he was brought up, and the Corps only reinforced it, even though the circles Joe traveled in meant he rarely came in contact with anyone who required a "sir" response.

But George liked hearing "sir" from a young man. Having no sons of his own, only this daughter, George often fantasized about what it would have been like raising a boy. Baseball, boxing, throwing a football, fixing cars…all things a girl is not much use for.

"So what is a guy your age doing with a girl Georgie's age?" he continued his line of inquiry.

"Well sir, I'm only a year ahead of her in school. I spent three years in the Marine Corps out of high school so when I arrived at college last fall, I was ready to start dating. But the girls my age didn't want anything to do with me. Half of them wouldn't date me because I was only a freshman and they were seniors, and the other half wouldn't once they found out I'd been in Vietnam. They thought every guy over there was a baby killer.

When I met your daughter this summer, I thought she was older than she is. She's very mature for her age and she has a good head on her shoulders, sir."

George responded, "You know, I was in the service too. The Army during WWII. Served in France and North Africa. The service will make a man out of you. Change you in ways you never thought you could change."

"Yes sir."

"You know, I only have one child. I love her very much. She is everything to me. Nothing, and I mean nothing else matters to me. You seem like a good young man, but if you ever hurt my daughter, in any way, you're going to think your days in Vietnam were like a picnic. Are we clear?"

"Yes sir." Joe felt like he had dodged the bigot bullet.

Finally, as if on cue, Georgie appeared in the family room, fresh and happy as if she were oblivious to this scene that Joe believed must have been scripted and played out many times before. Joe wondered how many of his predecessors were freaked out by George's scare tactics. How many guys lacked the balls to get back in the batter's box after being brushed back by a high-and-tight pitch? To amuse himself as Georgie and her father acted out her pre-date goodbye ritual, Joe continued with the baseball analogies.

Joe was going to hang in there and get some good cuts at bat. No bunting or walking tonight....although a "base on balls" did have a certain appeal to it. No, Georgie was clearly a major leaguer so Joe was up there swinging for a hit. He was pretty sure if he could at least get a single, he could steal a couple more bases. Maybe she would even wave him home? Just as long as Georgie didn't throw any curve balls.

"Are you coming?" Georgie's long goodbye to her father was finished.

"W-What?" Joe returned from baseball fantasy camp.

"Are you ready to go? You look like you're way out in left field somewhere."

Joe smiled. *She's speaking my language!*

Joe needn't have worried so much about the interrogation by Big George. In Georgie's fundamentalist Baptist church, it was not uncommon for girls to be encouraged to date men several years older. Dating, or "courtship" as they preferred, was goal directed, not recreational. Girls were discouraged from dating boys (or men) who were not seen as potential marriage material. It was easier for fathers to gauge older men for marriage potential as most older guys were further along their way to being good providers. In a small town environment, by their twenties, men should already have developed a reputation for being righteous, or conversely, abusive. A teenage boy, while seen by society in general as more age appropriate for dating a teenage girl, is too much of a wild card to enter into a courtship with a daughter of a fundamentalist Christian family. Still, Joe never fully believed Georgie's family would ever accept her marrying a half-black man.

This was Joe's first time back to Riverside Park in four years. Before Nam, there were certain things about amusement parks he liked and some things he disliked. In the "like" column were the roller coasters, crowds of people having fun, and the excitement of the lights and music emanating from the various attractions. In the "dislike" column were the heat of the summer sun on the blacktop and the greasy fried food. Now it seemed everything was reversed. Once you've had a ride in a military helicopter hovering a few feet over a rooftop trying to pluck a few desperate people out of a sea of writhing arms and heads, all the while expecting sniper rounds, the thrill of a roller coaster pales.

And once you've survived the intense, steamy heat of Vietnam, the worst heat of a New England August day was nothing. And greasy fried food? After three years eating MREs and mess hall food, and a year of college dormitory cafeteria food, a sausage wrapped in fried dough was near Nirvana.

This was their third official date and things were progressing as well as could be expected. Even better than would be expected. Joe really liked Georgie, and Georgie really seemed to like Joe, which surprised him. She was so far out of his league in the looks department that he found himself a bit on edge, like this was a dream that was about to end at any moment. And when he was on edge he frequently said stupid things that inevitably ruined evenings. Maybe it was a way to diffuse tension or deflect the awkwardness of being with a member of the opposite sex. But tonight he kept his edgy mouth shut and Georgie seemed to like his quiet way, filling the void with her own soliloquy.

On the ride home they were both quiet. Joe instinctively went to turn on the car radio to break the silence, but Georgie, softly touching his right hand, asked if they could just drive listening to the wind through the open windows.

So they held hands and drove on in silence for a time.

Sniff, sniff.

"Are you OK?" Joe asked

Sniff, sigh, soft moan.

"What's wrong?"

 "I'm having such a nice time with you I don't want it to end." Sniff, sniff.

"That's OK. We can go out again on your next day off. Or I'll come see you after work." Joe offered.

"No, not just tonight (she would, months later, call him a concrete thinker). I mean us. I don't want *us* to end."

"Who said it has to end?"

"Well, Hope said you told her last summer when you were seeing her that you would have to split up when you went off to school. That you weren't going to do a long distance relationship." Sniff, sniff.

"Well that was Hope. She was 16 and going into her senior year of high school. I was 20 and going off to college. And besides, she's a nice kid and all, but I didn't have any special feelings for her like I do for you."

It was true that Joe had told Hope that he was not in the market for an HTH (hometown honey), but his recent openness to the long-distance-romance possibility with Georgie had as much to do with the dating drought he had endured during his freshman year as it did with his "special feelings" he had toward her.

More crying.

"But you're not going to want me for long…"

"What are you talking about? Of course I want to keep seeing you."

"But I won't go all the way. I'm a Christian!"

Lots of tears; the visible ones coming from Georgie!

"Who said anything about going all the way?"

Loud crying.

"Hope said that she and you….that you were doing it…and"

"Wait a minute! I never did it with Hope! I've never done it with anyone *(Marine Corps time doesn't count!)* She told you we did it?"

"She said you were close…..very close."

"Well, our bodies were close, and maybe she felt close to me, but we didn't do it. We didn't come close to doing it. I'm OK with not going all the way. I want to wait for marriage too. We can find other ways to please each other. I'm fine with that."

Joe was pissed at this point. *Is this what girls talk about? Good Christian girls? Guys talk about what they do with girls, or what they'd like to do with girls. But a guy would never talk about what he's doing with a girl he cares about. These females are a mysterious lot!*

At the same time, Georgie's mood lightened dramatically; so much so, and so quickly that Joe was a little startled. Looking back later he wished he had put a little red flag next to this mental note.

She leaned over and kissed him on the right cheek and caressed his hand resting on the shift knob. "I'm so relieved. I thought I was going to lose you." They drove the rest of the way back to her house; her softly singing harmony to a melody only she could hear.

Last summer Joe couldn't wait to go off to college. Three years overdue. He didn't view the Corps as a total waste, but it was a detour from the path he planned to take. College would be a fresh start for him. Any friends worth keeping from his shithole hometown were also off to school, and most of them were going to be juniors or seniors. He had heard them brag about all their exploits with coeds and Joe was anxious to get some at-bats.

There had been a few women, girls really, in Vietnam. With the slight Asian females, sometimes it was hard to pin down their actual age, though they all claimed to be eighteen. His friend Eric's AM/FM scheme proved to be a bust, and Asian girls really wouldn't give head just for chewing gum. But they did like American dollars! There was one special girl, Kim-Ly, but that had ended badly....tragically.

Certainly, a worldly older guy would be a big hit on campus. Let the games begin! Last year Joe was desperate to get away.

But this summer, Joe wished he could stop the clock. With a return to school only a few weeks away, Joe dreaded the end of summer. His new budding relationship was about to get a lot more complicated before it had a chance to flower. The relative freedom of summer, being able to see each other whenever their work schedules allowed, would soon be confined to weekends only. Aside from missing Georgie, which he was certain he immensely would, dealing with a distance relationship was a real pain in the ass. It's true there was only an hour's drive separating the two, but Joe didn't have a car. Georgie had a car, but that meant he would always have to rely on her to come visit him in Providence. And St. Domenic's College dorms were single sex and not welcoming of overnight visitors of the opposite sex. Overnight guests were not a problem at her public college. The state university treated students as adults, whether they deserved the treatment or not. But her dorm situation would be complicated in its own way: she planned to room with Hope, her best friend from high school, who also happened to date Joe the previous summer.

Hope was a nice New England girl, full of spirit, positive attitude, and enthusiasm. She was the kind of girl you either really liked, or really resented. But most other girls were not threatened by Hope, the way girls are threatened by rival girls. Hope, with her plain-Jane good looks and unassuming manner made her just as easy to be friends with as to take advantage of. Georgie was different from Hope; different from any other girl he knew. Georgie was an only child, which was a rare thing in the 1970's. Joe didn't recognize that being an only child was the red flag that it is. Georgie had a wholesome beauty, the kind she might grow out of someday. But for now, she was definitely a beauty. Joe knew it. All the guys who saw her knew it. She knew it too. She had enough talent for two people, and she was going places in life. She radiated light and Joe was desperate to have her brighten his dark places.

So, whatever the hurdles he had to clear, it was worth it to Joe to figure out a way to keep this long distance love affair alive. The plan was to alternate weekends. One weekend she would drive to Providence. The next, he would find a way to Connecticut. And they would write every day and talk on the phone once a week, on Wednesday nights.

The first weekend got off to a rough start. Georgie was late getting to St. Dom's and she was worried that Joe would be worried (and he was) and she had no easy way to let him know she'd be late. When she arrived at his room, where he was waiting by the phone, they embraced and she immediately burst into tears. Between sobs she said, "Something terrible's happened!"

Unable to imagine what could possibly have befallen this lovely creature who appeared to be in one piece, Joe implored, "What happened?"

Georgie blurted out, "I have my period!"

Joe couldn't suppress his laughter. "That's not a bad thing! That's a good thing. A bad thing is if you told me you missed your period!"

This brought on a soft, relieved laugh and the cessation of tears. "But we won't be able to fool around and this is your birthday weekend."

The relationship had become physical over the last few weeks of the summer. It had gone from zero to nine (but not ten!) almost overnight. Joe was perfectly satisfied with their "other ways to please each other." This made the weekdays without her back at school agonizingly long. Joe had never before been with a girl (unpaid) who seemed to want it as much as he did. Georgie gave herself openly and freely, with none of the hand-checking he used to encounter with high school girlfriends. If this is what it's like to be with a Christian girl, Joe wanted to be born again……and again and again!

So Georgie's unwelcome periodic friend did not impact the birthday weekend in any noticeable way.

That is, until the long goodbye. On Sunday, with two hours left before Georgie needed to leave so Joe could get to his work-study job, the tears started to flow again. This time there was no stopping them. Joe hoped this was just a side effect of menstruation, but as with most things related to females, he was really just guessing. *If this was just due to her period, then most weekends should be fine, and maybe they should just take every fourth weekend off. Was it just four weeks ago that she did the mood roller coaster on the way home from Riverside Park? Well, there's no way I'm going to give up every fourth weekend. I'd miss her too much.* Joe wanted to cry too, but he wasn't a crier. He could only remember crying twice in his life: the day his dog Buddy had to be put down and the day he had to tell his mother he was going to Vietnam. He hadn't even cried on his last day in Vietnam, with everything that happened that day. *If I didn't cry then, I'll probably never cry again.*

Joe finally had to get out of her car and have faith that she could pull herself together enough to drive back to her school. He assured her that they had survived one week without each other, and the first week was always the hardest. Like the first week of boot camp. He had arrived at basic training in excellent physical shape. He was running five miles a day and doing 250 sit-ups and 100 push-ups in preparation. He never dreamed how different it would be running in combat boots, carrying a pack, all in the heat of South Carolina. After two days, his quads and calves were on fire. His pecs and shoulders ached, and his tongue was perpetually stuck to the roof of his mouth. His ribs felt cracked. But he survived. And by the second week he was in the best shape of his life, just like his father said he would be.

Heading west on Route 44, Georgie tried to keep her mind on driving, and off Joe. But it was a straight shot for the next 40 miles. Once she crossed over the state line she couldn't chase the thoughts away. Although it wasn't her thing, she clicked on the Ford's AM radio. Joe had programmed the pre-sets to stations he liked, since he was usually driving when they were together in the car. The two buttons on the left were for Providence stations; the three on the right were for Hartford. She pressed the one on the far right but it was all static. She was only fifteen miles outside St. Domenic's. She pressed the one on the far left. As soon as she heard England Dan and J.F. Coley oozing out the words to "We'll never have to say goodbye again" she completely lost it. She pulled to the side of the road and for the second time that day she was inconsolable. She cried so hard a mixture of tears and snot flowed from her face to the olive green vinyl seats of the Ford Torino. She clicked off the radio and looked at herself in the rearview mirror. *Joe's right. I really need to get a grip.*

11

September 28, 1978

Dear Diary,

I wish I had a sister, or even a different best friend I could talk to. I can't talk to Hope about Joe since they had been "close" when they were going out last year. She seems cool with everything and she says she is happy for me, but I don't want to rub her face in it. They never were serious, but still it's a little awkward.

I suppose if I had a sister I'd have to be careful too, because if she ever told Mom how serious we were getting, there would be trouble. Mom warned me not to get "involved" so soon after Alan. What does she know? She got married at 19 to the only guy she had ever dated!

Since I have no one to tell this to I am writing it here. It was really only a few weeks ago (hard to believe because it seems like I've known him forever!) that I told Joe I wouldn't go all the way, and now we're not, but we are doing everything else. It feels great and I love being close to him. He never pushes me to do anything I don't want to do. I know we are falling in love but neither of us has said it out loud yet. Joe said we should try to take things slowly because I'm "on the rebound," but we can't seem to slow it down. It just feels right and natural. He's all I think about and I can't wait to see him again just as soon as we leave each other. I LOVE JOE!

GF

Joe quickly settled into a routine at school. He prided himself on his ferocious self-discipline. Although the G.I. Bill was largely paying his tuition, he was not about to squander this opportunity, mostly because he didn't want to lose any more ground than he already had with three years in the Corps. The few bucks that he earned in his work-study job as a desk security monitor was reserved for necessities (books, soap, laundry detergent, stationery, notebooks, postage stamps), and for weekends with Georgie. He had virtually stopped drinking because he spent every weekend with a born again Christian who avoided alcohol as if it were distilled from Mormons. He gave himself an allowance of thirty-five cents a week so he could buy a Pepsi for a quarter out of a vending machine in the student union on Thursday night after work and have ten cents left over in case he needed to use a payphone somewhere.

He revived his pre-marines habit of setting his watch 10 minutes fast so he wouldn't be late for anything. This naturally caused friction with others who were late, or were presumed by Joe to be late since they were operating on standard time. The Corps had broken him of this habit as he learned the danger of being out of synch with others one night when on embassy roof guard duty he had been instructed to flash a light signal to the air traffic control tower at Saigon airport at precisely twenty-one hundred hours. His beacon signal, ten minutes premature, caught the tower off guard and made them question their own time bearings and ultimately lead to an aborted departure of a colonel. No lives were lost but the FUBAR situation caused a dust-up that quickly found its way back to the embassy roof. From then on, for the rest of his active duty, MSG Davis was meticulous about synchronizing his watch.

Every Monday morning (on the weeks he would be traveling to Connecticut that weekend) he went to the student union and posted a "ride wanted" card on the bulletin board. There was considerable interstate travel as rich St. Dom's students headed back to Connecticut and New Jersey for weekend rendezvous with their hometown honeys. Usually by Wednesday or Thursday he had something lined up in time to let Georgie know his ETA on Friday. But not all the time.

Hitch hiking was never a safe undertaking. As much as he learned to conquer his fears in Vietnam, he felt vulnerable hitching a ride from strangers. American strangers. Without his M16 Rifle, nightstick, or flashlight, or any other suitable means to defend himself, he felt uneasy and exposed. He even stopped carrying his knife that he used to wear, skin diver style, on his left leg. He had a criminal record after all, and he didn't think the civilian authorities would be forgiving of a concealed weapon on a Vietnam veteran with a record of civilian assault. And a black hitchhiker with a knife would never be able to explain himself out of a misunderstanding on the road.

Some Fridays when he hitched, he got lucky and hooked a ride most of the way to Georgie's school in just one lift. Sometimes he had to piece the trip together in two or three rides. He used to see hitchers walking along the road with their thumb out. He never understood the walking part. If it was close enough to walk, just walk! If it wasn't, just wait for a car to stop. Walking was a waste of time.

Georgie's college was located about six miles from where the major Hartford route turns west. Invariably, Joe was on his own from there. Hitching the one hour trip often took twice that long, so there was really no easy way to meet him at the turnoff without one or the other waiting for who knows how long. So, Joe would run. Compared to his pre-dawn twenty mile boot camp runs, with a full pack, in boots in the South Carolina heat, these six mile runs in his Adidas and sweats on paved New England roads were a piece of cake. Arriving on campus, Joe was a sweaty mess, a condition that was quickly rectified in the shower of a relaxed morality public university dormitory.

The weeks in between were long and sometimes lonely, if Joe let himself think about it. His only social outlet was playing in the college jazz band and pep band. Joe ate dinner most nights with his roommate before heading over to the library to study. He often sat by himself in the cafeteria for breakfast and lunch. Sometimes when he was sitting alone at a two person table, a pretty girl would approach and, pointing to the empty chair, ask, "Is anyone sitting there?" Joe would reply "No" and the girl would take the chair and go join her friends at some other overcrowded table. *Well that settles it. I'll be eating alone today.* It would drive Joe crazy when middle aged men would tell him, "You must be having a great time in school. College is the best time of your life!"

Last year, as a twenty year old freshman, Joe had been assigned a single room in the dorm at the far reaches of the fenced in campus. As a minority, the college wasn't going to take a chance with getting a complaint from some white kid who didn't want to room with a black kid. The only other African Americans, with a few exceptions, were on the basketball team. He hung out with some of them a couple times, but he went from standing out because he was black when he was with white kids, to standing out because he was a foot shorter than the basketball players. In high school, as one of only a few black kids, everyone expected Joe to excel at basketball. He still remembered the incredulous looks on the coaches' faces when they observed just how mediocre Joe was on the court during tryouts. No one on a college campus would mistake Joe, at five-nine, for a basketball player. "He must be a scholarship student," they all thought.

There were a few black students at St. Dom's on MLK scholarships, or so the rumor went. It was impolite to ask someone if they got into the school on account of being black. Most of the white kids Joe met felt compelled to comment, "You're so well spoken." It was as if they were surprised a black man wasn't speaking Ebonics. He made friends with one black student, another freshman living in a single room, from Washington DC. Ronnie had a portable TV that he would bring over to Joe's room at 11:30 some nights so they could watch Johnny Carson in color. Ronnie joked, "What kind of TV did you expect a colored guy to have?" Joe and Ronnie felt musically and culturally superior to the white kids who were just discovering 'punk rock' in the form of Blondie, The Cars, and The Police. Joe and Ronnie were bonding over Chuck Mangione, Spyro Gyra, and Gil Scott-Heron.

This year, Joe was determined to live with a roommate even

though he didn't know anyone well enough, besides Ronnie, to know if they would get along. And he didn't want to live with Ronnie as he felt it was more important that they both assimilate into the campus a little more. Joe had a few friends in the band, but most of them lived off campus. Joe knew he would be happier off campus, as he was a couple years older than most of the guys living in the dorms. Living off campus would help him pass as an upperclassman. But living off campus in a city, as a black man, also came with risks. He would no longer enjoy the protections of the campus walls, separating him from the real world outside the gate. At a school like St. Dom's, a black student was an interesting and non-threatening curiosity; almost exotic. Off campus, he would be seen as just another black guy to be feared when he happened to be walking down the street. Other than his trips to see Georgie, he didn't spend much time off campus anyway. He ventured off campus for his Child Psychology practicum down the street at the Chad Brown Public Housing Project. When Joe showed up to observe the children and engage them in a group activity, he was mistaken as one of the drug dealers who canvassed the project. The prospect of living off campus was a moot point anyway: Uncle Sam was only going to pay his room and board if he lived in a dormitory for the first two years.

Joe never missed a meal, no matter how bad the food looked or tasted. Joe's mother was never much of a cook, but compared to the USMC and dormitory hacks, she was a master chef. But this crappy chow was paid for by his prior service in the Corps and he was going to eat it. He couldn't afford to buy better meals, and he couldn't afford to miss a meal for fear of losing weight, especially now that he wasn't drinking any more. And he ignored the rumors that the priests had ordered that saltpeter be added to the cafeteria food. It didn't seem to be affecting Joe even if it was true. These were the same rumors he'd heard in the Corps and it didn't seem to have any effect on him then either.

As he ate in the crowded cafeteria, Joe would eavesdrop on the other tables. He was struck by the staggering inanity of the conversations coming from both male and female tables. (Having attended a co-ed public high school, Joe could never understand why guys and girls kept themselves apart from each other at this college. *Why bother attending a co-ed college if you weren't going to spend any time with the opposite sex? Was it because most of his classmates had gone to single sex high schools and were never socialized in a mixed setting? Was it something to do with the uptight Catholic culture that permeated everything on this campus*?) The boys talked about sports (they had played in high school) and girls (they were too afraid to talk to). The girls talked about hair styles (part it in the middle or on the side?), clothes (preppy only), and shoes (never enough). The girls never seemed to notice the boys.

Joe wondered what college would have been like had he gone right after high school. It was only a few years ago, he remembered, that there were campus protests about the war, revolution, and equal rights for women. Then there was the whole Watergate and Nixon impeachment thing that wiped away any lingering trust Americans had for their government. Now, stupefying apathy ruled the day.

When the college announced tuition increases for next year to fund a new fitness center to be built that no student, then presently attending, would ever be able to use, no one made a peep. Maybe it was because most of the students weren't concerned about money. But maybe it had more to do with protest fatigue. Even when the Dean of Student Services, Father O'Callaghan, wrested editorial control of the student newspaper, no one cared.

If I had gone straight to college, without the little detour to Vietnam, maybe there wouldn't be so many points of distinction. The most visible difference between Joe and the majority of these college guys (other than race) was their clothes. When did guys trade in their jeans, t-shirts, and flannel shirts for khakis and alligator shirts? Or maybe it is just the world of difference between attending a rural public high school and going to a prep school with spoiled rich kids. Even when Joe finally found an Izod shirt on the clearance rack in Marshalls, he couldn't bring himself to wear it with the collar turned up.

Why am I even at this school? Joe had been the victim of several of the decisions he had made while in high school. St. Domenic College had been suggested to him by his local parish priest, Father White, when Joe first had his "light bulb" incident on the tobacco farm. *Why would anyone put someone who was having trouble playing by the rules in a place that has the most rules….like the Marine Corps….like St. Dom's? Wouldn't it make sense to put that kid in a place where there were fewer rules to break? Were they just trying to break my spirit? Or were they just trying to turn a sinner into a saint?*

Except for watching their basketball team on TV, Joe's only other exposure to St. Dom's had been through the visiting priests who came to his parish to help out Father White on weekends. Joe and his siblings would laugh out loud at the sound of their Rhode Island accents. *"If today you heah his voice, hodden not yaw hots!"*

Still, the culture at St. Dom's was not totally foreign to Joe. Having been brought up a Catholic, he made sure he practiced his faith for one hour a week, taking in the 10:30 mass Sunday nights when he returned to campus (after a weekend of sins of the flesh)!

12

One late fall Friday Joe surprised Georgie with an early visit to her dorm. On their regularly scheduled Wednesday night call, Joe let her know he had found a ride to her school and should be getting in around suppertime on Friday. He couldn't wait to get there. Dorm sex was so much better than the back-seat-of-the-car sex they were having last summer. Even the college-issue twin bed was much more comfortable than a vinyl bench seat.

It didn't happen often that Joe could get a ride all the way to her campus so he was psyched to have lined this up. They would leave around 3:00 as soon as bio lab was done. Most of the students in bio lab griped about the twice-monthly Friday afternoon lab requirement. Joe knew, had he not served in the marines, he would have been bitching too. But putting in a full day of college will always be easier than a full day of Vietnam. He knew a lot of the other kids hoped to be doctors someday and a late Friday lab was only a small inconvenience compared to the hours they would later log if they continued their medical training. For Joe, bio lab was just a science elective for psychology majors.

Joe had witnessed enough medical treatment during his brief assignment in the surgical unit in Germany after the Evacuation that he knew he didn't want to be a doctor, but still he found this elective interesting.

After his 9:30 Religion class was dismissed, Joe ran into Kelly who was to drive him to Connecticut later that day after bio lab. "Hey Joe, glad I bumped into you. Did you hear bio lab got cancelled today? Dr. Benson is out sick. Any chance you'd be ready to leave earlier?"

"I can leave right now!" Joe excitedly replied.

"Awesome! I'll meet you in the quad in ten minutes. I just need to grab my bags and car keys."

All the way to Georgie's school Joe could not suppress his grin. He was going to surprise her! No one likes to be surprised but everyone likes to be the surprise. He was anxious to get there quickly too because, he thought, Kelly was interested in him. He could never figure out, when girls were flirting, if they were really interested in some action, or were bluffing as a way to exert control. A young woman, literally in the "driver's seat" was in control. *She might just be teasing me*, he thought, *so she can make a fool of me when I mistake her "innocent" comments as something else.* Joe even blushed a little, his brown skin taking on a burnt orange hue when Meatloaf came on the radio singing "Paradise by the Dashboard Lights."

Instead of the late afternoon arrival she was expecting, Georgie was stunned to see Joe striding through the cafeteria to her table as she ate lunch with her dorm mates. Ah, the warm embrace! How did they ever survive the five days since last weekend!

"Oh my God, I can't believe you're here! I thought you said you were coming at supper time? Have you eaten?" Georgie asked.

"I had a couple apples on the way down."

"Sit down. I'll get you a sandwich."

Joe would have been happy to go right up to her room and worry about eating later, but Georgie was already up fetching a sandwich. When they spent weekends at his college in Providence, Joe never brought Georgie to the dorm cafeteria. Between the guest fee and the shitty food, it just wasn't worth it. But at Georgie's school, the administration wasn't so uptight and no one cared if a friend stopped by and shared a quick lunch.

The sandwich was inhaled; Joe was eager to get upstairs. They practically ran up the three flights of stairs and down the hall to room 315, second to last on the right. Joe was thrilled to see Georgie sprinting ahead as they approached the door. *There goes my eager beaver!* Joe laughed to himself.

She flung open the door and quickly crossed the room to her desk where she grabbed something and shoved it in a drawer. She hoped she had enough of a lead on Joe that he would not notice the evasion. But Joe was right behind her.

"What was that?"

"What?"

"The thing you threw in the drawer right now," Joe added accusingly.

Before Georgie could answer, Joe was already opening the drawer to find Alan's picture. In an instant Joe's initial apprehension about this relationship returned. Other guys had warned him not to get involved with a girl on the rebound.

When Hope first called Joe and asked him to take Georgie out for some fun, it was because Georgie was crushed by her recent breakup with Alan. In the three months since they started seeing each other Georgie had never once mentioned Alan. Joe and Georgie's relationship had progressed so quickly and strongly that Joe never gave the whole "rebound" thing another thought. Georgie really seemed to be over Alan. But now, Joe was faced with the reality.

Tears now flowed; hers, not his. "I'm so sorry. I didn't want you to see that. I'm sorry, I'm sorry!" she sobbed.

Joe tried to soothe her (he hated crying) at the same time as he wanted to set his expectations of her. "You're with me now, and I can't…"

She cut him off, "I know, I know, it's just that I was missing him a little. I love you. I want to be with you. It's just that Alan and I were together for four years and I miss him sometimes. I'm so sorry. I'm putting his picture away. This won't happen again; I only want to be with you."

Glenn Frey's *The One You Love* was playing softly on the stereo that Hope had forgotten to turn off when she left for class.

Holding Georgie close now, her sobs ending, Joe really wondered if this was par for the course when dating a teenager. She seemed so mature for a college freshman, but still she was just a teenager finding her way through her first adult romance.

"Alan…..fucking crazy guy!"

"Why would you say that?" she shot back defensively, pushing herself away.

"Anyone would be crazy to break up with you. You are wonderful. You're a terrific girl." He was trying to build her back up, and he meant it too. "I tell you right now, I will never break up with you."

By now they were embracing again on her bed where she proceeded to prove to him that he was the only guy in the world who mattered. She never gave a thought to her Friday afternoon class.

They slept off their emotional and physical exhaustion for a couple hours. When they got up and dressed, reflecting on their earlier conversation, she said, "Sometimes you have an odd way of talking. You seem a little different today."

"I'm not talking different than I ever do."

"OK," Georgie replied skeptically.

Changing the subject, Joe asked, "You wanted to go get a bite to eat? What did you have in mind?"

"Anything would be fine."

Sometimes Georgie's malleability drove Joe crazy. It meant that he had to make all the decisions. Where to eat, what movie to see, where to go, what to do…It seemed strange that an only child would not want to be making all the decisions.

"How 'bout we get a grinder? We can cut it in half," he

suggested.

They headed over to the pizza shop diagonally across from her dorm.

Joe prompted her, "What kind you want?"

"I guess meatball or sausage?" she offered, knowing that these were Joe's favorites.

At the counter now, Joe ordered: "OK, we'll have a meatball grinder, por favor. Can you cut it in two?"

"Large or small?" the counter clerk asked.

"Big, por favor."

"See? Like that," Georgie pointed out. "All of a sudden you're speaking Spanish? And he asked you if you wanted large or small and you said 'big.' That's what I mean you have an odd way of speaking sometimes."

"OK, I'm a little odd. Deal with it." Joe laughed. Inside though, he realized that he had slipped back into his old speech pattern without noticing it. From the time he first learned to speak, Joe had a rather pronounced lisp. The family doctor blamed it on having been bottle fed as an infant. A common practice at the time for feeding premature infants was to enlarge the hole in the baby bottle nipple to allow more formula to flow. More food equals more growth. But a tiny baby can only take in so much at a time, and uses the tongue to stop the flow while attempting to swallow without choking. The doctor had called the resultant tongue action a "reverse swallow." The protruding tongue interferes with speech development, especially in the formation of the "s" and "sh" sounds.

Upon entering first grade (kindergarten had not yet been introduced in his little town), Joe was plucked from his classroom once a week and escorted to the speech therapy room, through the special services classroom. The special classroom had kids of all ages and sizes, and had carpeting on the floor. And there were tables instead of desks! He saw children he had never seen before. They weren't in the cafeteria at lunchtime. And he never saw them outside at recess. Some had wheelchairs or metal crutches, and some talked or looked funny. He actually did recognize one boy, Peter. Peter lived just a few doors down the hill from him and they had played together many times before entering first grade. Peter wore two large hearing aids and talked like he had marbles in his mouth, but he could play a good Indian when they were playing Cowboys and Indians. Peter was a good tree climber. But since he wasn't on the regular school bus in the morning, Joe didn't even know they went to the same school.

The speech therapy room was small with just a table and three chairs, two on one side and a bigger chair on the other side. Miss Russo would sit in the big chair facing Joe and Steven. Steven was Joe's neighborhood pal and they played every day after riding home together on the school bus.

Miss Russo was a speech therapist. Joe called her the "thpeech therapitht." It was fun being with Steven (Thteven) and repeating words after "Mith Rutho." Following Miss Russo came: Miss Carmel, Miss Kozlowski (call me Candy), and finally Miss Carpenter when Joe and Steven (now Steve) made it to the eighth grade. The two neighborhood pals progressed through elementary school, but both still had their lisps.

During these first seven years of speech therapy, Joe inexplicably found it easier to change his speech pattern than to learn to make the "s" and "sh" sounds properly. As he got older, what was once a cute little kid with a sweet lisp became a pre-teen with an embarrassing speech impediment. So Joe decided, whenever possible, not to use any words with the "s" or "sh" sound. He wasn't too fond of "z" or the "soft g" either! He could go days without uttering these sounds. It even appeared to his parents that his lisp had gone away.

The preselection process forced Joe to be a slow talker. He very rarely got in trouble for blurting out words in anger. And he developed a good alternate vocabulary. But he often felt exhausted by the expenditure of mental energy that such linguistic vigilance required. When he could, he spent many quiet hours without talking at all.

Since eighth grade when Miss Carpenter finally had a breakthrough and "cured" him, he rarely employed his "s" avoidance tactic. When he was stressed, as he was today, or when overly tired, he went back to "talking without uttering that letter." There were periods in his young life when it was especially important not to lisp, whether or not he was stressed or tired. A lisp in high school earned you the label of "queer," "fag," or "homo." In boot camp, a single "Yeth Thargent!" could earn you a beating, or worse.

Today, Georgie noticed this chink in his armor; the only one ever to notice. He had been avoiding words with the "s" or "sh" sound all afternoon. *Was she the first person who really listened to me? To really see through me?* he wondered.

On the quiet walk back to her dorm, there were no words with the "s" or "sh" sound uttered. There were no words spoken at all.

13

November 14, 1978

Dear Diary, Well Happy Birthday to me! Today was my eighteenth birthday so I am finally legal! The day was actually a little strange, not at all what I expected. I decided to play hooky and drive home for the day. Mom said she would invite my aunt and uncle and the five of us would have dinner to celebrate.

I told Joe I would be at home so he could call me there to wish me a happy birthday. But instead of calling, he showed up at 11:00 this morning. I was shocked and that's when the day got strange. Joe thought I would be thrilled to see him, and I was, but I was acting weird and he wanted to know why. I screwed up and there was no escape. I had to tell him. Alan had called me a few days ago and said he wanted to come see me on my birthday. I had spent every birthday with him since I was fourteen, and he sounded so sad and lonely on the phone I figured, since there was no way Joe would be coming on a Tuesday, it would be OK for Alan to come. I never figured Joe would come all the way back home to see me. I hadn't seen Alan since we broke up in July. I was curious more than anything. So I really messed up. It was only a couple weeks ago that Joe surprised me at my dorm a few hours early and he saw Alan's picture that I forgot to put away. I promised him it wouldn't happen again and now this!

So I had to tell Joe that Alan was going to stop by. Joe got real quiet but his eyes got so angry it scared me a little. All he said was: "Call him. Tell him not to come." I tried calling his house but there was no answer. We figured he was already on his way so I suggested to Joe we go out to lunch so we wouldn't be home when Alan got here. That way my mother would tell Alan what was going on. Joe didn't have any money (he never does) so I had to buy our lunch, on MY BIRTHDAY!

The rest of the day was better. Joe didn't mention Alan except to say, "So in the future, if I want to surprise my girlfriend, I have to call her first to make sure she's not with another guy?" I got his point. Joe hated skipping school and it was a big deal finding a ride and hitching to come 75 miles to see me in the middle of the week.

After lunch we went to the state park and made out for a long time. After we make out my face always gets red because no matter how close he shaves, Joe's beard stubble is so sharp it makes my cheeks break out. So, of course, in front of everyone my dad asked me what was wrong with my face. That only made me turn redder.

So now I'm an adult and I just hope I stop making adolescent mistakes like I did today! I never want to see that anger in Joe's eyes again.

Oh, I almost forgot. Joe bought me a beautiful gold serpentine bracelet for my birthday! I'm never taking it off!

GF

14

That Sunday at the Baptist church Pastor Johnson delivered his sermon:

"My Christian brothers and sisters, I want to talk to you this morning about love. Jesus' love. Jesus' love for all of us and for everything in this world. But I also want to talk to you about hate. Now Jesus, as divine, is incapable of hate. Jesus could get angry; remember, Matthew 21 tells us that in anger, Jesus overturned the tables of the money changers in the temple. So he is capable of anger, but hate does not reside in His heart. Hate is the domain of mortals, like us.

My friends, the worst kind of hate comes disguised as love. Over the last 20 years or so, an insidious form of hate has been seeping into our culture, disguised as love. This hate has been inflicting, and yes, infecting our young people.

Any thoughts or actions that go against the teachings of scripture and the Ten Commandments are hateful. In alarming numbers, teenagers and unmarried young adults are falling victim to this form of hate disguised as love. Let's call it what it is: carnal relations outside of marriage is fornication. It is a sin against each other, and a sin against Jesus."

Oh boy, here we go! thought Joe as he sat with Georgie in the seventeenth row. Facing front, the only person who could have possibly seen him roll his eyes was Pastor Johnson, if he could see that far. And it seemed to Joe that Pastor Johnson was looking straight at Georgie and him. After all, he knew the pastor didn't quite accept him as he was darker and shaggier than his regular congregants. And the Marine jacket didn't help.

Pastor Johnson continued: "And fornication feels like love at the time. But what do our young people know about real love? Mature love? The blessed physical love that can only rightfully be expressed through marital relations? Sure they see the fine examples of marital love their parents have shown them. And with their flawless young bodies full of hormones, they can't wait to experience this "love" for themselves. But wait they must, for as scripture says, 'A man will take a wife and the two shall become as one.'"

A couple muffled "amens" could be heard coming from some of the more senior members of the faithful.

"So you ask, how did this wave of love disguised as hate happen over the last twenty years? It's not your fault as parents. You didn't cause it. You did the things you were supposed to do. You went off and fought in WWII and Korea. You ladies kept everything going stateside. You led your children by example; doing all the right things and fostering a love of Jesus in your homes. So what was it that infected our children?

It is Rock and Roll music!"

HOLY SHIT!! Joe screamed inside. He squeezed Georgie's hand but she sat perfectly still and didn't return the pressure. Georgie had once asked Joe to turn off the radio when the Eagles "One of these nights" came on. He asked her why, and she said it was because the Eagles were "devil worshippers." Joe laughed out loud, incredulous. He said all he knew about the Eagles is that they made great music, liked to drink, and liked to fool around with young women; all the things that he, himself, was fond of doing. She said the proof was right there in their song: "Weren't they *searching for the daughter of the devil?*"

"And what about Witchy woman?" Georgie added.

"Give me a break!" Joe replied.

Pastor Johnson continued:

"Yes, Rock and Roll has degraded our culture, our society. It has eroded the moral foundation of our young people; a foundation you parents have worked so hard to build up. But there is hope! We all remember that wonderful Christian singer Pat Boone? His lovely daughter, Debbie, has the number one single so far this year. *"You light up my life!"* What a beautiful song with a beautiful message. I just know that she is singing about the light that is Jesus' love.

Yes there is hope, my friends, but there is a lot of work to be done, and Debbie Boone can't do it all on her own. So I had a couple ideas that we're going to try, right here in this holy place. After He closes a door, the Lord always opens another.

So let's close the door on hate and open the door of love! Next Sunday, I want all of you families to work together and bring all of your Rock and Roll records and tapes and drop them off in a barrel we will set up outside the entrance of this church. We wouldn't want to bring that filth inside this holy house of God." This induced a few chuckles from the congregation.

"Then after our service, we'll all go outside and read from the Good Book as we burn up all the dirty music."

Joe couldn't believe what he was hearing. He wondered if he was in some kind of time warp back to the '50s. Or worse, a space warp where he was thrust into the deep South! He wanted to get up and leave or to shout out, but he guessed that the humiliation to Georgie would have caused a terminal chasm in their fledgling relationship. He wondered where it would end. *Rock 'n Roll this week; miscegenation next?*

Pastor Johnson continued: "So we'll close the door on hate and we will open the door to love. Young people, would you search inside your soul for inspiration and open the doors of your heart to love? I would love to hear your poems about love, written in your own hand. Those of you that have a boyfriend or girlfriend, how about writing a love poem to the person you fancy? We can read these at our little bonfire next Sunday."

After the final prayer and (non-Rock 'n Roll) hymn, the members filed out; the adults uplifted, the children morose.

Back at his dorm to begin the interminable five days without

Georgie, Joe sat at his desk and began tapping on a notebook with his pen while his mind wandered. Only three hours ago he was kissing Georgie goodbye. Already he was missing her terribly. With the discipline that was drilled into him in the Corps, he cracked open his Abnormal Psychology textbook to prepare for tomorrow's exam. He knew he was taking a risk with his study-free weekends. He knew he had to work that much harder from Sunday night to Thursday night if he wanted to visit Georgie every weekend. As much as he had enjoyed spending weekday afternoons with his dad watching reruns of Hogan's Heroes, Gilligan's Island, and McHale's Navy, he now wished he had spent more time reading as a kid so he wouldn't find his current reading load so burdensome. He had no desire to go out partying with the other guys during the week. He felt that if he could cram all his studying and his part time job hours in during the week, weekends with Georgie was his reward. He really didn't have many friends anyway. Something had to give and the other stuff (Georgie, school work, job) was always more important than partying and friends.

Maybe it would be different (of course it would be different!) if he hadn't spent three years in the Marines. Then he could take his time. Maybe if he wasn't three years older than his peers he could relate better. Maybe if his peers had been through some of the shit he experienced in Vietnam, they'd take school a little more seriously.

Not able to concentrate on his Abnormal Psych with his roommate listening to talk radio, he said, "Hey Don, mind if I put some music on instead of that radio?"

Joe flipped the switch on the stereo over to FM. He scanned

the dial for the two stations with decent reception. He landed in the middle of Queen's "Fat Bottom Girls" and listened for a few seconds. Joe felt a special kinship to Freddie Mercury because they both had a lisp. He wondered why Mercury had never overcome his lisp. Or was it just that he once had a severe impediment and what one could now hear on the radio was just the residual lisp after semi-successful speech therapy? As much as he loved Queen, this song just wasn't doing it for Joe. He fingered through his pathetic album collection. *Quality, not quantity*, he thought, landing on a classic.

Joe slid the LP out of the sleeve. It was one of the few albums he owned and he only owned it by "acquiring" it when his brother left it behind when he went off to college. Somehow, between 1968 and 1978 the liner notes and lyrics sleeve of the classic Spirit Logic album had gone missing, but the music was still alive. The sound was even more raw now with ten years of scratches across the vinyl. As soon as he heard Billy Hansen belt out the opening lines, "My love is like a birdie, flyin' into your cage" Joe was able to settle into his chair and concentrate. He opened his spiral notebook and began feverishly writing, looking up only during the guitar solo. As soon as *Two Love Birds* was over, he jumped up and reset the stylus and played it again. Again his attention turned to the notebook and the obsessive note taking resumed. By the time the needle reached the center post, Joe exclaimed, "OK, I'm ready. I'm going to bed." He packed his notes and book in his backpack for tomorrow.

The following Sunday morning, Joe and Georgie emerged from her dorm room, fully clothed yet in need of redemption, and ready for services at Oakville Baptist Church. They drove the half hour from campus to the rural obscurity of the village of Oakville. (Joe never did find out what town Oakville was actually situated in.) The church was standard-issue New England: small white chapel, with a squat, squared-off nub where the steeple would have been on a less self-righteous temple. After the service the assembly gathered around the old oil drum outside the church. Joe was pleased to see there were only a handful of records, cassettes, and eight tracks in the barrel. He was sure the Pastor would interpret this as a testament to his saintly parishioner's relative contempt, compared to society in general, for pop music. Joe felt he was walking a fine line between being a silent objector to this whole outrageous spectacle, and being complicit in it, just by being there as a witness. In Joe's gut he had the same sick feeling of moral dissonance he felt when he saw other marines mistreating prostitutes in Saigon, when he stayed silent. But he did have to chuckle a little when he saw the Bee Gees and other disco records in the can.

Pastor Johnson said it was only fitting that the choral director, Mrs. Clark, do the honors. Mrs. Clark doused the pile with lighter fluid, ordered everyone to stand back, and struck a wooden match and flicked it into the drum.

Instantly a fire roared to life and acrid smoke filled the air. Joe immediately flashed back to Vietnam when embassy staff on the "burn crew" incinerated paper and vinyl tape files in the last hours before the evacuation, the black and grey smoke mixing with the yellow rain in the blue-green afternoon sky. Pastor Johnson picked out a couple of Bible passages whose relevance were so much of a stretch that Joe was convinced the pastor must have forgotten to look them up in advance. Once these were dispensed with and the fire died down a little, Pastor Johnson called for anyone who would like to read a love poem they had written.

Much blushing ensued among the dozen or so "young adults" and only one hand went up. Georgie volunteered. No one was surprised as she was the shining star of the whole church. She was the prettiest, most talented, and most graceful of any of the girls raised in the congregation. She would surely be a great catch for some righteous Baptist young man among them. "I'd like to recite a poem that my boyfriend wrote for me."

"That's wonderful Georgie!" the pastor gushed, "Somehow I knew you would be the one to start us off." By now the roaring barrel was just a smoldering, foul trash can spewing noxious fumes and chemicals into the crisp autumn air, spoiling an otherwise pristine New England scene.

Georgie cleared her throat from smoke and began speaking slowly, clearly, almost theatrically, as was her inclination.

"Two Love Birds," by Joe Davis

My love is like a birdie,

Flyin' into your cage.

My love's a little birdie,

Flyin' into your cage.

Your old birdie's gone now,

It's time to turn the page.

Open up your shutters,

> Open your windows too.

Open up your shutters,

> And your windows too.

If you let me in baby,

> I'll fall in love with you.

Your front door is locked-

Your back door too-

If I have to baby,

> I'll come down your chimney flue

> -Why don't you

Open up your shutters,

> and your windows too.

If you let me in baby,

> I'll fly the coup with you.

Let's fly away Tweetie,

We'll fly cheek to cheek.

Gimme a kiss Birdie,

Let's go beak to beak.

I want to peck you Sweetie,

Till you peep, peep, peep.

Open up your shutters,

Open your windows too.

Open up your shutters,

And your windows too.

If you let me in baby,

I'll fall in love with you.

Let's build a nest together,

Where we can stretch our legs.

Let's build a nest together,

To stretch our wings and legs.

I want to ruffle your feathers,

And fill our nest with eggs.

Open up your shutters,

  Open your windows too.

Open up your shutters,

  And your windows too.

If you let me in baby,

  I'll fly the coup with you.

Georgie smiled as she looked through teary eyes at Joe, and he clasped her hand in his and smiled too; a different kind of smile. Maybe, just maybe, he had introduced Spirit Logic to a whole new audience!

Pastor Johnson broke the pleasant silent tension by leading the small group of rejuvenated Christian sheep, with fresh wool pulled over their eyes, in a round of applause. "This is exactly the kind of love I was talking about. That was a beautiful poem and I can tell you have a deep and abiding love in your hearts and you are yearning for something that will be worth waiting for. Thank you for sharing your love and your faith with the group."

Joe hustled Georgie to the car so they could drive back to campus where he knew he would be opening her shutters and flying head-first into her cage all afternoon. He kept the car radio turned off, not taking any chances that "Two Love Birds" might screech across the airwaves.

15

Joe thoroughly enjoyed their lovemaking. The fact that they didn't "go all the way" did not bother him in the least. Receiving oral sex was perfectly fine with him. His USMC buddy Eric had been wrong about "all the gook girls giving head." Kim-Ly had thought the idea of it was disgusting, and only after some coaxing, consented to "normal" sex.

Joe didn't dare refer to oral sex as "sex" because Georgie was determined not to have sex until marriage. So occasionally, during the afterglow, Joe might say, "I look forward to when we are married and can have sex." He was building the case that what they were doing now was something less than sex; something he would have to settle for, for the time being. Georgie was glad Joe was willing to settle for "oral pleasure" because she would have resented the constant pressure to "go all the way" like there was with Alan.

Alan, also a few years older than Georgie, always made her feel like she was playing catch-up in the three years they were together. When they split up, seventeen year old Georgie was finally feeling OK about things he had wanted her to do when she was fifteen. But, upon turning seventeen, there was near constant pressure to have "sex." Georgie's heading off to college would be putting extra miles between them, and it meant his captive, sheltered girlfriend would soon be exposed to thousands of guys, all of them older than a freshman with a late-in-the-year birthday. More than just the miles, Alan was foreseeing, quite accurately, the psychic and social chasm that was, or would soon open between the two of them. He knew if he could get the ultimate commitment from her, he could hold it all together. And he was willing to risk pregnancy, and her sense of honor, if that's what it took to seal the deal.

Whether out of fear, religious conviction, or a sense that opportunities in her life would soon be knocking, she shoved Alan off the cliff into the first-love abyss.

None of Georgie's history mattered to Joe. He never asked her about Alan, or why they broke up. He never questioned her about how physical their relationship had been. He knew she was good at giving head and he didn't care how much she had practiced, or with whom she had perfected her technique. "Maybe she's a natural at it? Beginner's luck?" he mused. It didn't matter. She was with Joe now, and she was good!

16

November 22, 1978

Dear Diary,

I miss Joe so much! It's only Tuesday and I have to wait until Friday to see him again. Last weekend I drove to Providence because he couldn't get away because of a band concert. He made his roommates stay away all day so we could be alone (at night I had to stay in his friend Kathy's room.) Joe is always so afraid of breaking the visitation rules. He says he's been in enough trouble in his life and can't afford any more. He told me about the trouble he got into on the tobacco farm which landed him in the marines. In a way, I'm glad that happened to him because if he had gone straight to college without going away for a few years, we probably never would've met and he might be married to someone else right now.

Joe doesn't talk too much about past girlfriends and he doesn't ask me about Alan. He was the only other boy I ever went with. Joe said he likes to look toward the future and not dwell on the past. When I asked him if he wanted to become a born-again Christian, he said he felt like he already was born again the first time I kissed him! He can be really sweet.

I'm glad he never asks about how it was with me and Alan. I'm not going to lie to him but I want Joe to think he is the first guy I've ever done those things with. I only did that to

Alan because we thought we were going to be together forever. Stupid, silly girl! Now I really feel like I found my forever guy, but I still want to save something for our wedding night. I'm so glad he doesn't pressure me to go all the way.

GF

December 10, 1978

Dear Diary,

I just got back to my dorm from the weekend in Providence. When I visit Joe at St. Dom's I can't stay over in his dorm. Stupid Catholics! I have to sleep in one of his (girl) friends' rooms. When he wants to come up to see me, they call from the front desk to see if the girl wants to accept the visitor. Joe gave me the codename "Mo" when he calls because he said there are so many Maureens, called Mo, that the security guy won't know I don't live in the dorm. Pretty smart! There are no Georgies there so I go by Mo and now that's my nickname. I like it.

Last night we went to a mall in Rhode Island and went to a jewelry store and looked at engagement rings. Joe said he just wanted to get a "ballpark" of how much it would cost him for a "decent" ring. When I tried one on I was so excited (and scared too!) I wish he had the money now, but Joe said it would probably take him a year to put that much money away. Next Christmas maybe? We are so much in love!

GF

17

"Do you really think your father will let us get married?"

"You mean, because you're black?" Georgie knew there would be no other reason. "He doesn't seem to mind us going out. I even think he likes you. You made him laugh once, and he doesn't ever laugh."

"Yeah but going out and getting married are two different things. Do you think he knows I'm staying over in your room?"

"If he knew that, he'd kill you, black or white!"

Joe was not so sure Big George was so oblivious to what seemed obvious. He thought it was more likely willful ignorance. Most people are afraid to look at what they don't want to see. Maybe George feels like, if his daughter knew he didn't mind her sleeping with her boyfriend, as long as he was treating her right, she would lose respect for her father as if he were derelict of duty.

George knew Joe didn't have a car. How could he explain the fact that Joe was already in Georgie's room when he and Georgie's mom stopped by campus for a visit that Sunday after church? With Joe's gym bag on the end of Georgie's bed? Did he think Joe had hitched a ride all the way from Providence that morning just to turn around and go back a few hours later? Really?

But even as George was tacitly overlooking his daughter's discreet "courting" behavior, Joe knew that letting your white daughter marry a black man, even in 1982 (when they hoped to be married) was a lot to swallow. This thought always gave Joe a greater appreciation of what his own parents had dealt with a generation earlier.

"I think he'd be more OK with me marrying a black guy than a Jewish kid," Georgie offered, trying to lighten the mood. "At least you're some kind of Christian."

She turned suddenly serious. "You're going to ask him for his blessing, aren't you?"

"Of course I am," Joe answered defensively, "but not now. I see that as a courtesy, a formality really. I'll ask him when we're ready to get engaged. I mean, we're talking about getting engaged a year from now."

"But what if he says no? Do we really want to wait another year to find out he won't let us get married?"

"Are you saying you wouldn't marry me without your father's blessing?"

Georgie's face flashed red, then flushed. "I don't know. I don't want to think about that. I'm his only child."

"Sounds like he's got more to lose by saying no than you do." Joe was not sure his last comment helped much. These were the times when Joe felt their age difference most acutely. It was only four years, but it was more about which four years they were. Joe was just old enough to have caught the tail end of the Vietnam era "generation gap" when adolescents patently rejected the attitudes, morals, and decisions of their parents without regard to the presence or absence of any wisdom nuggets contained therein. Georgie just missed most of that rebellious spirit and was coming of age in a time of apathy and complacence when kids ignored their parents, or at the very least, went along to get along.

"Are you saying we should get engaged now?" Joe was trying to stretch a single into a double.

A still stunned looking Georgie now became annoyed. "Why did you bring this up now? Are you afraid that if a year from now my dad says we can't get married this will all have been a waste of time?" Georgie asked Joe, projecting her own fears at the same time.

"No, I'm not wasting my time. As far as I'm concerned, I'm going to marry you no matter what," Joe proclaimed. "Our parents will just have to learn to accept it. I know my parents will. And yours will too, over time, just like my grandparents did." He softened his tone, now more encouraging, "I can't imagine splitting up then any more than splitting up now. I want to spend the rest of our lives together."

Reflecting on this conversation later that day, Joe found it odd that it hadn't culminated in a round of lovemaking, instead of what actually took place: a silent walk through campus.

18

January 1, 1979

Dear Diary,

I am so filled with hope right now. Hope for this new year and hope for forever! Joe and I had the most wonderful New Year's Eve last night. We were at his high school buddy, Grande's house. There were people smoking pot in the kitchen so we mostly stayed in one of the back bedrooms that had a TV. Joe wasn't drinking (I'm sure because of me) so we pretty much stayed to ourselves. As the ball was dropping in Times Square he held me tight and we could hear the countdown as we looked into each other's eyes. We kissed from 1978 to 1979! This will be our first full year together and the first full year of the rest of our lives. Joe said he has never been happier in his whole life. I said I couldn't imagine ever being happier. Joe said he can only imagine being happier when we are married and have our first kid. That made me want to marry him right then! I can't wait to see what our babies look like! I think they'll be cinnamon colored with wavy light brown hair. I learned in genetics class that one of our kids could even have blue eyes because Joe's mom and I both have blue eyes. This is going to be a great year! I am so much in love!

GF

January 14, 1979

Dear Diary,

I have to write this down tonight because if I wait until tomorrow I'll think I had dreamed the whole thing. Joe and I were coming back with his parents from visiting Joe's grandmother. Joe and I were in the back seat and I was feeling sleepy though it was probably only about 8:00. I put my head down in his lap and fell asleep. He nudged me awake and unzipped his pants. I could feel Joe was "in a manly state" (in fact he was as hard as a stick) so I looked up at him and he just nodded. So I did it to him right there, with his parents in the front seat! I can't believe we did that. When we were done we both fell asleep with Joe stroking my hair. When I woke up later I thought I had dreamed it, but I still had Joe's taste in my mouth. I can't believe we did that!

GF

January 21, 1979

Dear Diary,

Well I'm back at school and I can't believe I am actually happy about being back at my dorm. It was a little hard being home for Christmas break because I don't have as much freedom (or privacy) when I'm home with my parents as I do at school. It was great seeing all of my friends from high school, but the truth is, most of them go to college with me. Joe and I thought we would have so much time together since we only live twenty miles apart, but he worked full time at the drug store all vacation. When we did see each other, it was hard to find a place to be alone. He has a large family and his mother is ALWAYS home. One afternoon, we snuck into my Granny's house since she is in the hospital. A couple times we drove up to my school to my dorm room since it was open for the international students. We told my mother we were going to the movies. "Grease again?" she asked. "Didn't you already see that?" Joe told her it was so good he wanted to experience it over and over again. We enjoyed our private joke!

I'll miss him now that I'm here and he's in Providence, but at least when we are together we can be alone together. I can't wait to be together with him forever!

GF

Joe and Georgie, once again, found themselves in her bed fooling around. Joe didn't find a ride this weekend so he ended up taking a Greyhound from Providence to Willimantic on Saturday, then Georgie picked him up at the bus station. In a way it was easier on him because he could tell her what time to pick him up and he didn't need to hitch a ride from some psychopath on the last leg of his journey. Coming in on Saturday instead of Friday only served to stoke their sexual fires and they had some catching up to do tonight.

Tonight seemed different; there was a surreal feeling to it. They both felt it. No words were spoken; they communicated with their eyes, their hands, their lips. Georgie felt like tonight was the beginning of forever. She felt that if Joe asked, she would let him go all the way. She knew that was a crazy idea, but she didn't care. It was almost like she didn't have control over her body. She would never have asked him to, but she would let it happen. Joe didn't ask, at least not in so many words. Foreplay was brief. He was rounding third even before she could lose her flannel nightgown. They made eye contact, and absent any objection, Joe entered her and continued his involuntary rocking. Not all the way at first; there was an obstruction. She was expecting it to hurt. Although she had never had a direct conversation about it with anyone who had actually had intercourse, all her virgin friends seemed to instinctively know it was going to hurt. It didn't hurt. It was more like a feeling of pressure, then release, then euphoria. He was all the way inside her now, thrusting and thrusting. Was she rocking intentionally, or was she just being moved with the natural flow of Joe's powerful primal spasms? She couldn't tell, and it didn't matter. Her pillow was brushed aside and she felt her head knocking against the bookshelf next to her bed in the cramped dorm room. She didn't care.

It was over in just a few minutes but he stayed on top of her and inside her for several more. Georgie didn't feel shame. She had never considered that she might lose her virginity before her wedding night so she never imagined having to feel bad about it. She and Joe were one being now. If he asked her to marry him right now she would say yes. She even wanted to ask him! But there were no words spoken. None were needed. This was the most magical night ever. She fell hard into a deep slumber, Joe already snoring softly in her embrace.

She awoke feeling moist and sticky in her nightgown, clutching her pillow. *I can't believe we did that last night.* She looked across the room at the still snoring Hope. *What is Hope doing here? Where is Joe?* The mind fog lifted, revealing an otherwise unremarkable Thursday morning. Joe was waking up forty-five miles away in his dorm, having gone to bed early, battling his own dreams, but with less happy endings.

19

Looking around him in the cafeteria, Joe didn't see one, solitary guy worth making an effort to become friends with. And looking at the girls only made the weeks seem longer.

Joe started thinking about the friends he did have. He wondered if he wasn't such a good judge of character. In high school he mostly hung out with Eddie. Their friendship was a remnant of the days before either had a driver's license; when proximity dictated who one's friends would be. And now, with the freedom to choose friends from varied backgrounds, Joe was still having trouble connecting.

After dinner he went back to his dorm room where he found it empty, and that was OK with him. When he wasn't with Georgie he didn't mind being alone. He just hated being lonely. He pushed the power button on his stereo. From his south facing room he could only pick up two FM stations; easy listening and easier listening. He fiddled with the dial until he got a decent signal. … *How deep is your love?*

I'm glad Eric isn't around to hear the Bee Gees singing or he'd smash the shit out of my stereo, Joe laughed. *I could never admit to him that I really like this song.* But he really wished Eric was around to help snap him out of this funk. Anytime Joe heard *Rich Girl* by Hall and Oates, or Al Stewart's *Year of the Cat,* memories of Eric and their post-Vietnam time in Germany invaded his consciousness. College friendships seemed so trivial and superficial compared to the bond between brothers in the Corps. That isn't to say that just being around Marine Corps brothers led to easy friendships. When he first got to Germany to serve out his three year commitment, he met up with other black Marines who were being cycled through Germany on their way home from Vietnam. When they found out he had been assigned to guard the embassy, they referred to him as a "house nigger" because he didn't serve in the "jungle" as they had.

It would be great if Eric moved east and he and I could rent a house near Georgie's school. I could get a full-time job and be with Georgie every night and every weekend. She could keep her dorm room just for show when her parents came to visit. The rest of the time she could (unofficially) live with me. I would even hook Eric up with one of Georgie's friends. Maybe even Hope. No, that would be too awkward. It's awkward enough that I've dated both girls. What kind of job could I get with three years of military training and a year and a half of college? Maybe I should just finish out this year and see if St. Dom's will grant me an Associate's degree? I'm sure I could get a job with an Associate's degree.

Joe emerged from his free association with an actual viable idea. He decided he would transfer to Georgie's school at the end of this school year. He was sure his veterans' benefits would transfer with him. *Hell, it would even save Uncle Sam some money if I transfer to a state school.* He became aware of Paul

McCartney's voice singing *With a Little Luck*....

For the first time since April 1975, Joe was starting to believe in luck...just a little.

February 3, 1979

Dear Diary,

I was reading back through some of my diary entries and it made me realize that every single one was about Joe (and before him they were all about Alan). It's like I have no life outside of him. All I do is drift through each day during the week, just existing till I can see him on the weekends. Although I love him, I feel like such a pathetic high school girl hung up on a guy I can't live without. I really need to start living my life!

GF

Georgie was beginning to see the nascent buds of her childhood dreams starting to bear the anxious fruits of womanhood. She began to realize that eighteen was just the springtime of adulthood. She was spooked. She was an adolescent girl checking off the boxes of the adult goals she was yet unprepared to accomplish. She was wary of the adult roles and constructs that would confine her if she continued down this path.

February 6, 1979

Dear Diary,

I never thought about it before but "Dear Diary" sounds so cliché. I mean, who am I writing to? Myself. But "Dear Me" makes me sound like an old lady…"Oh dear me!" And "Dear Georgie" sounds so formal. I could use "Dear Mo," Joe's nickname for me, but that just sounds like Joe is writing to me, not me writing to me. So I guess I'll just stick to Dear Diary for now.

Joe called me tonight at 7:00. Not 6:55; not 7:05, but 7:00 (or nineteen hundred hours as Joe calls it). He always calls at 7:00 on the dot on Wednesday night to tell me what time he is coming on Friday. I know he is sitting by the phone for ten minutes waiting to call me because he sets his watch ten minutes fast so he won't be late for anything. Joe said the Marine Corps tried to break him of that habit, but he can't stand being late for anything. Joe can be really intense at times (all the time). Sometimes that's really good, like when we're making love he's very passionate. But other times it's not so pleasant. He can be a real nudge and it's hard to relax around him. But mostly it is great because I know he really cares and loves me intensely.

Some weeks I drive to Providence for the weekend if Joe has a band commitment Saturday or Sunday. But usually he comes here because we can sleep together at my dorm, not his. (My father would kill me, or both of us, if he knew Joe was sleeping over.) I love sleeping with him. I love how his skin feels next to mine. He's so warm we don't even need a blanket! I love the way he smells. I love the sound of his breathing. Most of all, I love waking up next to him knowing we have the whole day to spend together. I dream for the time we can sleep together every night.

It's so hard waiting for Fridays to come. But that's enough of that for now. I have a bio exam tomorrow so I need to get some sleep. Goodnight.

GF

20

March 3, 1979

Dear Diary,

Sometimes Joe makes me feel stupid. I always thought of myself as a smart girl but he seems to be constantly correcting me. I know he is a few years older than me, and has seen more of life, but still I don't like it. The other day I made a new bulletin board, but I wrote on it "bulliten" board. He said, "That's why you go to this school and I go to St. Dom's." He said it in a teasing way but I think he meant it.

I told him he makes me feel dumb sometimes and I want him to love me for who I am. He told me he loves me as a woman with so much potential. "When you think I'm correcting you, I'm just challenging you to grow and be the best you can become." I wish he'd stop "challenging" me and love me for who I am now, not for someone he hopes I will become.

GF

Joe and Georgie never developed a healthy repartee. She was easy-going and pliable. He was more on edge. Georgie noticed this difference but believed that "opposites attract."

She had no brothers or sisters so she never had to compete with siblings for attention, love, or familial supremacy. There was no one pushing her and no one to push back on. Her only desire, common to most only children, was to succeed and please her parents.

Joe didn't recognize his demeanor as being competitive, but that was his style none the less. As part of a large family, he was accustomed to challenging those he loved, and to being challenged by them. With Georgie, he mostly enjoyed the respite of having a compliant girlfriend, but at times he wished she would stick up for herself and not be such a pushover.

They lay there on her bed, under the covers, naked and a little sour smelling from their nocturnal activities. Neither wanted to emerge from their warm cocoon, but both had to pee. Peeing was going to be a team effort because she had to guard the bathroom door when he was in there, inside this all-women dorm. But for now they were staying put on this chilly morning.

"Cut it out. You're tickling me. You're gonna make me wet the bed," Georgie giggled.

"Wow. You are ticklish," he teased as he ran his fingers over her torso. "Why are women so ticklish?!"

"Maybe because we have an extra rib."

"I beg your pardon?"

"Who talks like that? You sound like you're fifty."

He pretended to ignore her dig because of the shame he felt. He knew nobody his age used the expression "I beg your pardon?" in place of "excuse me?" but it was just a relic of his time when he was avoiding speaking the letter "s."

"You have an extra rib?"

"All women do."

"Where'd you hear that?"

"It's in the Bible. In Genesis. Eve had an extra rib."

"It doesn't say she has an extra rib."

"What do you know about the Bible? You're a Catholic."

"I'm also a Marine. When we shipped out to Vietnam, they gave everyone a Bible. I actually used to read it when I was doing overnight watch and there was nothing to see. Why don't you show me where it says Eve's got an extra rib." Joe's tone was playful, but with the edge of incredulity.

Georgie reached for her dust-free Bible on the book shelf above the bed. King James version, of course. She deftly opened to the correct book, chapter, and verse. Had this been any other Bible passage, Joe would have been impressed *but Genesis is on page 1 for Chrissake!* Joe thought.

"Here it is: Genesis 2:21," she began reading, "And the Lord God caused a deep sleep to fall upon Adam, and he slept: and he took one of his ribs and closed up the flesh instead thereof; and the rib which the Lord God had taken from the man, made he a woman, and brought her unto the man. And Adam said, This is now bone of my bones, and flesh of my flesh: she shall be called Woman, because she was taken out of Man.''

"Hold it right there" interrupted Joe. "Just stop. Listen: Number one: you can't take this stuff literally. The Bible was written as a bunch of stories to be told orally to a bunch of illiterate people in a way they could understand. Earth as we know it, and all the animals, weren't created in six days. It took millions of years. Even Jesus spoke in parables. Do you really think camels pass through the eyes of needles?" (He didn't wait for an answer.)

"Number two: Even if you took the story literally, how do you know the rib God took from Adam wasn't an extra rib? Which leads me to number three: Whether you believe the Bible or not, the fact is, men and women have the same number of ribs. And number four, you skipped right over Chapter One. Here, let me see that." Joe grabbed the Bible from Georgie. "Read this; start right here," Joe said, pointing to Verse 27.

"So God created Man in his own image, in the image of God he created him; male and female he created them." "Hmmm," she paused.

"Keep going," Joe pushed as he read along over her bare shoulder.

"And God blessed them and said to them, 'Be fruitful and multiply.'" She kept reading to the end of the chapter; the end of the Sixth Day.

"So you see, how could God have created Eve out of Adam's rib after the seventh day when he already created them both on the sixth day? You're a smart girl, I mean you're pre-med for

Chrissakes. You should know men and women have the same amount of ribs. If you said that in class someday, they would laugh you straight out of the lecture hall."

Now, feeling ashamed, confused, and really pissed off, Georgie closed the Bible, got up, put on her robe, and headed to the bathroom.

"Wow, that went south in a hurry!" Joe said to himself. He won the battle but knew this was a war he was bound to lose. In his mind he was back on the tobacco farm wondering how being "right" could be so wrong.

He made a mental note to himself; a pledge really*: when you're in bed with a woman, don't bring up anything controversial (read: keep your fucking mouth shut!)*

21

He had been in her room all of one hour. The usual Friday afternoon. Finish classes, eat a quick lunch, meet his ride behind the student union, get dropped off at the Route 44 turnoff, try to call Georgie from the payphone (no answer), hitch the last six miles, run up the stairs, make love, relax/snooze, and think about supper. It was one rut Joe didn't mind getting stuck in. Of course, it would have been better if they were at the same school and could see each other all the time. Joe had been working on this plan for a couple months since the idea popped into his mind one lonely Monday night. If he was going to transfer, he needed to make a decision soon as the deadline for next year was quickly approaching. His brother, Eldon, had done the same thing when he was in school. After two years of conducting a long distance relationship he'd had enough and decided to transfer. Only problem was, he hadn't told his girlfriend until after he made all the arrangements. He had wanted to "surprise" her. Well, she'd had enough too….of him. As much as she feigned loneliness while they were apart, she secretly enjoyed the arrangement; the flexibility it gave her to fool around on the side. So there was a surprise when he broke the news to her, only the surprise was on him. He ended up staying at his original school but lost his housing for the next year, and his girlfriend forever. He did learn a valuable lesson in communication that he was generous enough to impart to his younger brother, Joe.

So, as they relaxed in the afterglow, Joe was set to tell Georgie of his plans to transfer so they could be together full time. *With all our talk about being together forever, why not start now?*

Georgie got up to turn on a light before they both fell asleep and missed supper. Taking her robe from the back of the door, she wrapped herself up and sat down at the desk and looked over at Joe, still naked on the bed. Usually she would make them both a cup of cinnamon tea on her hotplate, a taste Joe had acquired on humid mornings in Kim-Ly's Saigon apartment. Today there was no tea….Georgie looked away from Joe and cast her unfocused gaze at the beige carpet.

"I have to tell you something."

Just by the tone, Joe knew it wasn't a casual "I want to be with you forever" something. No, there was a gravity in her voice that made his stomach clench and in the three or four second eternity he went from afterglow bliss to *Holy shit, she's breaking up with me!*

"Somebody kissed me."

"What do you mean someone kissed you? Did you kiss him back?"

"No, I told him I have a boyfriend."

"Who was it? How did it happen?"

"I feel really bad. He said he wanted to get my notes from biology and asked if he could come by and pick them up. I was showing him the notes and he just kissed me."

"Who is he?" Joe asked more strongly this time.

"His name is Ira. Ira Benjamin Shapiro."

"He's a Jew?"

"How did you know?"

He shook his head. "Wow. You have led a sheltered life! So, you even know his middle name? Ha, his initials are IBS! Irritable Bowel Syndrome! What a shitty name!" Joe regained his focus and turned serious again. "Have you been seeing him?" His gallows humor, so finely honed during his rooftop watch duty in Saigon, belied the anger and dread that was beginning to creep in.

"No. I told you. I told him I already have a boyfriend so we could only be friends."

"Did you tell him we're serious? That we've been talking about getting engaged?"

"No."

"Did you tell him he can't be coming over here to get notes...or anything else?"

"No. I'm really sorry. Are you mad?"

"No, you did the right thing. You just gotta realize guys are gonna do or say whatever it takes to be with you. You're beautiful and this is going to happen all your life. You need to be looking out for this kind of thing.

Tomorrow morning you and I are going to go over to his dorm, together, and tell him we are serious and we're going to be together forever. OK?"

"OK."

"You promise? Are you strong enough to do it?"

"Yes, I can do it. You really don't need to come."

"Yes I do! I am going to be there. I need to meet diarrhea man. He needs to hear this loud and clear and there can be no doubt in his mind. If he is a good person, he'll back off. Is there any doubt in *your* mind?"

"No, I love you and I want to be with you."

"OK, let's get drethed and get something to eat. Someday we'll laugh about thith." Joe could feel himself slipping.

Joe knew, even though the transfer deadline was quickly approaching, that this subject had to wait for another time. Right now he had a whole head full of other shit to deal with. He could hardly believe she had agreed to go see Ira Benjamin Shapiro in the morning. He had really just thrown that out there to test her. *She passed the test! Maybe she wasn't the weak teenage girl she appears to be. Extremely naïve, but maybe not so weak.*

121

After supper they went to see "Grease" for the fifth time at the campus cinema. Back at her room they fooled around again and went to sleep for the night. Usually, after a couple rounds of sex, Joe slept like a corpse. But this night was different. He couldn't get comfortable in the narrow college-issue twin bed. Every time he moved, his arm or leg brushed against her naked body. He listened to her soft sleeping breaths. He could see the outline of her breasts and thighs under the sheet in the dim green light given off by the mercury parking lot lamps outside her curtain-less window. He found himself getting aroused all over again and he wanted to do it one more time.

It reminded him of their first night they spent together last October. They had only been seeing each other a couple months. They had been fooling around every chance they could, but had not spent the night together. It was her weekend to visit Joe at his college. Because of the archaic parietal rules at St. Domenic's, she was not permitted to stay over in a men's dorm. Joe would always arrange to have Georgie sleep in one of his female band mate's rooms.

They had gone to a "mixer" and were having a good time, but Joe really wanted to get some alone time with Georgie. She looked so wholesome and pure in her handmade dress. She was so unlike the girls who went to St. Dom's, with their designer clothes and makeup. And Billy Joel was right about *Catholic girls starting much too late!*

Over the noise of the music, Joe asked, "So, what's Hope doing this weekend?"

"She went home to see some friends and go apple picking."

"Let's get out of here!" He led her up the stairs and out the main door of the student union.

Once out in the crisp New England air Georgie asked, "What do you want to do now?"

"Let's drive back to Connecticut. Hope's gone and we'll have the room to ourselves. Are you ready to do this?"

She gave him an excited hug. "I'm ready!"

They arrived late back at her dorm. In their fever to get inside her room, they forgot her suitcase in the hall, where it remained until the next morning. (She wouldn't need the change of clothes anyway for what they had planned.)

They immediately did it and crawled under the covers. Neither of them slept all night. Usually, regardless of the time of day, sex induced sleep. Each time one or the other moved or turned over, the skin on skin contact only aroused them again. Even after three times they still could not fall asleep. The newness of the situation was just too new.

Tonight was different from that first night together. Their lovemaking was even more spirited than usual. Joe suspected that Georgie was giving it a little extra effort to prove to him he was the only one. Joe recognized the ominous threat for what it was: he had a tiger by the tail and he was losing his grip.

22

April 4, 1979

Dear Diary,

I am so unhappy. I'm confused and really don't know what to do about Joe. It has only been a couple weeks since he made me go with him over to Ira's dorm and tell him Joe and I are hoping to get married someday so Ira needs to back off. And today, Joe was home on his spring break so he was going to pick me up after rehearsal. He was parked right in front of the auditorium as Ira and I came out. When I got in the car he had that same look in his eyes as he had on my birthday when Alan almost came to see me. He was so pissed. He said, "I thought this was settled. I thought he was going to back off?" I told him Ira and I are just friends; nothing more. Joe said, "You might want to be friends, but he wants to get into your pants." I hate it when talks vulgar like that to me.

I didn't dare tell Joe that while we were walking out of the building Ira asked me to go to his grandfather's ninetieth birthday party with him. I didn't tell Joe anything. He dropped me off at my dorm without speaking and didn't even kiss me goodbye. I just don't see why he doesn't want me to have guy friends. I cried most of the afternoon and didn't go down to supper. I just don't know what to do.

GF

Joe was also feeling out of sorts. Really out of sorts. He was home on spring break. He wasn't one who could afford to go to Bermuda or Florida for spring break. Even if he had the money, he would have put it away for Georgie's engagement ring. He hoped to spend as much time as possible during break with Georgie. Since their school breaks didn't coincide, it afforded them the chance to visit privately in her dorm room and not have to hang out at either one's house.

Joe felt that if he could spend some quality, concentrated time with Georgie, it would help solidify their relationship, having been recently rocked by the Ira Benjamin Shapiro kiss. So the goal for spring break was to get the love affair finally back on track without outside influences or distractions. Joe was waiting outside in her car when he saw the two of them coming out of the auditorium and he felt heat building up behind his eyes.

It also gave genesis to a feeling he had never had before, anti-Semitism, and that made him feel even sicker. Joe didn't know a lot of Jews in his life, having grown up in a small farm town in Connecticut. But the few he did know, including Attorney Goldberg, he liked very much. They were even his friends in high school. Joe knew about anti-Semitism of course, but it was an affliction that had never plagued him before. He hated that it was seeping into his psyche now. Even his best USMC buddy, Eric, was Jewish and he would have defended him with his life. But this new ugly feeling was powerful and he felt it with every thought of "IBS." He thought, *Next time I see him, I ought to kick him right in the matzo balls.*

He told Georgie when he saw her coming out of the building with IBS, he couldn't help feeling all their good days together were behind them. He was enveloped by a sense of doom.

Earth, Wind and Fire's *"After the Love Has Gone"* was playing on the car radio.

He had always hoped his relationship with Georgie would change him as a person, but he was hoping for positive change, not bigotry. He was hoping for a second chance at love after losing Kim-Ly in Vietnam; not looking for a new way to hate. The thoughts of Kim-Ly and Eric brought him back to boot camp.

23

1975

They sat on the ends of their adjacent cots polishing their boots to that "new car shine" that Sergeant demanded. The fading light from the orange sun made it almost impossible to find every scuff and ding accumulated from a day of punishment. But they kept polishing because tomorrow, under Sergeant's critical oversight, the morning sunlight would betray a young marine's best efforts and set the tone for the whole day. Each new marine knew this was just one of a thousand things they must do, not for any real reason, but just because Sergeant ordered them to do it.

This morning they were instructed to take the bowl from their mess kit, fill it with water from their canteen, and shave using their boots as mirrors. Then they promptly laced up their boots and marched-ran a five mile loop through the red South Carolina mud.

"So, what kind of name is Sklar?" Joe asked, never taking his eyes off his boots.

"It's Jewish," replied Eric.

"Oh."

"Is that a problem?"

"No, just wondering is all."

"What kind of name is Davis?" Eric returned the volley.

"It's a slave name."

"Oh, OK."

"Is that a problem?"

"No, it was a stupid question," Eric admitted.

Eric and Joe had each experienced some degree of prejudice because of his name and complexion, respectively. But both felt they had not had to deal with the amount of hate one might expect for a Jew and an African American living in a white, Christian society. Eric always felt lucky his name wasn't Goldberg or Silverstein, or any 'berg or 'stein for that matter. Joe grew up in a small rural town in New England where there were so few blacks that no one seemed to pay attention….as long as he stayed in line and ignored the occasional slur. (Joe and his brother climbed the neighbor's trees until the neighbor cut off all the lower branches, telling Mrs. Davis that was the only way he could keep "those monkeys out of the trees.")

Joe and Eric compared slurs: kike, hymie, dirty Jew, Jew boy, Yid, hook-nosed bastard, and Eric's favorite, Christ killer. Joe contributed: tar baby, coon, jungle bunny, shine, spook, nigger, and the all-purpose "boy." They had a good laugh, then laughed a little harder when Eric suggested it was a good sign when a friend used a racial slur. "It just shows they're comfortable around you," he offered half-heartedly.

Race was never again discussed in all the time these two marine brothers knew each other.

24

1979

It was a rainy, sloppy, spring Sunday in Connecticut. The well-worn footpaths on this normally bucolic New England university campus today reminded Joe of the Vietnamese tidal rice paddies he had flown over on his farewell chopper flight out of country.

Joe and Georgie had huddled (but not cuddled) in her dorm room most of that dreary day. She was as affectionate in spirit as a person could be without having actual physical contact. "The things we did together I did because I thought we would be together forever. Now I'm not sure and I don't want to lead you on," she would tell Joe whenever his advances became too overt. This recent stance was confusing and frustrating to both of them. Joe was trying to be understanding, giving Georgie the needed time and space. Joe felt he had to be on his best behavior all the time, suppressing his real desire to shake some sense into Georgie. He wondered which feelings were his "real" feelings. Isn't it just as real to want to change to be acceptable to your mate? But maybe the change wasn't real, only manipulative. If she fell for it, would she be loving the real Joe, or the adapted, fake Joe? In any case, it didn't feel real.

He had arrived on campus on Saturday and they spent the day walking hand in hand all around campus. It was a lovely spring day. To the casual observer, they looked like any other young couple in love. Saturday night they went to the University Movie House to see "Hair." Joe figured that "China Syndrome" might be too heavy for a couple already saddled with emotional baggage, and he thought the full frontal nudity scenes in Hair might induce Georgie to be more receptive to physical intimacy later that night.

After the show they went back to her dorm; Georgie singing the production numbers in the car on the short ride. When they arrived at her dorm, she asked Joe not to come up. Joe was incredulous and sat in stunned silence in Georgie's car for several minutes after kissing her goodnight and watching her slender figure ascend the four steps to her dorm. Joe drove twenty minutes to his parents' house as he was out of other viable options for the night (there was no way he was going to drive all the way back to Providence only to have to come back tomorrow with Georgie's car. And as a black man with a criminal assault record, he thought sleeping in a car outside a women's dormitory was just plain asking for trouble).

There were still a couple lights on at his parents' house at 11:30. Mr. and Mrs. Davis were not party people. A more likely reason for the life signs was that this was probably Mrs. Davis' "on" weekend as the 3-11 ER nurse. Joe's mom welcomed him home with suspicion, not surprise. Nothing surprised her anymore, and after a weekend night shift in the ER, nothing phased her.

Joe had never acknowledged he was spending his weekend overnights in Georgie's dorm, so he casually explained he was in for the weekend to see Georgie and he needed a place to crash. Mrs. Davis had never acknowledged she knew full well that Joe was sleeping with Georgie almost every weekend night, but she didn't challenge Joe's impotent claim.

Joe arose early Sunday morning and drove Georgie's car to campus to pick her up to drive to Oakville Baptist Church. He was in a foul mood having spent a ridiculous night in his childhood twin bed. Georgie was waiting in the lobby of her dorm, Joe having arrived promptly on schedule at 0-900 hours. She had even gotten to the lobby a few minutes early to eliminate the need for Joe to come up to her room (there were some Sundays in the past when they just skipped church altogether and decided to stay in bed).

They embraced and kissed good morning as Georgie launched into the car, trying her best to avoid the downpour. She scooted over (out of habit?) to the center of the bench seat. As they drove to the church, Joe instinctively reached down with his free right hand and rested it on her exposed left knee and lower thigh. He was so glad winter pantyhose season was over! Joe gave her knee a squeeze and Georgie leaned in and placed her left hand on his right hand, but did not attempt to remove it.

After the service, these once-and-future fornicators drove back through the washed out secondary roads of north eastern Connecticut, each with wildly different assessments of where their relationship was, and where it was headed.

That Sunday afternoon they napped. Well actually, Georgie napped while Joe lay awake with an hour-long, unrequited erection. They had plans to meet Georgie's parents for dinner, so Georgie got up and dressed in front of Joe. This act just added to his frustration and confusion. *Is she just teasing me? Is this a signal that she wants me to stay tonight? I hope so since I don't*

132

have a ride back to school.

Joe and Georgie were ready and waiting in the lobby when Big George and Georgie's mom pulled into the parking lot. As the young couple ran out to the car, Georgie splashed in a large puddle/small pond, soaking her high-waisted polyester slacks.

"Oh, I can't believe this! I just bought these pants! I need to go change."

Joe stayed put as it would have been a scandalous acknowledgement if he were to accompany Georgie to her room while she changed. Georgie's mom offered to go up with her, but she was summarily shot down by her daughter. Joe was trapped in the backseat of the blue, Plymouth Fury wagon. An ambush that would have made the VC proud commenced immediately, as if on cue.

She started, "You've been seeing a lot of Georgie."

Oh, if they only knew how much of Georgie I have seen! "Yes, I see her as much as I possibly can."

George jumped right in: "So Joe, what are your intentions with my daughter?" These nine words may have been the most Big George had spoken to Joe since the pre-third-date interrogation.

"Wow. OK. Well, since you asked I will tell you," Joe responded, almost relieved that he could get this off his chest and possibly enlist the help of other adults who had Georgie's best interests in mind. "But the answer I give you might be different than if you'd asked me a month ago. My intention is to marry your daughter and to spend the rest of our lives together."

There was a brief, unsurprised silence as this registered with her parents. Then George asked, "What did you mean your answer might be different if I asked it last month?"

"Last month I would have said the same thing, and Georgie would have agreed with me. But right now, she's not sure she wants to spend the rest of her life with me."

"Did something happen? You seem to be getting along fine," chimed in Georgie's mom.

"Yes, something did happen. Georgie met another guy. He kissed her and now she's confused."

Joe earnestly conveyed the situation to them, not understanding that there could have been any augmenting issues for which he bore responsibility which could have deepened Georgie's uncertainty.

"Didn't she tell this other boy about you?" she asked.

"Yes, we both confronted him. He said they just want to be friends, but now they can't seem to stop bumping into each other all over campus, and Georgie even went to his house a couple weeks ago for a family birthday party!"

"What's his name?" George inquired, almost menacingly.

"Ira Benjamin Shapiro."

"He's a Jew?" was the response from both front seat occupants.

"That's exactly how I reacted!"

"Should we talk to Georgie?" asked her mother.

"No, I think this is something she just needs to figure out for herself. School will be over in another six weeks and I think, once I get her home and away from him, she'll come to her senses. What would you say to her anyway?"

"I don't know," she continued, "I guess I would tell her to be careful and not throw away something special."

"That's very nice of you. I have never asked you, or Georgie, what you two think of me. Or us."

"Well, we're both very fond of you. Isn't that right, George?" George nodded. "We think you're a nice couple."

Joe knew this day would come, or at least he hoped it would. When he pictured it in his mind, it was a long way off...not today, maybe a year from now. He and Georgie had even talked about it back during their argument about what she would do if her father said no. Joe thought he would have plenty of time to plan and obsess about what to say and when, how, and where to say it. Joe would be in control of all these factors. He had a vague idea that it would take place in George's converted breezeway family room, the only place Joe could picture finding George alone. He would have to get Georgie to take her mom into another room on some pretense. It might be awkward. It might be strained. But it would be over quickly. Joe had not even been thinking much about it lately, given the state of affairs with Georgie. In any event, Joe believed it would be several months before he even had to worry about it, if at all. Until now.

Joe cleared his throat. "This is a conversation I intended to have with you eventually; many months from now. But since you brought it up, I wanted to make sure I understand you. Are you saying, sir, that I have your blessing to ask your daughter to marry me?"

For a mini-eternity, the only sound coming from the front seat was from bodies squirming and changing positions on vinyl upholstery. George was realizing it was much easier to talk around the subject than to address a direct question. But this conversation was of his own making and it was one for which he was preparing/bracing/dreading for the last eighteen years. Georgie's mom thought they had answered the question already. Joe wondered how long it takes for a young woman to change her pants!

George and his wife looked at each other, then George, looking in the rearview mirror at Joe, spoke: "You have our blessing."

"Thank you, sir. That means the world to me. But it sounds like you have some reservations?"

"She's too young to get married," was his quick reply.

"I agree, and I wasn't planning to talk to you about this for a long time," Joe reiterated. "We wouldn't get married until we both graduate and I get a job. And I don't even know if she would say yes if I asked her now. I need to give her some more time. Thank you both. I promise I will always put her first and will never mistreat her."

Joe reached over the front seat back and shook George's hand just as Georgie returned to the car; clean, pure, and lovely.

"OK, I'm ready, let's go," blurted out this only child, oblivious to the possibility that anything could have transpired in her absence.

Conversation at dinner centered around Georgie, as usual. Except for a few furtive glances between Joe and his prospective parents-in-law, nothing seemed out of the ordinary. While Georgie talked, Joe was occupied with two goals he was trying to objectify:

1) Get Georgie to let him stay over tonight; and
2) Tell her about his conversation with her parents without jeopardizing his authorization to sleep over tonight.

After dinner the young couple was deposited back at the dorm just as the rain let up. Georgie's mom punctuated the evening by rolling down her window and saying directly to her daughter, "You two make such a lovely couple." Georgie smiled at her mom and said goodnight. She turned to Joe and flashed a sweet, sad smile. Joe knew his night, at least, was over.

"I know you don't have a ride back to school tonight so you should just take my car for the week and come back next weekend for Easter," she said preemptively. Joe decided not to bring up the conversation he'd had with her parents. Nothing could help him tonight. With less than a dollar in his pocket, he drove back to Providence, wondering if an eighth of a tank would get him there, all the way testing the upper limits of the Torino's single AM radio speaker as it distorted Paul Davis' voice singing *I go crazy*.

25

She was weepy the entire twenty minute ride home from Joe's parents' house. For a little distraction, Georgie clicked on the car's radio to one of the preset buttons assigned to her by Joe (in her own car!) The soft-rock station was playing Lobo's "Don't expect me to be your friend." She burst into sobs. She knew it was not going to be easy delivering the fatal blow to the relationship, but she had no idea it would be so gut wrenching. She had rehearsed it over and over during the last two weeks. She knew she had to do it, maybe even a month ago. She had stopped sleeping with him (except once during a weak moment) about six weeks ago during her "just not sure anymore" phase. But timing was important too. She knew it would be devastating to Joe when the final breakup came. She wasn't about to do it during finals; for his sake and for hers. *If we can just keep it together until we get home for the summer*, she hoped.

At times during the lead up to the breakup she grew frustrated. This was not a "nobody could have seen this coming" moment for Georgie, but it was for Joe. All the red flags she held up and red lines she crossed seemed to go unnoticed by him. He could not feel the continents shifting beneath his feet. No matter what she did (stopped having sex with Joe, going to another guy's family party as his date, saying she needed space, not being as available on weekends, toning down the intimacy in her daily letters), he didn't seem to catch on. He seemed as desperately in love with her as ever (she had no idea he had already been granted her father's blessing to marry her, Joe never having found the right time to tell her). *If only he could get mad at me and it could blow up into a big fight causing a breakup, it would all be so much easier!*

But he didn't get mad. He listened, was understanding and patient to a fault. She perceived his calmness as pure cruelty. He gave her no other reason to break up with him. She had to do this by herself. For herself.

The only thing that gave her the confidence to complete this difficult task was the knowledge that, when it was over, they would move forward as friends. She knew she could count on Joe to comfort her even at a time when he would be upset about the breakup. When she told this patient, understanding young man she wanted to remain friends after the breakup, she really meant it and believed he would agree. She knew she would be returning home that afternoon without a boyfriend. She never considered she would lose a great friend in the process. She was stunned.

When the words "still be friends" came out of her mouth, Joe's reaction was swift and strong. He knew she wasn't saying it just to soften the blow, and he appreciated that fact. But he realized, again, just how naïve Georgie was, that she would think two former lovers could be friends. "Absolutely not! If we can't be boyfriend and girlfriend, we can't be friends. We were never friends. We were always lovers."

In the coming days, he would grow to regret saying that, even though he knew he was right. Anger started to build in her over the sudden and unexpected loss of her friend, even as her sadness over the breakup dissipated.

Joe girded himself for the long, lonely summer ahead. At 22, he was out of touch with just about everyone in his hometown. Most of his friends from high school, if they were still in college, didn't even come home on school breaks anymore. And those who did were involved with their own girlfriends. The only reason he had come home this summer was to be near Georgie. *If we can just keep it together till we get home for the summer,* Joe's mantra for the last month, came back to eat at him.

Georgie never once felt an ounce of guilt over the sex while they were together. She didn't really consider it sex, but whatever she considered it, she felt no guilt. The only compunction she experienced was from the feeling that she *should* have felt guilt and didn't. In truth, she missed the sex. While "pleasing each other" there was oneness, warmth, love, excitement, danger, acceptance, exhilaration, satisfaction, release, power, vulnerability, and the sense that she had achieved womanhood.

Now she felt despair, disillusionment, sadness, anger, humiliation, frustration, shock, and depression. "This is all self-inflicted. How could I have been so stupid?! Why can't we just be friends?" she wrote in her diary. She had the power to undo everything she had done. She knew Joe would take her back immediately; no questions asked. She believed he would swallow his hurt feelings and never hold this transgression against her. He told her so, many times. She knew if she did go back, it would need to be forever. He would never let her go again.

She felt nauseous and foggy, like the time she had two beers at a friend's birthday party one Thursday night in her dorm. She couldn't concentrate. She even thought she might be losing her hearing since she couldn't tune into what others were saying. She couldn't concentrate enough to read a book, or even watch TV.

She felt this way before, briefly, last summer after she and Alan broke up. But Hope had put her in touch with Joe, and well, here we are again.

Something kept her from running back to Joe and begging forgiveness. *I did nothing wrong!* Was it pride? No, she had cried out all of her pride already. Was it weakness? No, it took much more strength not to go back to him. Was it Ira waiting in the wings? No, she had convinced herself that this had nothing to do with Ira. She just needed to "find herself" and she knew she could only do that in her own wilderness.

Joe had said the whole "finding yourself" concept was "bullshit." He said that "dropping out and finding yourself was so 1969, not 1979. How can you find yourself when you don't have a clue where to look? You're probably on the wrong road anyway! All the road signs are pointing this way, and yet you always head the other way!" He, too, was feeling nauseous and foggy, but some of that could have been due to his recent rediscovery of beer, and finding a few leftover three year old red pills in a pocket of his knapsack from his time in Saigon.

26

June 6, 1979

Dear Diary,

Well, Joe and I broke up a couple weeks ago. It was awful. I don't know if it is forever, or just for now. It is strange but I feel more attracted to him right now than I did all spring. We've seen each other a couple times since and both times we made love. Joe cried the last time when I later told him it didn't mean we were back together. That really broke my heart to see him cry. Now, without his daily letters and his phone calls, I miss him so much. I am just trying to get through each day.

My mother has been acting strange lately too. Last summer when we started going together, my mother didn't seem to like Joe; probably because he is black. But now she thinks I'm crazy to have broken up with him. She said Joe is really going places in life. I don't want to be just going along with someone who is going places. I want to be the person that is going places and have someone going along with me.

GF

Joe surveyed the local female talent pool and saw that it was pretty well picked over. He spent some time with the ex of one of his friends, but that was just to keep from being alone. He liked her Fiat convertible as much as he liked her.

He saw Georgie three more times that summer, each time having sex. Each time, Joe was transported back to their relationship and his hopes for the future were all restored. For Georgie, it was just a moment of pleasure without the burden of Joe planning out the rest of her life. He wanted to become a couple again; lovers. She wanted to salvage a friendship. She wanted to keep him close, but "on ice." She wasn't completely sure she had made the right decision to break up with Joe, and she really didn't know how long it might take to "find herself." At the end of each encounter, when it was time to part and go back to being a former couple, Joe was, each time, devastated anew, and Georgie left bewildered that Joe couldn't "just live in the moment."

Joe felt pathetic that he couldn't just enjoy the sex when he could get it because it sure was hard to come by. One thing he knew for sure: this was killing him from the inside out. He likened her to eating a perch: the meat was so sweet and lovely, but you wonder if it was all worth it as you try to dislodge the tiny fish bone that is stuck in the side of your throat hours later. Georgie, too, struggled to reconcile their sporadic interludes. *How can I be going to bed with my former boyfriend when I had stopped sleeping with him while we were still a couple?* Maybe she wasn't the person she thought she was.

They had just enjoyed a couple hours together, holding hands through Monty Python's Life of Brian. "Almost like a date,"

Joe snarked. On the ride back to drop Georgie off at home, out of habit Joe clicked on the AM radio in his mom's new Chevy Chevette. They were greeted by Gloria Gainor's *"I will survive."* Georgie blurted out, "Oh, I love this song. It has really helped me get through this tough time."

"Are you serious!?" Joe was incredulous. He clicked off the radio. "Have you listened to the words? You broke up with me, remember?"

"It's been hard on me too, you know. You were the center of my life and now we're just struggling to be friends. I'm heartbroken over this. I didn't want us to break up and not see each other anymore. It was just something I needed to do until I can figure out who I am!"

"First of all, I was not the center of your life. You are." Joe regretted saying this as soon as it left his lips. "There's an easy way for the pain to stop: all you have to do is take me back. No questions asked, and no looking back, only forward. All you have to do is say yes."

"I can't. I need this time."

"Well, I'm not worried about you surviving. You'll be just fine. You have all the control. You get to decide if you want me, or any other guy. You're completely in control. I'm the one who should be worried about surviving. I don't know how I am going to go on." He paused, his voice softened, almost inaudible now. "You are everything to me. I'm completely lost. And this going out as friends is just killing me. Please, let's get back together."

With each make up/breakup session she became more and

more convinced that Joe was right: former lovers just can't be friends. She wasn't just sad they couldn't be friends. She was distraught about how badly she hurt him. They rode the rest of the way in silence. Joe the non-crier, looked out the driver's side window, surreptitiously wiping away his tears.

Two weeks later they found themselves back in Joe's cramped bedroom at his parents' house in Valley Park. As they lay on his bed after the final time they would ever make love, Georgie asked Joe: "If you could do it all over again, what would you change?"

"Do what all over again?" Joe was hoping she was talking about the sex they just had.

"You know….us. If you and I were just starting to go out together, what would you do different?"

Why is she asking me this? And, doesn't she mean "differently"? Does she want to get back together? Is she trying to blame me for breaking us up so she won't feel so guilty? Or is she fishing for pointers on how to conduct herself in her next relationship?

"Are you asking because you want to get back together and you don't want us to repeat the same mistakes?" Joe asked hopefully.

"No, I'm not asking you to get back together. I just want to know if there's anything you would do different." She was hoping Joe might be able to identify the flaws in their relationship that she couldn't see, but could only feel.

This seemed to Joe to be the kind of question a third party

would ask. *"So, what happened to you guys? You seemed so happy and so much in love. Is there anything you could have done to stay together?"* It seemed like the kind of question a concerned friend would ask, but not a former lover. And if she was going to be asking this, right now seemed way too premature, when everything is still so raw. Joe wondered if he would ever be ready to be hearing this question from Georgie. *We just had sex! Is it really over?!*

"I think we were nearly perfect together and I wouldn't change anything about the way I acted. I didn't do anything wrong. I would change what you did, if I could. You were the one who decided to leave me."

Joe, blinded by righteous indignation, paralyzed by grief, and confused due to his own lack of introspection, was unable to provide a strategic answer. Georgie didn't know what the right answer was either, but she was pretty sure she would have recognized it if she had heard it. But then, she had no idea what to do next. All that remained to their love-fire were a few smoldering embers, too burnt out to be reignited, yet still too hot to walk away from. They lay there silent and naked, too drained to even look for answers on the blank, white ceiling, while the humming window fan dried their perspiration. Neither of them could imagine that this was to be the last time they would ever touch, smell, taste, or see one another.

July 29, 1979

Dear Diary,

Well, it happened again yesterday afternoon. I stopped by

Joe's house after work and we ended up in his bed. I had no intention of fooling around *(Georgie knew this was a lie when she wrote it but she desperately wanted to believe it.)* I just wanted to talk to him to try again to start a friendship. But it seems every time we're together we end up in bed. This has to stop! It's too confusing for both of us. But I want to keep him close because I don't know how long it will take for me to figure this whole thing out… GF

What did Joe miss about her the most? Was it the sex? Well yes, he certainly missed that! Attending a Catholic college meant that was one thing that could not be easily replaced. But it was more than that. Much more than that. He had built his whole future around her. She was his second chance after Kim-Ly. Marriage, kids, and lifestyle: it had all been lined up. Now, gone in an instant, or so it seemed. Now everything was in flux. His plan was shattered. It is one thing to start over, tabula rasa, if there is such a thing. But it's a whole other thing to have to start over with all the pain left behind from what could/should have been. It was almost easier to accept losing Kim-Ly. She really was gone in an instant and there was no chance of bringing her back. She was not to blame.

He was so miserable he wished there was a war on so he could re-enlist. He would volunteer for the front line! Dying for a just cause seemed like a sensible way to relieve his misery. He felt hopeless, and yet he continued to have thoughts that they would end up together someday; somehow. The alternative was just too hard to bear. While they were both away at school, and still a couple, they each wrote the other a letter every day except for the days they were actually together. It was a daily half hour agonizing ritual that reminded them just how lonely they were when they were apart from one another. But now, this summer, after the break up, Joe yearned for that kind of longing that lovers know will be satisfied instantly upon sight of their beloved. Joe's loneliness now seemed unquenchable. And yet he continued to write, albeit sporadically, in hopes of maintaining some kind of lifeline (love-line?) to Georgie.

August 1, 1979

Dear Georgie, I wish I could be saying "Happy Anniversary" to you today (today would have been one year since our first date). I miss you so much. The few times we saw each other this summer were the best three days I've had in my life (except maybe our first overnight together last October!) but they were followed by the worst three nights of my life. It really messed me up even more afterward. It was like breaking up all over again and I just can't understand how we can have such a great time together all day (including fooling around), and then just go back to being broken up when you leave?? This is killing me! But I don't want to not see you at all because I know if we don't see each other, we'll never get back together. And the longer we wait, the harder it will be to get it back to where it used to be. I know you're going to get sick of me writing these sad letters (you probably already are?) And every day without you that my heart literally aches, I'm afraid I'm going to build up resentment for all this pain we are causing each other. You say you still love me, and I know I still love you. So what do you say? For our sake, on our anniversary, can we get back together? PLEASE? Love, Joe

27

Joe's mom had been urging him to get out of the house, see some girls, and stop moping around. "God never gives you more than you can handle," she liked to say.

"Mom, I know that's not true. I was in Saigon. I saw men jump off buildings as the VPA was approaching," he answered.

"That was during war. This is a teenage girl we're talking about. Get a hold of yourself!" Thus ended his encouraging talk with his mother.

Joe's friend from freshman year, Ronnie, came to visit one weekend to escape the oppressive humidity of D.C. His "Black Experience" was completely different from Joe's, having been brought up in urban Washington where whites were the minority. He convinced Joe to drive them into Hartford to find a bar that would be hospitable to young black men. The "dance club" reminded Joe of the discos he went to in Germany, but in Germany, the distinction was American/non-American; not black and white. In this Hartford bar, it was only black. Ronnie, Joe later learned, had cajoled Tanya (or Tonia, or something like that) to dance with Joe. Joe was

149

drinking like he was back in his post-Nam days in Germany. Anita Ward kept singing "You can ring my b-e-l-l-l-" and Tanya kept spinning Joe. Round, and round, and round….Joe ran out to the sidewalk and puked between a Buick and a Chevy.

They returned to Cityside Club the next night, but everything looked different. There was a line of white guys coming out the door. The raucous sounds of The Village People singing *Y.M.C.A.* spilled out onto the sidewalk. Joe and Ronnie approached the line and were met with surprised expressions. "What's up?" Joe asked the leather-attired, last guy in line.

"Hello girls."

"What'd you call us? You're gonna be standing out here a long time. There's only black brothers and sisters in there. We're goin' in," proclaimed Joe.

"Last night was negro night. Tonight it's queer night. But you'd be welcome here, if you like to party. We don't care."

Ronnie seemed unfazed. Growing up in D.C., he was used to seeing all walks of life. But in a big city, each group had its own bar. They didn't need to alternate nights. They drove back to Valley Park and stopped at a package store and got a couple six packs and sat in the Little League dugout near Joe's house. "No offense, Joe, but Hartford is a lame city. We gotta get you back to school and get back in the game."

Joe agreed.

The crop of girls around Joe's age in Valley Park was fairly depleted, but Joe figured he would take another look through the leftovers.

Early one August morning in 1979, Joe drove his mom's car to the other side of town. New Towne Acres was developed on land that was once tobacco farms and cornfields. The relatively well-off families, in their early 1970's-built raised ranches and Cape Cod style houses didn't know it then, but only years later learned that the groundwater that fed their wells was contaminated by all the farm pesticides that had been sprayed on the crops for decades. So whether you smoked the tobacco, or merely lived on land where it had been grown, chances were, you were going to get cancer.

There was one girl Joe knew from high school; they'd played together in the band when he was a junior and she was a freshman. Each year there were always a few cute little flute players coming up. He'd seen her around town a few times that summer and was surprised she wasn't spoken for already. He went over Stacy's house a few nights earlier and they grabbed a couple beers from her dad's garage refrigerator and went down the terraced back yard to the in-ground pool. She had a new rectangular pool illuminated by a single underwater spot light right under the diving board. They turned off the pool light, undressed, and slipped into the shallow end of the pool. Joe had never skinny dipped with a girl before. The only time that he had ever swum naked was on a hot night after a Little League game when none of the boys had their bathing suits, and didn't want to get their baseball uniforms soaked. Even at boot camp, they swam in their boxers. This night would be a totally new experience!

Joe and Stacy made out and tickled and felt each other up, but that's as far as they went. No sense getting carried away while Stacy's parents were still up watching TV in the living room with the windows open on this balmy summer night. Her parents were open minded enough to let Stacy date a black kid a few years older than her, but no parent wants to witness their daughter having sex. But that was a few days ago.

Today Joe was headed back to New Towne Acres, in his mother's car, to pick up Stacy so they could drive to the beach. They were destined for Misquamicut beach in Rhode Island as there was not a single decent beach along the entire hundred mile Connecticut shoreline, from Greenwich to Groton, due to the presence of Long Island on the southern side of the sound.

Joe hoped Stacy would still be sleepy at 6:30 AM as he wasn't in the mood for two hours of small talk on the ride to the beach. But Stacy was her chirpy, bright self when she bounded out of the house to see Joe. "Wow!" he thought, "What will she be like after we stop for coffee!" Joe didn't get to turn on the radio for the entire trip to Misquamicut. Stacy kept the one-sided conversation going without so much as an "um-hum" required from Joe. *How could she have this much to talk about after only three days since I saw her?* wondered a cranky Joe, although, to be fair, they hadn't talked very much that night in the pool.

Joe marveled about his own ability to tune her out. *How am I able to recall, almost verbatim, a college lecture weeks later, when I don't even remember what this girl said five minutes ago!* He wasn't happy about driving without the radio; that was an issue he thought was resolved when Georgie dumped him. But he had plenty of noise going on inside his head to keep him occupied, without having to listen to Stacy.

They made good time and arrived at the beach parking lot before 9, and had to wait a few minutes with bulging bladders for the bathhouses to open. Needless to say, at that hour they had first choice among all the private places between the dunes. They found a secluded spot and spread out their blanket. Joe kept his USMC issued wool blanket in his knapsack when he saw the nice bed spread Stacy had brought. His blanket was practically new, having never been needed on the muggy nights Joe slept in the Embassy in Vietnam. *Maybe someday*, he thought, *I will go camping in the Connecticut woods and put all my bush survival training to good use!*

They each brought a cooler too; Joe's filled with beer; Stacy's filled with sandwiches, chips, and potato salad. Right away, upon seeing the cooler contents, Joe judged a stark difference between Stacy and Georgie. A picnic with Georgie started with bread, condiments, lunchmeat, chips, potato salad, and plates, utensils, and napkins. Stacy's feast featured pre-assembled sandwiches, already soggy from the melting ice in the cooler, and forks to eat from the shared container of potato salad. Joe re-confirmed that he needed to move away from his little hometown.

The morning passed OK with occasional dunks in the frigid Atlantic followed by drying naps on the blanket. After a soggy lunch and another avoidance nap, Stacy made her move. She began by stroking Joe's arm, then his shoulder. She moved closer and started kissing Joe but soon realized he wasn't into it. Stacy rolled away. Joe sat up and looked at his hands playing with pebbles in the sand. He felt worthless. *How can I be here at the beach on a beautiful day, with a pretty girl in a bathing suit, she's putting moves on me, and I don't feel anything?* he wondered.

"You can't stop thinking about her," Stacy said flatly, breaking the awkward silence.

"I'm really sorry," answered Joe, still looking down at his pile of pebbles.

"Do you want to talk about her?"

"No. I want to forget about her! ….I'm really sorry. I feel terrible. You're such a sweet girl and I'm sure we could have fun together, but I can't be with anyone right now. My head's really messed up. It's not fair to you."

"Do you want to stay, or should we go?"

"I'm really sorry to have ruined your day. We should go home."

They packed up their towels and blanket, and picked up the empty cooler, and the almost full cooler of beer, and headed to the parking lot.

"It really is a beautiful day," offered the always bright Stacy. Joe brooded on, seeing only the dark storm clouds in his head.

Joe switched on the radio as soon as they got in the car. He was greeted by the sound of Little River Band playing *Lonesome Loser*.

Joe was amazed at his ability to get through each day. He was busy all day working as a cashier at the drug store. About the only excitement he had at the store was after hours when they were cleaning up all the cigarette butts and spent scratch tickets dropped by the low-lifes. Joe or one of his mates would get on the PA system and say, "Good evening shoppers, come on over to our lingerie department for a great sale where we have our bras and panties half off." The boys would roll around laughing at the blushing girls. Great fun for frustrated young men.

During the daytime hours he challenged himself by looking at all the items the customer placed on the checkout counter and calculating, in his head, the total price, including tax. When it was busy, he wouldn't close the cash register drawer between customers. When someone came in and only bought a Pepsi for thirty-five cents and handed Joe a dollar, he would give the customer two quarters, a dime, and a nickel, without ringing up the soda. He liked selling single packs of cigarettes. Marlboro in the box was fifty-nine cents so for change he gave the customer one of each type of coin and didn't have to think about it. He would put the dollar in the drawer and put a little hash mark on the pad next to the register for every sale he didn't ring up. At the end of his shift he would remove from the drawer one dollar for every two hash marks, usually five or six per day. Since the sales were never rung up they wouldn't be counted as missing at the end of the day. The inventory erosion was too small to be detected.

Joe took his stolen "tip" money and mailed it to the bank in Providence each week, enclosing his "Christmas club" coupon. Even with no engagement ring for Georgie to buy, he still had to fulfill the deposit contract of the bank's Christmas club. Joe didn't try to justify stealing the money. He just stole it.

Most evenings were tolerable too as Joe found things to do. On the nights he wasn't playing softball in the men's league, he umpired women's softball games. Looking at the women, aged eighteen to whatever, Joe was struck at how plain and unattractive they could be, even the pretty ones, when dressed for softball and sweating out in the field on a clammy night.

But the nights with little to do were torture for Joe. Without the distraction of work or sports, Joe's mind defaulted to Georgie. Wondering *where is she, what is she doing, who is she doing it with, why did she dump me?* He perseverated himself to a restless sleep every night. There were emotional triggers all around him: the empty mailbox with no letter from her, the silent phone on the wall, a passing green Ford sedan that looked something like her car, or a girl on TV that looked something like her (why did Georgie have to look so much like Marsha Brady!), a song on the radio that they had listened to as they used to fall asleep together. Or worse: that insidious Paul McCartney song (Don't Say Goodnight Tonight) that was such a hit on the radio when they were in the last excruciating weeks of their relationship. All these triggers sent his mind reeling when all he wanted was to sleep so he could forget about her for a few hours.

Sleep, when it did come, was never restful. Dreams of Georgie didn't replace his Vietnam dreams so much as they became entangled with them. Instead of reaching down through the open helicopter door to grab Kim-Ly's outstretched hand, it would be Georgie's face with Kim-Ly's black hair, wearing Kim-Ly's dress. The suicidal South Vietnamese officer, so prevalent in his dreams, now had Joe's face, and Georgie was holding the gun.

One of the recurring dreams that Joe hated most had been revisiting him for the four years since the evacuation of Saigon.

In it, he sees a fat Vietnamese business man wearing a plaid leisure suit, clutching a safety strap inside the last helicopter to leave. Joe is disgusted with this man, as he took a seat that could have gone to Kim-Ly. In the four years of enduring this dream, it had changed very little, until recently when the business man is seen wearing a yarmulke.

By the end of the summer, Joe had had alcohol-induced dates with several girls but none were, in his eyes, the caliber of Georgie. His final date of the summer fizzled as soon as it started. Joe's ever-helpful mother was determined to drag him out of the doldrums. There was a "pretty young nurse," she reported to Joe, who worked at the hospital with her. Mrs. Davis had been working on her for months, even before the breakup between Georgie and Joe. Annette was only a year younger than Joe, having finished her three year RN training last year. She didn't have a "steady guy" and….she was Catholic. Joe both appreciated and resented his mother's meddling in his affairs but, desperate as he was, finally relented to a blind date. He shaved, put on his best clean jeans and the Izod shirt he bought at Marshalls so he might "fit in" better with the preppies at St. Dom's. Mrs. Davis gladly relinquished her car for the night so Joe could take Annette to see *Life of Brian,* a movie Joe had already seen with Georgie, but also the only decent movie showing at the local cinema. Annette still lived at home with her parents a few miles from Joe's house, but in the next town. They hadn't known each other during their high school years. Annette most certainly would have remembered him!

Joe parked in her driveway behind a maroon 1978 Buick Century. He wondered if this was Annette's car from her nursing salary, or if her dad was home. It looked more like a dad car than the Datsun or Toyota he pictured Annette driving.

He walked up the slope of their grass front yard, with inlaid slate pavers, to her cheerful yellow, Cape Cod style house. The wooden front door was open but the screen door was closed. He didn't get a chance to knock before a girl's face materialized. She looked young. She was young. "Are you Joe?" the girl asked incredulously.

"Are you__" Joe began before being interrupted.

"Annette! Joe is here to see you!" yelled the sixteen year old Amber. Joe was invited to stay on the front stoop while he waited. After a few minutes (he was well accustomed to this game) Annette appeared. "Hi… Joe?" she asked, seeming genuinely unsure it was really him.

"Hi Annette, it's nice to meet you," he mustered, wondering who else she might be expecting.

She opened the screen door and stepped out, more to get a better look than to properly greet him. Her shocked look was something Joe had seen before but for some reason hadn't expected tonight. He had let his guard down. He thought this date had been thoroughly vetted, from both sides. Apparently his white mother had not mentioned to Annette that her son was black. It hadn't occurred to Annette to ask. Joe offered his hand to break the awkward three second eternity. Joe wanted to call it a night right then, but he knew his mother would want a full accounting later and he wasn't willing to expose Annette's bigotry. He suspected it would rear its head at some later date at the hospital when Mrs. Davis could witness it live. They rode together to the cinema in Joe's mother's car. The AM radio was turned on but Joe's mind was turned off.

Near the end of August, Joe was busy ringing the cash register at the drug store. He was on auto-pilot as he checked out the winos with their half pints of Gallo White Port and their Pall Malls. Her familiar voice snapped him to attention. Joe had dated Donna for a couple months in high school. She had been one of his cross-border conquests, newly accessible once he got his driver's license. It had never progressed beyond hand holding and brief, tongue-less kisses; not for lack of effort on Joe's part. Donna was just a nice, sweet, wholesome girl. That's not what Joe was looking for, at least not back then. They had drifted apart as Joe searched for someone else who could give him a reason to be homesick once he got to Vietnam. Although five years had since passed, they each, in their own way, regretted the earlier parting. Their relationship had felt like friendship, rather than courtship. Joe couldn't think of anyone who had ever adored him the way Donna did. Donna saw something redeeming in Joe, beyond the pressure she felt from the experiential sexual imbalance in their relationship.

"Hey Donna, how have you been? I haven't seen you in so long."

"I know. I used to write to you when you were in Vietnam but I never heard back from you so I wasn't sure if you were even getting my letters. I gave up after a while." She had a tendency to talk without stopping to breathe.

"What are you up to? Did you ever go back to school?" Joe

asked.

"I've been busy. I got my Associates Degree from the community college. And..."

"That's great! I'm proud of you. I'm in school now too. It's a little weird...being a few years older than everyone. Where are you working?"

"Oh, I'm just helping out my mother at the florist's shop, but on Friday and Saturday nights I've been singing with a group at the Holiday Inn. You should come by sometime!"

"I'm only home for a couple more weeks, but I'll definitely stop by to see you."

Donna took her feminine hygiene products to another register, already blushing as she did so.

True to his word, as he had absolutely nothing else going on, Joe went to see Donna and her trio on Friday night. The lobby of the Holiday Inn was already tired and dated in 1979, with its garish, cheap chandelier and floral print carpeting. As soon as he cleared the lobby and headed toward the bar, he heard her reedy voice belting out Carole King's "I Feel the Earth Move..." The trio consisted of Donna on keyboard and lead vocals and two guys in their early forties wearing brown corduroy vests and blue Chinos; one playing guitar and one on drums. The guy without the wedding ring had a severe comb-over. Donna was wearing a dress that would have been more at home in the hotel ballroom, if there had been a high school prom that night. (Joe wondered why he hadn't asked Donna to the prom five years ago. Maybe that was the dress she would have worn?)

The trio worked their way through their repertoire, mostly Donna Summer hits (which magically started the disco ball a-spinning), another Carole King song, some Linda Ronstadt retreads, and an ambitious rendition of the James Taylor/Carly Simon *"Mockingbird."* Donna had noticed Joe as he walked in; it was hard to miss the only black man in the joint. Joe thought Donna was singing directly to him when she sang *"You Light Up My Life."* Joe laughed to himself that if his Marine Corps buddy Eric were here, he would have smashed all the all the musical instruments after that song!

Donna and the boys finished the night with Olivia Newton-John's *"Would a Little More Love Make it Right?"* Joe answered the question to himself: *Yes.*

Joe stayed until the end and accepted Donna's invitation back to her parents' house for a nightcap. Her parents were already in bed as Joe and Donna quietly made their way to the family room, each carrying a Busch beer. Donna was still in her prom dress, showing more skin between her bust line and neck than Joe had ever seen on her. Joe had been in a good mood as he watched her up on the stage, but his demeanor returned to its new normal, general malaise, as they sat hip-to-hip on the orange tweed couch.

"Are you feeling OK?" asked Donna in her chirpy way.

"Yeah, I'm just a little tired, that's all," he responded unconvincingly.

"I heard about you and Georgie. I know you took it kinda hard."

"I guess that's true," he said flatly, not caring where she would

161

have heard about it.

"You know, I could be your girlfriend. I'd like that."

"Really, you'd want to be my girlfriend?" he asked incredulously.

"Well, why couldn't I?" She feared it was the same reason they had never gotten off the ground five years earlier.

"You really want to be my girlfriend? I'll show you what it's like to be my girlfriend." He swiftly put his hands on her shoulders and pushed her over on the couch. He leaned over on top of her and kissed her hard on the lips as he moved his right hand to her left breast and gave it a squeeze.

"Did you forget who I am? You know I don't do that! Get off me!" She was firm and brisk, but did not raise her voice for fear of waking her parents at the other end of the ranch style home.

Joe sat up and looked at his hands. He couldn't look at her, and he didn't speak.

"I think you should leave."

Joe arose and headed for the door, certain that he would never see her again, and feeling lower than even his "new normal."

On Saturday night he was back at the Holiday Inn. He stayed in the lobby listening to Donna and the vested men, hidden from view by the plastic ficus tree. He waited until the first set finished, knowing the last notes of "*Like a Heatwave*" were his cue to move in. Donna seemed completely unsurprised to see him. Really, she had expected him to appear at any moment that day, knowing he would apologize.

"I feel terrible about what happened. I can't believe I did that to you. I really regret it. I truly regret it." Joe was now in full no "S" mode. She listened silently, patiently, without speaking, sipping her sloe gin fizz through a straw. Her eyes were intently locking on his. "I can't quite find the right word," he admitted.

"Is 'sorry' the word you are looking for?" she offered.

Joe swallowed hard. "Yeth. I'm Thorry."

She forgave him immediately.

He never did.

28

FALL 1979

Joe didn't seem to benefit from the extra three years of maturity from his time in the Marine Corps. A younger man puts a lot of importance on any single year but usually this sentiment is gone when he gets a little older and realizes that time goes by so fast any single year is insignificant. Joe was trying to make up for lost time and believed any 'wasted' year was a tragedy. He was dying to get back to school where he could immerse himself in a campus half-full of co-eds. Maybe as a semi-exotic upperclassman, the odds would be better this year. Georgie was also anxious to get back to campus where her process of self-actualization could begin in earnest.

Georgie settled into the large wooden desk chair in Ira's room. She felt comfortable, safe, and relaxed in his room. He was so different from Joe; not tightly wound and intense. She didn't have any brothers or sisters, but she imagined Ira was what a brother would be like. He was fun, playful, easygoing, and relaxed. Sometimes maybe a little too relaxed. He watched a lot of TV and was a little soft around the middle. But that didn't matter. She really shouldn't compare him to Joe, she thought, since they were just friends. She liked having a guy friend; Joe said it would be impossible for a guy and a girl to be friends because a guy would always be "trying to get into your pants. If he's not trying to get in your pants, he's a homo." The only other guy's dorm room she had ever been in was Joe's, and that was mainly spent in bed. She could go to Ira's room to study and actually get some studying done. The first few times she went there, Ira had tried to kiss her again. But since she set him straight that she was only interested in friendship at this point in her personal identity quest, Ira backed off. Sometimes she wished he wouldn't back off so readily. She enjoyed the ability to relax with Ira, but sometimes she yearned for the feeling she had with Joe. Just riding in the car next to Joe, or sitting in a movie theater holding his hand made her lubricious. She never once had to change her damp panties after hanging out with Ira.

Tonight she sat cross legged in her blue jeans reading her biology textbook on the chair by the window, looking like a Carole King album cover (all she needed was a cat!), while Ira sat on the bed. Ira broke the quiet calm to say, "Mind if I put on some music? I can't study without something on."

Georgie replied, "I like it quiet when I'm studying. Do you have something quiet?"

Ira chuckled to himself. He didn't have any Debbie Boone

handy. "Can I just put it on low?"

"Don't you have any headphones?"

So Ira got up, put on the record, and plugged in his headphones. It was quiet once again, except for the occasional yellow hi-liter tapping his notebook to the 2-4 blues shuffle beat. She could live with that, she thought. Better than actually listening to his rock 'n roll music.

Minutes later the tapping got louder and faster, as Ira started singing along to the refrain, his headphones internally masking his true volume.

Georgie sat there stunned as Ira belted out the lyrics to a Spirit Logic song. Just as he was getting to, "If I have to baby, I come down your chimney flue" Georgie was on her feet screaming at Ira.

"Stop singing that! Stop that! How could you! How dare you! Where did you find that?"

Mystified, and returning to the world beyond his headphones, he shouted back, "Take it easy! Sorry. I didn't know I was singing out loud. No problem, I'll turn it off."

Georgie, still hot, shot back, "You read my diary. I can't believe you would do that! Are you mocking me?"

Confused, Ira asked, "What are you talking about. Find what? I never read your diary. What are you talking about?"

"Where'd you find my poem? That was special to me. You had no right to go through my stuff!"

"Honestly Georgie, I don't know what you're talking about. Calm down. I was just singing along to the record."

"That wasn't the record. That was the love poem Joe wrote for me: *"Two Love Birds"*

Ira smiled widely. "He didn't write that. That's Spirit Logic. You thought he wrote that?"

Georgie, now angry at Ira's smile, proclaimed, "He wrote a whole poem for me to read at church. It goes:

My love is like a birdie,

      Flyin' into your cage.

Your old birdie's gone now,

      It's time to turn the page.

Ira was laughing now, "Oh my God! Holy shit!"

"Stop laughing at me!" Georgie cried, still furious, but a little confused now.

Realizing he couldn't talk his way out of this mix-up, Ira reset the needle on the third track of Spirit Logic's classic eponymous album, and pulled out the headphone jack. He turned up the volume so all the world could hear Joe's love poem!

As Billy Hansen sang out: "Open up your shutters, open your windows too" Georgie stood there, her head spinning, too shocked to cry. Ira stood in his doorway as she ran down the

167

hallway from his room, her ears ringing from the crescendo of "If you let me in baby, I'll fly the coup with you…with you…. with youuuuuuuuuuuuuuuuuuu." She was halfway across the expansive rural campus before she realized, wild-eyed, sweating, and gasping for breath in the chill of the early autumn night, that she had left her coat, books, and pocketbook in Ira's room. Upon reaching her room she gave Hope a real fright. Hope hadn't seen Georgie in such a disheveled state since the final days of her relationship with Joe. Hope, her roommate once again for their sophomore year, would later that evening be cajoled into retrieving Georgie's belongings from across campus, sparing her friend, not for the first time, nor the last, the humiliation born of her naïveté.

29

Joe committed to himself that he would keep an open mind about the women at St. Dom's. Returning to school in September as a junior, he felt his chances at getting women would be incrementally better. Given that he'd spent time in the Marine Corps, this year's incoming co-eds would be just too young for him. Last year he had Georgie, and she was just marginally acceptable, age-wise. Now, a year older, the age difference between him and the freshmen crop was getting a little creepy. Maybe, as an upperclassman, he'd have a better shot with junior and senior women, especially now that they've seen him around campus for a couple years and were starting to believe he might not be a Vietnamese-baby killer.

Last year he had traveled to Georgie's college so many weekends, abandoning any chance of developing friendships on his own campus, that he became a virtual stranger to everyone except his bandmates, with whom he'd spent three afternoons a week. This year, without a reason to travel on weekends, he was determined to (or stuck having to) look for some action at St. Dom's. After about a month of dating drought, what Joe called "house arrest," he decided to go back to Connecticut and meet up with his high school friend, Eddie, and go to a 21st birthday party of another hometown friend on Friday night.

"I heard Kathy's roommate Oona is going to be at the party," Eddie said excitedly as he drove Joe to the party.

"Did you say 'Oona?'"

"Yah."

"What the hell kind of name is Oona?"

"I guess her family's Irish or something." No one had ever asked what nationality Joe was. Everyone figures that a black person is just African, as if Africa is just one big country, not a continent. In fact, Joe didn't really know which African country his father's family came from. But he did know his mother was Irish.

"Do you know anything about her? Other than she's Kathy's Irish roommate?"

"Kathy said she's pretty, that's all. And she's single." Those were Eddie's only two criteria.

"Well, if she's pretty, she should be pretty easy to spot at the party." The two self-imagined studs shared a good laugh. Joe sarcastically wondered why Eddie would, all of a sudden, care about looks. "Pretty" apparently hadn't been a longstanding criterion for him!

Later, on the way home from the party Eddie bragged, "I found out Oona's last name!"

"Congratulations," Joe said sarcastically. "I've got a date with her tomorrow night." In the dark car, Eddie couldn't see Joe's wide grin, but he sure could sense it. Joe could smell Eddie's seething humiliation.

Joe didn't see Eddie as a serious competitor. More of a clumsy buffoon than anything else. But theirs was a default friendship. Just a guy to hang out with when Joe was between girlfriends. Joe's dad worked evenings so his car was never available and he couldn't always count on his mother not needing her car. Eddie was almost always available and had his own wheels. Their friendship was a remnant from their high school cross country running days, before either of them had a license or a girlfriend. Really, their friendship was a relic from their childhood, a time in life when geography is greater than character as a determinant of friendship. It wasn't doing Joe's self-esteem any good to be back hanging out with good ol' Eddie. Joe was more convinced than ever that the answers to life's tough questions weren't going to be found back in Valley Park, Connecticut.

Oona lived a few towns over from where Joe grew up, in the general vicinity of the tobacco farm where Joe's trouble with the law started. Driving down those rural back roads, Joe was transported back to the sights, sounds, and smells of his short stint as a tobacco picker. He had never before driven down these roads at night and the bent posts, naked this time of year without their summer shrouding of gauze netting, resembled an endless group of unoccupied crucifixes. *There's no Jesus here either,* Joe thought.

Joe didn't have high expectations of his date with Oona. Kathy was a good friend of his and he didn't want to drive a

171

wedge in their relationship by being overly aggressive with her roommate, at least not on a first date. And they would all be going back to their respective colleges on Sunday night. Joe had lost his appetite for long-distance relationships. Arriving at Oona's house after his godless drive through the farms, she greeted Joe at the front door. She stepped onto the stoop and hugged Joe in a perfunctory way. "Shouldn't I meet your parents?" Joe offered. "Oh, that's OK, they're not home." Joe was never sure when picking up a date if the parents really weren't at home, or if they just didn't know their daughter was about to go on a date with a black man.

It was a cordial, platonic date, the first and last for Joe and Oona. But it was a success in some ways for Joe. Finally, after several months of self-flagellation, Joe was able to spend an evening enjoying a young woman's company without feeling miserable about Georgie. The only miserable person that night was Eddie, home alone and imagining wild sexual escapades between Joe and his stolen date, Oona.

30

Joe was already emotionally numb when he returned home from the Corps. His final day in Vietnam, watching Kim-Ly die just beyond his grasp, hardened him to the type of emotions a man needs to have to maintain successful relationships. Now, after the break with Georgie, he sometimes felt, not just numb, but dead inside. Other times he struggled to keep a lid on his temper, his anger, and his despair. He started to resent Georgie because she could go on with her life unburdened while he was stuck with his own crazy thoughts for (he feared) the rest of his life. He convinced himself to never write another letter to Georgie, but, like so many of his other self-promises of late, his convictions were as empty as his emotional reserves. Being unable to conjure up the emotions necessary to write a love letter from his heart, he took to plagiarizing pop songs that he knew Georgie was not listening to.

Georgie was just about the only person he knew who wasn't listening to Fleetwood Mac (*rumors* of drug use), so Joe felt safe lifting one of their songs for one of his last desperate letters to her.

October 7, 1979

Dear Georgie, It was a year ago tonight that we first spent a whole night together. Remember how we left the Oktoberfest dance and drove back to your school? Remember how we could hardly sleep because our naked bodies kept brushing up against each other in your bed? That night will always be special to me. In honor of that night I wrote you this poem:

Sleep easy by my side
Into gentle slumber you can hide
I'm waiting for the sun to come up
I can't sleep, with your warm ways

Forever
Forever love
Together
Together love

You made me a man tonight
Sleep until the morning light
I'm waiting for the sun, to come up
I can't sleep, with your warm ways

Forever
Forever love
Together
Together love

Please come back to me and we will only look forward, never back. Love, Joe

And then later that month, in what would be his final letter to Georgie, Joe "borrowed" from Andy Gibb, copying, word-for-word, the lyrics to "Don't throw it all away, our love."

31

For her part, Georgie wanted to rekindle a friendship with Joe so she could go off into her future life, whatever that might look like, with an unburdened heart, knowing there were no unsaid words and no unanswered questions or issues. And she wasn't sure if they might not be together again someday. Friendship was a way to keep him in her orbit.

Joe seemed to be doing much better lately. Whether it was initiating counseling with the chaplain, Father Foley, hanging out more with his bandmates after rehearsal, or just simply the time away from Georgie, he was now concentrating on his coursework better, and taking in the occasional hockey game on campus. He was in full "fake-it-till-you-make-it" mode, putting on his brave face every time he left his dorm room. A large part of him didn't want to be feeling better because, to him, it represented a wider separation from Georgie; almost a betrayal. *What happens if I get over her completely? Will we never get back together then?* Even without the counseling, Joe would have recognized that this view was not healthy. Every indication was they would never be together again.

All summer he had set deadlines for when he thought he should be over her. Even accepting the idea that he might someday "get over her," he couldn't grasp the concept that life experiences leave us forever changed. Week after week he had blown past these arbitrary roadblocks, each time feeling renewed shame that he was still torn up inside over a teenage girl. Accepting that this was a futile strategy, Joe gave in to Father Foley's advice to try to take life a day-at-a-time rather than trying to plan out his whole future. Still, he did have a little hope, and to give up all hope was tantamount to giving up his will to live. No one, least of all Joe, recognized how desperate he had become that fall after failing to shake his depression over the summer.

He felt he was strong enough to handle a cordial phone call with Georgie. He was weak enough that he had to make that call. He had been consciously holding off aggressively jumping into the dating pool to give Georgie some time to come to her senses. Conveniently, his passive approach to dating did not interfere with this pipedream.

He got her on the first try. He took a chance she would keep roughly the same schedule this year. It was 8:00 on Wednesday night. But instead of letting her know that he'd found a ride and would be seeing her on Friday, just like every Wednesday last year, tonight was just about reopening recently bound wounds. When she said she wasn't ready, and didn't know if she ever would be, he had either too much respect or too much fear to ask when she might know when she might be ready to maybe get back together. She sounded a little sad to Joe. He wasn't even sure if she ever thought about "the one that got away" and if she did, was she thinking about him, or was it her old boyfriend Alan? After all, Joe had swooped in to rescue her when she was fresh off the Alan breakup. *Everyone knows not to get involved with a girl on the rebound, but I just couldn't stop myself!* Joe asked if she had received and read the love letters he had recently sent. She had, and thanked him for them, although she was internally skeptical about their authorship since Ira had exposed Joe as a plagiarist during his rendition of "Two Love Birds."

She was just about to say he could call anytime and stay in touch as friends when he couldn't resist asking caustically, "So, how's the whole finding yourself thing going?" Although nothing more of substance was discussed, somehow the call lasted fifteen minutes and it seemed much longer. He later only recalled "not ready" and "if I ever will be" from her, and his own "So, how's the whole finding yourself thing going?" and "I still love you, Georgie." He knew this must be, and probably would be, their last call ever, or at least for a very long time. Sensing it was the end of the end, he wished he could have left both of them with a better final impression of him. He had now given up hope; not because there was no hope, only that having any hope at all was driving him crazy.

Joe would be headed back to Connecticut for the weekend, just not to see Georgie.

St. Domenic's had requested that all residents of McDonnell Hall go home or stay with friends in another dorm for the upcoming long weekend so the maintenance department could remove asbestos from the heating system in McDonnell. Since Joe didn't really have any friends in other dorms who he knew well enough to bunk in with, he ruefully decided to head home.

"If only I was still with Georgie," he thought, "this wouldn't even be an issue." Joe had only one friend left at home, Eddie. Eddie was Joe's standby friend that he would get in touch with when nothing else was going on. Nothing else was going on.

Eddie considered them friends who had been through a lot together. Joe didn't see it that way. Joe had been through a lot, and Eddie lived vicariously through him. In high school, Eddie would listen with rapt attention to Joe's tales of teenage mischief and romantic conquests. Later, as Joe related stories about his time in Saigon, Eddie could almost imagine himself being there taking heroic stands and risking his life to save young virgin "gooks" from that Embassy rooftop.

Eddie once asked Joe when he was stateside on leave, "So, over there, did you ever get to see Fu Manchu?"

"Fu Manchu? Do you mean Ho Chi Minh?"

Eddie stared back blankly.

"You're a fucking idiot, Eddie!"

They hadn't been in touch in about a month, and Joe was anxious to share the embellished details of his date with Oona. He knew how to get a rise out of Eddie. Eddie was in the driveway working on his car when Joe stopped by. Eddie was covered in grease and his eyes were ringed in red. They didn't shake hands.

"You don't look so good. You feeling OK?" Joe asked.

"Naw, I'm sick man. I musta gotten into some bad pussy last night."

"You wish," Joe chuckled, "more likely some bad cock."

"Get bent." Eddie's grin slackened. He was one of those who liked to joke around, as long as the joke was not on him.

"Are you still broken up about Georgie?" Eddie was ready to pick this scab even if Joe wasn't looking depressed. But he was looking depressed, so the question didn't seem out of place.

"Well yeah, I'm having a hard time shaking her." *I must be wearing her on my sleeve*, he thought.

"Well I saw her last weekend and she seemed to be doing OK…."

"You saw her? You saw her how?" Joe asked, feeling a combination of confusion and anger.

"I took her to the movies," Eddie peacocked.

"What are you doing taking her out? What are you trying to do?"

"I just figured she might need a friend to lean on."

"She's got plenty of friends," Joe barked. "You're supposed to be *my* friend!"

"Hey, you went out with my old girlfriend," countered Eddie.

"That was different. It was long after you two broke up and I came to you first to make sure you were OK with it. And she and I were just hanging out anyway. And that was like five years ago!"

"Georgie and I were just hanging out too, at least I thought we were, but she was very friendly. VERY FRIENDLY." Eddie goaded.

"You're a Lothario!"

"What'd you call me?"

"A Lothario."

"What's that?" Eddie had never heard the term but he was pretty sure it was worthy of a physical confrontation. Eddie was a big guy and not one to shy away from a fight, but ever since Joe came back from Vietnam, now a marine, Eddie wasn't so sure he really wanted to get into a scrape with him.

"A Lothario's a back-stabbing son of a bitch. That's what you are. It wouldn't kill you to crack open a book once in a while either. You're a stupid asshole," Joe added over his shoulder as he headed to his car. He hopped in, slammed the door, turned the key, jammed the shifter into first, popped the clutch and drove off without the slightest concern for Eddie's mother's flower garden under his wheels. It was the last time Joe would ever speak to Eddie.

Eddie continued to work on his car; his mother's flower bed now a complete mess. Eddie's mom arrived home a short while later, not noticing the ruined garden.

"Hi Eddie, how's the car coming along?"

"It's OK. A little slow but I'm almost done. Where you been?"

"I went to the hairdresser's."

"Was it closed?"

"Very funny. You know, you can be a real jerk sometimes."
No mother wants to call her son an asshole.

"So I've been told."

As she turned toward the house she spotted her mums, all
broken and scattered, not looking *hardy* anymore. "Oh my
God, oh my God!!"

"What?"

"Look at my flowers! Did you run over my flowers?"

"How could I run them over? I don't even have the wheels
back on my car!"

"Did you see who did it?"

"Yeah, Joe peeled outta here and tore it up."

"Why'd he do that?"

"I dunno. Girl trouble, I guess."

"Well you better get his ass back here and replant me a nice
bed. I mean it! And if he won't do it, you're gonna fix it!"

"I can't go up there now. I'm not done fixing my car yet."

"Then walk up there!" It was less than a mile up to Joe's
house, but once you have a license and a car, you would never
think of walking anywhere.

32

Even if Eddie hadn't been to Joe's house a thousand times before, it would have been easy to find his way there this time. All he had to do was follow the muddy tire tracks up the hill. There was Joe's car, with bits of broken mums in the wheel wells, parked at a funny angle, right up on the front lawn as if he had been in a desperate hurry to get in the house.

In the driveway was the ambulance, also looking like it had been parked in a hurry. Eddie approached the house and was beginning to size up the situation when he first heard the wailing. There's something primal about a mother's scream that requires no language to be instantly understood. Eddie watched the paramedics hurriedly wheeling the stretcher carrying Joe's lifeless body toward the ambulance. Joe's parents then emerged from the garage. As they hustled to their car to follow the ambulance, Joe's father staggered past Eddie, never seeing the devil in his midst.

A half hour earlier, a distraught and frantic Joe had arrived home to an empty house. Ever since the breakup he had been holding on by only a couple threads. He tried one final time to get a lifeline from Georgie on the call last Wednesday but she severed his hopes. Now the only thread was his friends, precious few as they were.

In this shitty little town in the late 70's, when people might spend their whole career at the same company, families bought a house and stayed there until the mortgage was paid off. They might even put a modest addition on their home but would never consider moving. So you better make friends with your neighbors because no one new is coming to give you a second chance at friendship.

Sure, there was his marine buddy Eric, but he was living 1,000 miles away in Kansas City. Joe was often amazed at how, after being almost inseparable for three years, there could be so little contact now. They were both discharged on the same day in June, 1977, flying back from Germany together and getting processed stateside. There was a visit that summer in Connecticut when Eric was so shocked to see that Joe's town looked so much like his own town in Missouri. From that point on, Eric always busted Joe's balls because that part of Connecticut was just as much a shithole as his own area outside of Kansas City. But Eric wasn't much of a letter writer and expensive long-distance phone calls were few and far between. They didn't much like talking about Nam anyway after what they'd gone through. It was just easier to try to move on with life; Joe off to college and Eric working in the family electronics store.

So Joe's friendship burden was concentrated on his hometown

friend, Eddie. Today he lost everything, including his friend. The thread that he was holding onto was getting taut.

Glaring out from behind wild teary eyes, his brain swimming in a lethal brew of rage, heartbreak, disgust, and desperation, Joe ran to the kitchen phone. Dialing his last lifeline to a life that once was, and could have been, he had to hear it from her. *Was it true? Did she get intimate with Eddie? How could she!* She had shown poor judgment in the past, but this was a new low. *Was she trying to hurt me or is she just so fucking naïve that she believed Eddie's bullshit!!*

Ringing…ringing…No answer. *Now there is no other choice. Only the final option left. Down to the basement. Need rope. Strong rope. Or a knife. No, I've seen enough blood in my life. Need rope. How can a house not have any fucking rope?* Then he spotted the lawnmower. Off the workbench he grabbed a jackknife. He grabbed the handle of the mower's pull cord, extended it all the way and slashed the cord at the source. He had no idea how to fashion a noose, but he had seen a few South Vietnamese men who hastily hanged themselves with just a slipknot as the VPA were approaching.

He placed a cinder block on end and stood on it to swing the cord over the main beam in the cellar. He tied it securely as if he were anchoring his tent to a tree. He made another small knot in the loose end and looped the cord through it. He got down from the cinder block and went back to the workbench where his cassette player stood sentinel in silence. Seeing that Queen was loaded, he turned the volume knob to 10 and pressed play. As the opening strains of Bohemian Rhapsody blasted through the single solid state speaker, Joe ascended his concrete pedestal a final time, slipped the corded cowl over his head and kicked over the block.

Time slowed down as he hung there suspended by the lawnmower cord. The physical part of his being was a chaotic mix of gasping, burning lungs, feet and legs kicking in random directions, desperately searching for elusive solid footing, and fingers digging at the rope around his neck. His mind was struggling too. He was filled with regret; not for wanting to end his life, but for realizing, at that time, he would never again see Georgie. Had he known he would never see her again, he surely would have stared at her face the last time he saw her to burn her visage into his consciousness. As his body struggled for life, his mind groped to conjure up her face, one last time, as his light was flickering out. He hadn't considered writing a suicide note until just then, as time slowed down. *Just as well*, he thought, *anyone will understand why I killed myself after losing such a remarkable girl.*

At the hospital, Joe's parents were whisked past the ER reception desk and brought to ER2. ER 1, 2, and 3 were all the same room, each part separated only by an olive-green canvas curtain. Joe's mom had watched this type of scene play out so many times before during her years as an ER nurse. But this time she was unable to maintain the cold detachment required in such a profession. This time the tubes and wires were being attached to her child. This time she recognized the duty nurse's cautious yet optimistic tone for what it was: a diversionary stalling tactic used to put off the emotional reaction she was sure would be warranted when the ultimate bad news arrived. Joe's mom had seen patients arriving in the ER following suicide and suicide attempts. She recognized Joe's ashen complexion and his lack of vital signs as characteristics of the former. She was disconsolate. Her husband was the same ashen color as her son, but he still had enough composure to request the services of the chaplain.

Father White arrived momentarily, having already been on site delivering Holy Communion to some elderly patients in the chronic ward. He seemed to have an uncanny ability to know when his services would be needed in the emergency room. This was the part of being a priest he hated the most. There were many parts he hated: having to whine and cajole parishioners to give more in the collection basket, counseling bickering couples who should never have been married, the loneliness of celibacy, and treating fellow priests with respect even when their soul-staining sordid pasts were well known within the rectory. He hated performing last rites even more than officiating at funerals. At least funerals had the advantage of taking place a few days after tragic deaths, after the families had a little time to recover from the initial shock. But here in the ER, no one is yet composed and the priest has to stand amongst the family, not able to avail himself of the buffer that is the altar.

As Father White parted the curtains in ER2, he embraced his familiar parishioners. He knew the family well and immediately surmised that it was Joe lying there, all hooked up to monitors, scanners, and other humming and beeping machines. Although Joe was not his actual "family," he always felt an affinity for the Davis family. He had hoped that one of the two boys would have a vocation someday. Joe's brother Eldon had gone in a different direction after college, leaving Joe as the only viable candidate. *Only the good die young*, thought Father White.

The nurses, having done all they could at this point for Joe, turned off the beeping monitors, and parted from his bedside allowing Joe's parents and Father White to assemble in close. Father White opened the book and began administering the Sacrament as Joe's parents wept quietly.

END OF PART ONE

PART TWO

33

1995

"Come on in, Moira." Father Martin was at the office door welcoming Moira with a hug. Closing the door behind the sophomore, he offered out in Mrs. Hennessey's direction, "Mary, since this is my last appointment, you can leave early today."

For some priests, being a college chaplain might be a dream job, he thought. *If I had any dreams*, he added. Still, there were many perks to this kind of assignment. At a small, non-denominational, liberal arts college in the scenic hills of New England, a Catholic chaplain could be his own man, flying under the diocesan radar. College administrators didn't know what to do with him so they left him alone. And his monthly check-in call with Bishop Flannery was largely a formality. Often, at the appointed time, Father Martin would call the Bishop's office only to learn that Bishop Flannery was "otherwise indisposed," as his secretary would say. Father Martin would end up having to chat with the auxiliary bishop (Bishop Douche Bag, Father Martin called him.)

For a priest, a chaplain's hours were almost ideal (there was nothing he could do about having to work Sunday mornings!) He kept regular office hours, Monday through Friday, carving out 35 minutes every morning to celebrate "express Mass" for the handful of students who might attend. He always wondered what drove these kids to attend mass during the week. Were the boys actually considering a vocation?

He figured the girls were there to cleanse themselves from some moral infractions occurring the previous night. *Why were my college nights so devoid of moral infractions,* he mused. *Surely not for lack of trying!*

As far as Confession, or Reconciliation as it was now referred to, in three years on campus only one student had ever shown up to unburden himself at a "Reconciliation Retreat." And his "sin" was such a contrived piece of bullshit Father Martin felt like he was wasting his time at best, or was the fool in some college prank.

So now, Confessions were by appointment only. Usually these Reconciliation sessions started out with a confession of some canonical infraction, but quickly morphed into a full blown cathartic counseling session.

Of all the college chaplains around, Father Martin was one of the most qualified, at least by academic degrees, to counsel students. Between the GI Bill and joining the seminary, Father Martin's education expenses were almost entirely taken care of. So he stayed in school….and stayed. After a few extra years of graduate school, concurrent with seminary, then, newly minted Brother Martin also became a licensed psychologist.

Although Father Martin's ecclesiastical training might have

taken a back seat to his clinical preparation, he always saw himself as a cut above his fellow priests. *At least I can do something useful*, he congratulated himself. *And if this priest thing doesn't work out, I can always make a living.*

So here, on this bucolic campus, amongst the elms and beech trees, he "makes a living" counseling (mostly) young coeds.

Beats the hell out of the drudgery that is the lot of the parish priest! With so many funerals, hospital visits and sessions with dysfunctional couples, it's no wonder priests are leaving in droves. And the constant harangue to fill the collection basket! Jesus! These were the realities they never told you about in Seminary! But Father Martin also felt dead inside. Or was he just detached from his emotions? Was this compartmentalization just part of his training as a psychologist? Or had he developed a way to tamp down his emotions following his traumatic adolescent and early adult experiences as a way of protecting his psyche from any future attack?

"Come on in. Have a seat right there, Moira." He motioned to the end of the couch nearest the tissue box.

Moira. Moira. Wow, that's really Irish! Back when he was an undergrad the Irish-American girls all had names like Maura, Maureen, Kathleen, Margaret, Sheila, or some combination of Ann and Mary (Annmarie, Mary Ann, …) Now, the children of the Michaels and Brians and Sheilas and Mary Anns are showing up with uber-Irish names like Oona, Caitlin, Brigid, Seamus, Connor, Sioban, and now Moira.

"Moira? Am I pronouncing that right?" he asked as he took the chair next to the couch.

"Yes, Moira," she replied just as she was starting to shake off the creepy feeling from the initial "welcome hug."

"So what brings you in to see me today?" He prepared his mind for some inane drivel about a campus romance on the skids, alcoholic parents, roommate problems, or yet another abortion confession.

"I had no one else to turn to."

"You can tell me anything. Whatever you say stays between you and me." He used to say: "Whatever you say stays between you, me, and the Lord," but he found the "Lord" part got in the way of people opening up. Anyway, he figured, the Lord keeping a secret was pretty much implied.

"This is my second year here and I don't seem to fit in."

Wow, this girl's a talker, he thought. She jumped right in. Sometimes it's like pulling your foot out of the deep mud of a clam flat at low tide.

"I can't make friends," she continued, "my roommates and other girls don't like me (projection). Boys don't pay me any attention (reaction formation)."

Father Martin's psychoanalytic training always kicked in. Although he only had one year of formal training in the Freudian method, it clearly had an impact. He analyzed every conversation, labeling emotions as various Freudian defense mechanisms.

He knew the actual content of what she was saying was unimportant, but the defense mechanisms were critical. Very rarely does a client reveal upfront the real reason they are seeking counseling. This preliminary dipping of the toe into the counseling water was just the way people begin to test and develop trust with the therapist, easing into an awkward, unnatural setting while protecting their ever fragile ego. Father Martin had been through this process so many times before and he wished there was a way to cut through this preliminary bullshit and get to the real issue. But he knew he had to wait until his client was comfortable enough to open up to him. Sometimes they never did. Father Martin attributed his failure to elicit the "real problem" to his client's discomfort due to sexual feelings toward him (counter-transference mistaken for transference!) He never entertained the thought that his (female) clients sometimes couldn't get comfortable with him as a result of his "welcome hug."

As Moira droned on, Father Martin periodically applied a psychological band-aid, interjecting his best Rogerian: "That really hurt you when she said that," and "you feel lonely and upset." And a few "um-hmms" sprinkled in for good measure. His mind went on a side trip, remembering a few snippets and trying to make sense of one of his dreams last night. *Why were the cemetery workmen removing the gravestones to clean them?*

"Father Martin, are you listening?"

"...Yes, of course....please continue."

Sometimes Father Martin didn't mind that it took a few sessions (or more) for his student clients to open up. Besides, he had to fill his day one way or another and counseling co-eds sure beat the hell out of visiting sick undergrads in the infirmary. It was just an uncanny coincidence that the most attractive young women needed the most sessions!

As he studied Moira's face, her hair, her body, her smile, Father Martin was able to formulate her diagnosis, prognosis, and treatment plan:

> Diagnosis: Lonely

> Prognosis: She'll get over it

> Treatment Plan: Come back and see me if it gets worse.

Plain looking Moira was not going to need additional visits.

On Thursday of that week, Father Martin spied a new face at his morning Mass. This young woman was a remarkable beauty. Usually at Mass, Father Martin read both the New Testament reading and the Gospel and had a student come up to read the responsorial psalm. Today he called up one of the regulars from the pews to read the first reading so he, himself, could sit and gaze at the beauty on the right side, eighth row back. Not hearing anything St. Paul had to say to the Corinthians, his mind churned to come up with some way to get this young woman to come and see him in the Chaplain's office.

Why had she come to Mass all of a sudden? She wasn't part of the usual pre-exam panic uptick in attendance, as finals were still weeks away. She looked sad but not distraught. Was that a tear or just the light of the altar candles reflecting in her glistening eyes?

Usually he stayed up at the altar after the final prayer as the students scurried off to their classes. Today he would create his own recessional, saving the final blessing until he reached the front doors of the chapel. "Go in peace to love and serve the Lord."

"Hi. Father Martin," he said, extending his hand to the newcomer.

"Good morning, Father. I'm Sarah," returning the handshake.

"How are you? I haven't seen you at Mass before."

"I'm OK. I just thought I'd like to come. I was afraid I would be the only one here."

"I have that same fear every day," he responded initiating a quick laugh. "If you ever want to come see me Sarah, I'm over in the Chaplain's office every day."

"OK, I might do that sometime."

It wasn't much, but "might" gave him a slight pang of hope. Hope, once blazing inside him, now was just a tiny spark in a cold, dark cave.

34

It was getting worse. The nightly visitations left him exhausted, sweaty, emotionally drained. How long had he been having these dreams? This dream really. It's always the same dream. Was this visitor an angel? The devil? His face is always obscured but he seems familiar. Father Martin had started sleeping with a light on by the bed. The light might keep the visitor away, or at the very least it could illuminate the mysterious face.

There really is no way to escape an unwanted visitor. For years after he left the Corps he had the nightmares. They all began in a different place but ended, abruptly, in the same place. He is on the deck of the helicopter, one arm bent through the safety netting, catching him by the elbow as he grasps for her outstretched hand while she falls away from the bird. The straps give way and he begins his slow-motion free-fall decent to the rooftop.

He awakens on his bed, always face down, exhausted and filled with regret that he couldn't save her, or even himself. Lately his helicopter dreams are replaced by the strange visitations of his mysterious ghost. On the nights the bedside lamp keeps him awake (keeping the visitor at bay), he often pays the price during the day. He sees glimpses of the visitor during mind wanderings during a run, a counseling session, or even in the middle of his auto-pilot recitations of his morning consecration of the Host. At times he felt like he had never left Vietnam (or Vietnam had never left him!) Of all the pills the Marines gave them, the "Reds" and "Yellows" were the only ones that seemed to do any good. The Orange anti-malaria pills never did any good, but if you were going to be up for all-night guard duty, you would definitely want a couple "Reds" (amphetamines) to keep you alert. Of course, the next morning you'll need a "Yellow" sleeping pill and a couple formaldehyde beers to bring you back down.

Father Martin had recently reprised his Red/Yellow regimen.

35

Father Martin had all but forgotten about the beautiful co-ed he met at Chapel two weeks ago. At a college of 5,000 students, with more than half being young women, there were always new, interesting targets. His regular running route through campus took him past all the columned administration buildings, brick classroom buildings, and student dormitories. If he timed his run just right, he would be crossing through the quad just as the classrooms were discharging hordes of co-eds right into his path. The classic architecture got stale, but the ever changing colors of the female student population never did.

Looking at his watch, hoping for a cancellation, he picked up the telephone. "Who's my next appointment Mary?"

"A Sarah Brennan, Father," replied Mrs. Hennessey.

Father Martin hated how Mary always said, "a Sarah Brennan" or "a Moira Collins" or "a Sheila Andrews." Couldn't she just say "Sarah Brennan?"

"She's here. Should I send her in?"

"Welcome Sarah. Oh, you're the Sarah I met after Mass a

couple weeks back. I hadn't seen you again at Mass so I thought I had scared you away."

"I'm just not a morning person, Father Davis."

"Please. Martin…Father Martin."

In the seminary, novices with a "past" were urged to leave their past behind and "create a new future" by adopting a new name and dedicating their new identity to a historical man of faith who inspired the new candidate. As the deadline for selecting a new name approached, Saint Martin emerged as a viable choice for the future priest. Walking from his dorm to Chapel every morning the young seminarian would pass the statue of Saint Martin, stopping to feed the squirrels on the mornings he remembered to bring peanuts with him. "If it took me six months to decide on a name," he asked the squirrels, "how did I make such a snap decision to enter the priesthood?" Later, most people assumed, because he was black, Father Martin had picked his name as a tribute to Rev. Martin Luther King, Jr.

Since boyhood, the future Father Martin wondered about this thing called "a vocation." It seemed that every Catholic family in the neighborhood talked about it for their boys. Especially the Irish, …and then the Italians. He never heard the Polish talk about it. In the big Irish families the parents hoped that one of their sons might become a priest. Growing up in the 60's and 70's, he didn't remember anyone asking his sisters about joining a convent.

But for the boys, a "vocation" was always on the table, even if you were only half-Irish. He never really seriously considered it when he was growing up. He did like all the pomp and circumstance that accompanies Sunday Mass. He liked the

great sense of tradition, the candles, the music, the
Communion bells, the incense. And he carefully observed the
level of esteem and respect (and power) commanded by
anyone wearing a roman collar. As a kid, maybe ten or eleven
years old, he fantasized about being able to dress all in black
and walk up the center aisle with a gun and pick one person in
each pew to shoot. It would not be personal; just one person
in each row. That would be real power. Power he imagined a
priest to have. He could never imagine that, years later, when
he was an actual priest walking up the center aisle of a church,
he would be fantasizing about picking out one woman in each
row he wanted to fuck.

But the young boy wanted the same things every other kid
dreamed about. They all wanted to be baseball players. And
when a guy named Yastrzemski won the Triple Crown, even
the Polish kids thought they had a chance to make it to the
majors!

A vocation was always in the background; a fallback position in
case life didn't turn out the way you hoped; in case you
couldn't throw strikes or hit a curveball, or form adult
relationships with women.

"Come right in, Sarah."

Her path to the couch was blocked by his well-rehearsed pivot
into the customary "welcome hug."

Sarah recoiled slightly, prompting him to hold her a little
tighter; a little longer. This was "just to calm the nerves of a
student who was visibly shaken" he would later explain to
college administration.

Seated now, her nerves apparently "calmed," she began to respond to the usual salvo of "What brings you in to see me today?"

Months later when he was asked for his version of the truth, Father Martin would claim confidential privilege as the reason he would not divulge why Sarah had come to see him. The truth was, he had no recollection of why she sought counseling.

Of course, that would not stop him from establishing a treatment plan:

> Diagnosis: Depression; unspecified

> Prognosis: Guarded

> Treatment Plan: Counseling 2X/week; open ended

Where his clinical notes should have been there appeared a pen and ink likeness of Sarah, drawn by Father Martin's hand in his notebook (counter transference).

By the end of the fifth session, Sarah was complaining that she felt more depressed than ever, and her friends had noticed this too. Father Martin had counseled that the beginning stages of the therapeutic process often felt like the hardest work, and discouragement was very common.

The welcome-hugs and good-bye "peace be with you" hugs continued. Somewhere during the course of five visits the "hug break" was introduced to "relieve the stress" of especially intense interchanges.

Not only did the frequency of the embraces increase, the duration increased as well. And the severity of the hugs progressed to the point they could only fairly be described as "bondage and groping" sessions.

Father Martin sensed he had broken new ground with this one. All of the previous co-eds had terminated the pastoral counseling relationship by the second buttocks groping episode. After all, anyone can have his hand "slip" *once*.

These sexual assaults gave Father Martin an adrenaline boost, not unlike the jolt Marine Security Guard Joe Davis felt every time he climbed the embassy roof stairs exposing himself to the unknown dangers of the Saigon night.

His nights and his problems sleeping were still the same, but Sarah now occupied his daytime mind wanderings. Father Martin even mused about the irony that his thoughts could be drifting, thinking about holding Sarah, even as she was sitting in his office. He thought about what it meant "to have and to hold;" words he recited many times while performing accidental weddings for students who had not yet discovered birth control.

To have and to hold. Did he have Sarah? He could certainly hold her. To have and not be able to hold is heartbreaking. He had been through that. Having without holding eventually leads to not holding or having. Who wants to have if you can't hold?

Because of his position, he can't have. *At least*, he thought, *I should be able to hold*. And he did hold; each time tighter, longer, lower. On today's good-bye hug with Sarah, which would turn out to be his last, he held her for (what seemed to Sarah, at least) a very long time. With his usual groping stance, perfect frontal alignment with one hand pressing firmly across her mid back and the other hand pressing/squeezing one or the other of her buttocks (he fancied himself ambidextrous), he could feel the contour of her breasts and pelvic area through his black priest suit. He was sure she could feel his interest in her too.

36

"Will someone answer the phone! Where is Mrs. Hennessey? So now I have to be the receptionist too?" Father Martin asked out loud to himself as he picked up the receiver.

"Pastoral Center, can I help you?"

"Oh, um, is this Father Martin?"

He did not recognize the voice. The voice obviously did not recognize him.

"No, but can I help you?" he lied.
"Oh, well, uh, I'm calling about Father Martin. I need to, …well, I need…..Let me start over. This is Mrs. Kerrigan. My daughter, Christy, is a student there, and she was seeing Father Martin for counseling, and, well, I have some concerns about his conduct."

"OK…." Father Martin got up from behind his desk and closed the door.

"Are you the right person to talk to?"

"Yes, of course," Father Martin replied. "I'm Monsignor Nitram Rehtaf."

Inverting his name, Father Martin decided to have some fun as he put out this fire. "What is it you want to tell me?"

"Well Father Martin, he, well Christy said that he….This is hard for me, Monsignor."

"It's OK. Just take a breath and start when you're ready."

"My daughter is really upset. She came home from school last weekend and she says she doesn't want to go back. She even started crying in church on Sunday."

"What does Christy say Father Martin did?"

"I didn't believe her at first because she has always been a bit dramatic. But she was so upset that I told her I would call Father Martin's supervisor…..She said he kissed her……on the lips. And he touched her buttocks, on two occasions."

"Oh dear. This is a serious accusation. I thank you for having the courage to bring it to my attention. I'll need to ask you some more questions. Is that alright? Obviously I'll need to address this with Father Martin. It's not that I don't believe you, or your daughter, but you know, the counseling profession poses as many risks to the counselor as it does to the client. It is not uncommon for a client to become attached to her therapist, often in a romantic way. This is usually one-sided and the counselor might not even be aware of the attraction. College girls can have vivid imaginations and with all the emotions flying around in a counseling setting, it's sometimes hard for them to tell fantasy from reality.

And when you add a good looking priest into the mix," (Father Martin especially enjoyed putting in that part!), "well, there's no telling where a college girl's imagination may lead!"

Father Martin did this a lot; asking if it is alright to ask more questions, then embarking on a soliloquy.

"So Mrs. Kerrigan, when did Christy say this kiss happened?" Father Martin asked while avoiding the groping accusation, for now.

Of course Father Martin knew precisely when the kiss had occurred and it was accompanied by one of the groping incidents. He wasn't surprised he hadn't seen Christy since that session. His clients (victims) frequently felt too much shame after kissing a priest to ever return. Those young women who did return for more sessions came back for one of two sets of reasons, Father Martin surmised.

They came back to see if it would happen again. *Maybe it was just a one-time thing? He/we had a weak moment. Maybe it was something I was wearing that day? Maybe I was giving off signals that it was OK to kiss me? Maybe it never happened and I imagined the whole thing?*

Father Martin thought a few of the women came back, and went further, for another reason: *they like being kissed by a priest. They liked the thrill, the adventure, just like Eve; the thrill of forbidden fruit. They wanted to boldly go where no woman had gone before. It was a way to have a relationship with a man with no strings attached. The sex was quick, fun, and drama free.*

The latter happened often enough that it seemed worth it to Father Martin if "*a few girls took it the wrong way.*"

"The kiss happened two weeks ago," replied Mrs. Kerrigan.

"OK, and it sounds like Christy has been quite upset about it. When did you say she came home?"

"Well, just last Friday."

"So she's been home for what, really about four or five days?"

"Yes, that's right."

"Did she say why she waited over a week to come home and tell you about it?"

Father Martin, the psychologist, knew it took a while for these things to fester before an abscess formed. Some abuse takes years to bubble over. During the incubation period so much other emotional baggage gets mixed in that it is sometimes hard later to decipher the trauma from the memory. What might have been resolved in a therapeutic setting if dealt with early on becomes an infection that seems to feed itself if left untreated. Garbage thrown into the trash and left there awhile becomes part of the rest of the garbage in the can.

He imagined Christy feeling stunned and ashamed when it first happened. Returning to her dorm and taking a shower, she would wonder whom she could tell. Who would believe her? Who would believe a priest would kiss a young woman on the lips? And why had he picked her, with her self-described plain looks? He knew she wouldn't want to disclose it to her friends for the shame of having needed to go for counseling.

Of all the girls I've been close with, why is this one so uptight about it? I've gone a lot further with some of the other girls and there's not been a peep out of them. Father Martin wished there was some way to

207

know in advance which "college girls" would take to his advances, and which would be repulsed by them. If he had known Christy was going to take it so badly, he would have limited his involvement to a short course of psychotherapy; a treatment plan more in line with her diagnosis: plain looks.

Over the course of the next ten days following "the kiss," Christy found herself increasingly sleepy. She stopped making her bed and it was so easy to just slip back under the covers after class. Her roommate was starting to worry, but Christy explained it away as "an unusually heavy flow."

During her frequent naps she would replay the kissing/groping event in her dreams. After only a few such days and nights she began to doubt whether it had really happened or if it was just dream material. *Am I awake right now, or is this all just a dream?*

"She had classes and exams she couldn't skip." Mrs. Kerrigan countered, explaining the delay. She immediately felt bad that her voice sounded so irritated.

"Mrs. Kerrigan, I am going to look into this with Father Martin and then get back to you. Can you give me a week or so to fully check this out? What is your phone number?"

Mrs. Kerrigan thanked "Monsignor Rehtaf" and provided her telephone number.

"Do you think you can persuade Christy to come back to school? And would she like a referral to another therapist?"

After they hung up, Father Martin took the top sheet off the pad on which he was doodling and threw it in the trash. He hadn't bothered to write down Mrs. Kerrigan's telephone number. "Monsignor Nitram Rehtaf" knew he would never have the courage to confront Father Martin with these allegations.

He glanced down at his planner and saw blank space for the rest of the day. He looked at his digital Timex: *time for a run.* These were the times he really appreciated being a priest assigned to a college pastoral center. *If I had a real job, or even if I were a parish priest, I wouldn't be finished with my day at 2:30!*

He arose from his desk and saw him inside the closed door.

"Did I startle you?"

"Well, yes you did, although I was expecting to see you in the light of day sooner or later. And so now you have a voice and a face?" Father Martin was relieved to finally identify his ghostly visitor, but disappointed as to his identity. "I thought you were dead. I killed you myself long ago."

"You certainly tried, but it turned out the spirit was weak and the flesh was strong."

"Why are you terrorizing me? I made a fresh start back in '79. I dedicated my life to the Lord."

The visitor let out a disgusted laugh. "You're pathetic, you know that? You didn't dedicate yourself to anything. You're hiding behind that Roman collar, avoiding healthy adult relationships, and using your position of authority to fuck up young women's lives with your molestations."

Father Martin shot back, "I need to get rid of you once and for all. You're a twenty-two year old punk who doesn't know anything about being an adult. You're not even real. I've got to find a different supplier. I must've gotten a bad batch. The reds were supposed to pick me up and you're bringing me down."

"You're the one who's stuck at twenty-two. You're still chasing co-eds, you live on campus, and you won't listen to any music recorded after 1979. You have no dreams and you've given up on even trying to grow personally, never mind spiritually. And you don't have the balls to try to kill me again!"

"Well, aren't you a skilled amateur psychologist!" Father Martin said sarcastically. "When you're not haunting me, you must be spending your time reading *Psychology Today*."

Father Martin looked up and studied his visitor's face to see if his lame putdown had struck a nerve. He saw the emotion filled eyes, the same color as his, but otherwise so unlike his own. He saw the scarred neck, exposed to the light without benefit of turtleneck. Father Martin looked away and down at his hands, feeling ashamed at the waste his life has been. He lifted his head and refocused on the door and saw that he was alone. Devastatingly alone.

37

The killing off of Joe Davis began with the suicide attempt.
By trying to eradicate Joe, he had effectively killed off Georgie.
He had felt regret, not for having tried to kill himself, but for
the failure of the attempt. What he couldn't kill physically, he
then had to psychically kill. He thought about the motivational
poster on the barracks wall in basic training: a picture of
Shackleton's gravestone with the Browning quote, "I hold that
a man should strive to the uttermost for his life's set prize."
Why, Joe wondered, *if I was willing to kill myself after losing her, was
I not willing to die trying to keep her? What does that even mean? What
could I have done to die trying? Was I supposed to lay down behind her
car so she couldn't back out of my driveway? Was I supposed to kidnap
her and get shot by the cops who would come to rescue her? Should I have
gone on a hunger strike until she took me back? Didn't I "strive to the
uttermost" just by begging Georgie not to leave?*

In school, Joe focused on his studies and grew distant from his
family. He forced himself, as best he could, to forget his past:
childhood, Vietnam, Kim-Ly, Eddie, Georgie. When not
studying he spent his time rehearsing and performing in St.
Dom's band, and went on occasional dates. He even had a

steady girlfriend for a while. During the four months Joe was dating Karen, he largely submerged thoughts of Georgie. Karen was his non-addictive painkiller, masking the Georgie withdrawal symptoms. When the Karen prescription expired, the old addiction came roaring back. This time there would be no Georgie-fix. There would be no suicidal cure. Joe was forced to detox alone, without the benefit of female elixirs. From all outward appearances, he had moved on. At the same time, his psyche was a shallow grave of repressed, rotting memories. He willed himself to extinguish all emotions for fear of having to confront those he had been willing to kill himself over.

The daytime visitation brought Father Martin face to face with Joe's decaying emotional corpse. The traumatic experiences of his earlier life had metastasized into a tangled bundle of malignant psychic worms. Emotions from unrelated experiences were now indistinguishable from one another. The flooding and racing of his mind now resembled his nightmares where all the traumas of his life became comingled. He was confused over new emotions that were contrary to some he had been clinging to in the past. One in particular was rising above the din. His dominant feeling after the breakup with Georgie had always been sadness. He would never allow himself to stay angry at her. To be angry, he felt, would have shown that he loved her less than he needed to believe he loved her. He needed to uphold his side of the love equation in the event she someday metamorphosed and emerged from her self-discovery cocoon and came back to him.

The sadness was being pushed out by the feeling of resentment. Joe had heard that Georgie had visited him in the

ICU twice in the few days he was in a coma. The nurses had told him Georgie had actually come by several more times, but seeing Mrs. Davis there at his bedside, decided it was best not to go in.

Eddie had called Georgie as soon as he figured out why the ambulance was in Joe's driveway. He confessed to Georgie that he might have caused Joe to harm himself after exaggerating the details of their date. Georgie raced to the hospital and kept a parking lot vigil, attempting a visit to Joe's room only if she saw no sight of the Davis' family car.

Once Joe regained consciousness, there were no more visits from Georgie. Joe figured she had only come to see him when it was safe for her to speak her mind, or say nothing at all, without fear of reproach from him. Maybe she was hoping he would die, now that she had said her peace. Real closure.

After he recovered and returned to St. Dom's, there were no visits, or even phone calls. But there were letters. Joe recognized her return address and handwriting. The stack of unopened notes accumulated over the next two years. Dead men don't read, and even if they did, they wouldn't be interested in reading the remorseful, cheerful, banal, justifying (who knows?) scrawls of a dead young woman.

Father Martin knew that without professional help, there would be no way to process this mess. All of the long distance running in the world could not sort this out. He was fairly certain he would never even try.

38

Others also had had their fill of Father Martin. The call from
Sarah's parents spurred Dean Drinkledge into action. He had
never really pursued the two previous complaints against
Father Martin. Although no fan of Catholics, he had enough
respect (and apprehension) of priests not to wade into the
murky confluence of religion and psychotherapy.

Besides, the previous allegations were more rumor than
substance and didn't rise to the level where Dean Drinkledge
felt he needed to do anything beyond "duly noting" the
complaints.

Sarah, as the daughter of an active Alumni donor, could count
on a higher level of investigation than did her equally worthy,
but less well connected predecessors. After learning the
similarities of the three co-eds' stories, Dean Drinkledge
wished he had taken the two previous complaints more
seriously. Armed with new evidence, and the fact that the
college president had been copied on the letter from Sarah's

parents, the dean knew he had to take action. (The president had commented that there was very little difference between "duly noting" and "doing nothing.")

How many more girls had been groped but were too embarrassed or ashamed to come forward? He wondered. *How does one go about confronting a priest? Firing a priest?*

Dean Drinkledge knew (now) that Father Martin was guilty and had to go. *But would others believe that a priest could do such things? Could he prove it without risking further trauma to these young women? And what about the inevitable scandal to the college? If this were any other college employee, the path would be clear: disciplinary hearing with the employee and their union rep, and a financial settlement concurrent with a letter of recommendation. Nice and tidy. Would Father Martin go away quietly? Wouldn't he be worried about the scandal to his church?*

On the advice of the college president, himself a Catholic, Dean Drinkledge decided the direct approach would be best, thus saving Father Martin any undue embarrassment with his diocesan hierarchy. Keeping the circle small and contained, he called the chaplain's office himself. Although Father Martin decried this intrusion into his busy schedule, he accepted the invitation to meet the following afternoon.

Father Martin arrived at Dean Drinkledge's office ten minutes early. Old habits die hard. Mrs. Griswold received him in the anteroom and ushered him to one of two tufted leather wingback chairs. She said Dean Drinkledge would be with him shortly, and offered Father Martin coffee. Declining, and reclining, he glanced at the array of reading materials neatly displayed on the coffee table: the college annual report, the school newspaper, "The News Beat," US News and World

Report, *Best Colleges and Universities* edition, and a curious, small hardcover book entitled "Short Poems" by Walter Drinkledge.

So, it appears our Dean Drinkledge is a poet. What a surprise a poet would have to moonlight as a college administrator! Father Martin mused to himself.

He opened the book to a random page about two-thirds through and began reading silently.

Flaccid Pink

I stare down at her left areola

And its centrally located nipple.

I brush it, ever so lightly

With the side of my thumb.

But it remains motionless.

It used to stand at attention and salute me,

Erect even at the suggestion of a touch.

Now the flaccid pink flesh

Just stares back at me,

Like the dead eye of a beached grouper.

What kind of wierdo is this guy! And he's the one questioning my morality! This book is right out in the open for all the world (or at least all the college) to see. And now I have to go in there and endure my own 'Father Martin's Diet of Worms.' This ought to be some meeting! Well, 'I cannot and will not recant anything' in front of this pervert!

Mrs. Griswold entered the anteroom and approached Father Martin. "Reverend Davis, Dean Drinkledge will see you now."

Father Martin could not remember the last time he had been greeted with such formality. The staid atmosphere hung in the air like incense during the entire brief meeting between the two intransigent parties.

The meeting did not go well. Dean Drinkledge was left with few options to rid the college of this "Catholic menace; this sexual predator." He realized he was at the bottom of the bureaucracy with Father Martin, and he would need to move up the ladder.

Dean Drinkledge, a dyed in the wool Episcopalian (*American Anglican*, he preferred), was astonished to learn how similar were the bureaucratic structures of the two rival churches. He had once attended a wedding at a Catholic church and, with the exception of a misplaced word here and there in the Nicene Creed, there was very little difference in the mass. He had dutifully sat in the pew and abstained from receiving Communion after the priest's admonishment, welcoming "Catholics of good conscience" to the altar to receive the "Blessed Sacrament." The tone was another difference from his more welcoming church tradition.

Unable to induce the resignation or replacement of Father Martin, the dean was left to track down Father Martin's boss. He had heard of "Mother Superior." Was there such a thing as

"Father Superior?" This was something he would have to do himself without involving his secretary (or *Administrative Assistant* as they now like to be called.) If he could contain the ring of fire to just those who were already involved (President Williams, Father Martin, Sarah, Sarah's parents, and anyone else any of them might have told) he could avoid an expanding scandal that would necessitate a public denial, followed by a public inquest, followed by a public apology (and maybe his own firing). And on and on through a period of increased scrutiny and "healing" all the while accompanied by the inevitable donor drop off and decline in new student applications.

So he pulled out the phone book. *Yellow or white pages? Oh forget it*, he groaned, picking up the phone and dialing 4-1-1. "Boston please?....Diocese of Boston?...OK, the Roman Catholic Archdiocese of Boston then....Yes, the main number is fine."

Starting with the switchboard on the outermost circle of the labyrinth, working his way to the center after several wrong turns and dead ends, he began to wonder if maybe a public scandal would be easier to endure than this maze that was the Roman Catholic bureaucracy.

"I need to speak with the bishop please."

"Do you know which one?"

"There's more than one?"

"We have six bishops."

"The one who's in charge of the Boston area."

"Well, we have six bishops in the archdiocese."

"Who's the most….in charge?"

"You mean His Eminence?"

"Who?"

"His Eminence, the Cardinal?"

"Oh, that may be too high for this matter."

"What is this regarding? Can you hold please?" The phone went to church hold music without waiting to see if Dean Drinkledge could hold.

"Thanks for holding. Who did you need to speak with?"

"A bishop?" replied Drinkledge incredulously.

"Which bishop? Oh yes, I remember. What is this regarding?"

"I need to talk to whoever is in charge of priests." Dean Drinkledge was starting to lose his respectful tone.

"Well, that's usually the parish pastor. Which parish are you calling from?"

"It's not a parish. I'm Dean Walter Drinkledge from Covington College."

"That's not one of the colleges on my list that falls under our jurisdiction. Do you need a priest to come to your school?"

"No, we have one too many!" He said sharply, revealing more than he had wanted. "No, what I mean to say is we have a priest here, and well, he's involved in a ….I just need to speak with whoever is his supervisor. Please."

"Is he a member of a religious order?"

"I don't know. I think he's just a priest."

"OK, what's his name? They are usually listed by their parish assignment but I have individual folders in my file cabinet."

"Father Martin. Father Martin Davis."

There was a brief silence on the other end of the line. He heard her take a breath.

"Oh yes, Father Davis. Let me pull his file and see who he reports up through." A minute later: "You'll want to speak with Mary, Bishop Flannery's secretary. Please hold."

At least they still call them secretaries in the Catholic Church.

"Bishop Flannery's office. How can I help you?"

"I need to speak to the bishop about Father Martin Davis."

"Maybe I can help. Bishop Flannery is out right now."

Probably sleeping off his morning Communion wine, Drinkledge wanted to say. "No this is a very private matter. This is Dean Drinkledge of Covington College. Would you please have Bishop Flannery contact me as soon as possible? It is urgent."

Within a week, a meeting was held. Dean Drinkledge was pleased that, except for having a bishop seated in the chair usually occupied by the union rep, the disciplinary proceedings went on in similar fashion. This time, however, there would be no severance package or letter of recommendation! Father Martin was out; no need to send a replacement for the chaplaincy. Any Catholic students in need of pastoral services would just have to visit the local parish off campus.

Father Martin was out; in vocational limbo, if you will. Bishop Flannery's decision was final. So, Father Martin Davis, the young, handsome, turtleneck wearing, running priest, now with the reputation as a lascivious, buttocks groping psychologist/chaplain, was at yet another crossroads in his life.

"Martin, if this was your first transgression, I could have easily looked the other way. We all mess up once or twice. I know the flesh is weak and all that, but this just can't keep happening. And we can't keep this inside the family now because too many people know. We'll be lucky to keep this under wraps now that Drinkledge and President Johnson know. I had them sign a privacy agreement, but you know WASPs like Drinkledge will always expose us when they have the chance. And you just gave him the chance."

Martin listened, a little distracted, half dreading his next assignment, half hoping to be kicked out of the priesthood.

"You know Martin, I'm tempted to just cut you loose. Decommission you."

"You would defrock me for kissing a young woman?"

"It was more than kissing, and it was multiple young women, but no, I'm not going to defrock you. I was thinking about taking you out of circulation for a while. Teach you a lesson maybe. But we need all the priests we have; even ones like you."

Father Martin braced himself for what he was about to hear. He knew he had just forfeited a prime assignment. He suspected there were not too many desirable posts available to him with his limited seniority and well-deserved reputation. *Anything but a parish assignment!*

"I made some calls." Bishop Flannery began. "Down in Baltimore they could use more priests like you."

"What do you mean 'priests like me'?" Father Martin asked suspiciously. "Is Baltimore looking for priests with women troubles?"

"No, not that. You know…like *you*. Your kind of priest. Someone with your background. I think you'd feel more at home down there."

"You mean because I'm black? You think I'd do better with *my own kind*?"

"I'm just saying."
Father Martin cut him off. "You should stop 'just saying' 'cause what you're saying sounds racist to me. I'm not going to Baltimore. I'm not leaving New England. Don't forget I'm half white too and I never had a problem getting along with any kind of people. If you can't find me a good assignment in this area, you can mothball me and I'll go find a job outside the Church."

Following the tense meeting with Bishop Flannery, Father Martin decided to take one last run around campus. His mind was the miasma of all the bad decisions and behaviors that brought him to this point in his life. Running was the only time Father Turtleneck, as the students called him behind his back, felt normal and healthy. Except for the occasional daytime apparition of his nocturnal visitor, he was alone to think on his runs. Sometimes he tried to think about nothing and just run. Inevitably his mind would race along with him. Other times he would try to focus on a particular thought or theme and "run" with it. He enjoyed his loop run through the hilly part of town. He told himself, *the down-hills giveth, and the up-hills taketh away.* On his running route, he saw the parallels to his own life. There were highs and lows, and no matter how far he went, and how much he saw, he always ended up back where he started. *Ashes to ashes*, he figured. On his final trans-campus jaunt, his thoughts were darker: *When did I become someone who doesn't care about other people? Other people who were created in God's image? Maybe I'm just angry at God.*

END OF PART TWO

PART THREE

39

1996

Ashes to ashes; shithole to shithole, Father Martin thought as he surveyed the landscape on the drive over to his new assignment. How much this town reminded him of Valley Park, the small Connecticut town where he grew up. *But that was over twenty years ago! This little town looks like it was frozen in time. And it is only fifty miles from Boston. How does this happen?* Assigned to a parish *(a "last-chance assignment"* Bishop Flannery had warned) was the least desirable job a priest could have, with the possible exceptions of hospital, army, or prison chaplain. *And to be back in a town that was right out of the 70's! Is this God's way to make me start over? Almost literally going back in time?*

Preparing a homily was nothing new for Father Martin., but most of his homilies, having been delivered in a small college chapel, were directed to a totally different demographic than abided in the pews of St. Margaret's Church in Thornton,

Massachusetts. Unlike the grizzled priests he had studied under at St. Domenic's and the seminary, where the same sermon that had been used for the last fifteen years could be dusted off on a moment's notice if it were your turn on the rotation, Father Martin had really to start from scratch.

Sitting at his desk on Saturday morning, trying to craft a sermon that his yet-to-be-acquainted-with flock could relate to, he opened the Bible to page one and "let the Lord guide" him.

First Homily at St. Margaret's

My brothers and sisters (should I say "my children" as is my habit?), today's first reading from the Book of Genesis tells us about the spiritual beginnings of the human race. As Catholics, we are not compelled to take the Old Testament as literal, historical fact. It was written down from the oral tradition to be told to an illiterate people with limited knowledge and understanding of science. But while the books of the Old Testament cannot be judged as scientifically, or even historically accurate, and the language used seems outdated, the spiritual lessons we can take from reading Genesis are as relevant today as they were 6,000 years ago when monotheism was introduced to the Israelites.

I like to meditate on Scripture. Now I know, many of us Catholics are not very familiar with the inside of the Bible, other than to record births, marriages, and deaths. When I was growing up, every good Catholic family owned a Bible. It was kept maybe in a place of honor on a table in the living room or parlor. Ours was kept on the top shelf of the coat closet. As a little kid, I couldn't even reach that shelf to read the Bible if I wanted to! Our family Bible was just the place where we inserted Mass cards after an old relative died.

Let's face it: the only exposure most Catholics get of the Bible are the three readings at Sunday mass. When I first found out, in college, that these three readings were only snippets of the full readings, I was shocked.

I really didn't start reading the Bible until I was in the Marine Corps, and then later when I began attending Sunday services with my Baptist girlfriend in college. Yes, that's right: priests can have girlfriends before becoming a priest. (He was sure this would get a chuckle when delivered.)

So yes, I like to meditate on the readings. This morning's reading in Genesis brings us back to one of my favorite Bible scenes: the Garden of Eden. This is what I think about when I read the story of Adam and Eve.

Roman Catholics are taught that the pain of childbirth labor is a remnant of Eve's original sin, which was giving the apple to Adam. Maybe it was really a pomegranate, but let's just call it an apple for now. Baptismal waters and oils are believed to cleanse the soul of original sin, yet two thousand years of Catholic women continue to experience pain in childbirth. And truly, non-Catholic women have experienced the same labor pain in the six thousand years since the Old Testament was written, and I submit, probably have for millions of years before religions were established.

I grew up in a farm town. I got to see animals being birthed. Truly, some have an easier time of it than others, but for many it is an exhausting, if not painful, experience. So can we all agree that childbirth labor is not punishment for Eve's original sin?

Before you report me to the bishop, hear me out.

I like to think that when Adam took a bite of that apple, a seed from the apple got lodged near his heart. It would be even easier to believe if it really was a pomegranate! That seed is the seed of salvation. All people, as heirs to Adam, are born with that seed in their hearts. At the sacrament of baptism, when we are cleansed from sin, what we are really cleansed from is that seed. The priest collects all the seeds stripped from the new little Christians and gathers them up and sends them to his bishop. The bishop, in turn, sends all the seeds he collects from all the parishes in the diocese, to the Vatican where they are locked away for safe keeping, and overseen by the Grand Master Seed Keeper. (He hoped he was not getting too esoteric for common parishioners.)

The first seeds collected two thousand years ago, indeed the Son of Seed, was deposited, yes planted, in Rome where it grew into a great righteous tree which originally provided shade to the first sacred followers and buildings of the Vatican Church.

These seeds of salvation are kept safe for each of us, away from us, until at last they are returned to each of us at our judgement day. All we have to do is ask, in the form of repentance, and our seed of salvation will be given back to us, pristine and free from sin, as it was on the day of our Christening, to accompany us to the afterlife.

Regardless of the abuse we heap upon ourselves, or endure from others, our seed of salvation will be safe and ready to accompany us at the end of our worldly life.

This seed is a gift from God we cannot reject. Everyone is born with this seed in their heart, and much of the joy and tenderness in this world comes from remembering our seed and longing for its eventual reunion with us. Much of the compassion in the world comes from remembering that others were also born with their own seeds, just like ours.

But many of us forget our seed daily. Maybe even for long periods. The seed is tiny. The space where the seed was is tiny, almost insignificant in comparison to the rest of us. Obviously if we are all running around without this seed, we don't really need it, right? Maybe we don't need it in this life, but we sure as heaven need it in the next.

And I submit to you that we do need it now in our everyday lives. Not to hold, literally, inside us, but to fill the void it leaves with faith. Faith that science can't detect, but faith that we can feel, and others can see. Remember St. Paul tells us: "They'll know we are Christians by our love."

Why do you suppose we should have our salvation seed removed at Baptism? If we were to keep our seed, we would be more aware of it, no? Maybe not if the seed were still in the heart, but you would certainly be aware of it if it was lodged under your dentures, or inside an eyelid!

No, the seed must be preserved in its flawless state to be worthy of eternal life. We should all remember our seed daily and make a spiritual visit with it at Sunday Mass, and repent often, until the Grand Master Seed Keeper determines it is time to return the seed of salvation to any of us.

And as we go through life, let us not forget the seeds that belong to our sisters and brothers in faith, and help them to stay worthy of such a precious gift. Let us also remember the opening verse of Genesis: In the beginning God said, let there be light. Go out and be the light of the world. God bless you. Let us stand and profess our faith.

During the Consecration, Father Martin became distracted wondering if he had blown his parishioners' minds with his abstract homily. He came back to the present just as the altar boy holding the chalice, also distracted, was overflowing the mingled water and wine onto Father Martin's black Florsheims. He asked the altar boy what happened, and the boy replied, "You were supposed to tell me when to stop." Father Martin could have made an issue about the boy's intelligence, but instead just whispered some joke about a cup that runneth over.

40

2000

Father Martin began moonlighting as Dr. Davis and hung out his shingle as a psychologist. Testing the waters of life after priesthood, he decided to see if he could actually earn a living without hiding under the clergy umbrella. (Four years ago Father Martin had been told explicitly that his St. Margaret's assignment would be his last chance.) As a young Marine, Joe had sent most of his pay home throughout his service in the Corps. His mother never asked it of him; it was just something he did, as did most of his marine buddies. Joe's family wasn't poor; they just didn't have any extra money. Extra money could have been used to buy the things they didn't have. But if they didn't have it, they didn't need it. The logic continued: if they had everything they needed with no money left over, then leftover money was "extra money." This way of thinking worked well unless the furnace or a car broke down (which they did).

To contribute money as a young man made Joe feel like a giver and not just a taker, especially after all he had put his parents through, emotionally and financially, during his teen years.

Even as a kid he remembered how good it felt to have a little money of his own from his own labors. When he was thirteen he gave his parents $200 out of his paper route profits so they could fly to Mississippi to attend the funeral of the elder Mr. Davis' favorite uncle. Joe couldn't understand why any black man would live in Mississippi if he wasn't born there, but he was proud to help his parents afford plane tickets so they could go, and then get out of there quickly without having to drive through any southern states as a mixed-race couple.

In 1970, $200 represented about four months of paper route savings. Now Dr. Davis could make that in a little over two hours, if he could find the clients. Earning a living now meant Dr. Davis had to accept any client who sought out his services. No more screening coeds to determine, by physical attributes alone, who might require multiple visits.

Bob Morgan was a regular guy. Regular in every way. He was married, had three children, worked full time as a claims manager and had put on 30 pounds since graduating college. He was a Protestant. Dr. Davis liked counseling Protestants as they seemed to lack the head trash that was part of the Catholic psyche.

Bob was at a crossroads in his career *(so, I'm doing career counseling now,* Dr. Davis thought.) After several years working for an abusive boss who wanted to be a "friend" to all his employees, Bob broke free and took the first position that became available to him at another insurance company. What relief he had found in his new job! No longer was he waking up nights going through mental lists of the tasks he had to get through before his boss made his mid-morning appearance. His new employer was supportive, patient, understanding, and gave Bob considerable autonomy. But now, a year into the job, Bob was not so sure he made the right choice to leave his old job. He had been making good money. Was he some kind of pussy that he couldn't withstand a little (much more than a little) harassment? Were things really that bad back then?

He really liked his new boss and the company seemed OK, but did he really have a future there? At 45, could he really see himself spending the rest of his career there? If he didn't make a move soon would his life just acquiesce? Would he be stuck there for the duration? But if he did decide to leave, there was no real clear path. He really couldn't go back to his old company. He could stay in the same industry doing the same thing with a new company, but what would he have gained? A new boss and a new company? No, he was fine with his current boss and his current company as well as any other. This was the time to really make a break for it, or spend rest of his career wishing he had.

Dr. Davis had, more or less, checked out at "a year into the new job, Bob was not so sure he had made the right choice." He was still quasi-listening, but he wasn't present with Bob. He was transported back to his break up with Georgie when he was in college. Had Georgie really started seeing Joe as an antidote for the break up with Alan? Joe had been "supportive, patient, understanding" too but had Georgie reached the point where she, like Bob, just wanted to go off on her own, "to find out who she was" as she put it, before it was too late? Was she afraid of the complacency of being stuck in a relationship that was neither bad nor one with a clear future?

If she had made no decision to leave they would surely have gotten married, by default. *How could she have doubts about our future together when I was so sure?* After all these years it was suddenly clear to him: this was just the natural progression of a relationship with an expiration date stamped on the label. *This is what you get when you ask an 18 year old to make a lifetime, adult commitment,* he thought. For the first time in his adult life, Joe felt like a huge weight had been lifted off his chest. *She left because of her, not me. We were just at different places in our lives. She didn't leave me because I was inadequate in any way* (although he later proved to be inadequate in so many ways). *She left because she was not ready, at 18, to forsake all other options, real or imagined, for the rest of her life.*

How many years had he beaten himself up, been the victim, when all along it was just the natural course of a young person not wanting to commit until considering all available opportunities! Ah, how the wisdom of an old man could have served him better when he was a young man.

Would he have become a priest? Would he have been so fixated on coeds? Could he have led a "normal" life if only he had recognized what was happening to him when it was happening?

"Are you listening to me? Dr. Davis, are you listening to me?"

"Yes, of course….Robert….Bob. A few questions come to mind: What would happen if you went back to your old job?"

"I was miserable there. I think it would only be a matter of time till I was miserable again."

"OK, let's pretend you stay at your current job. What would

that feel like in a couple more years?" As many times as Martin tried to get Bob to "feel" something, Bob could only "think."

"I think, as much as I like my boss, I would always be wondering if I could do better somewhere else or on my own. It's not really fair to him if I'm not fully engaged in my work for me to continue on there."

The 20 year old Joe would have encouraged Bob to hang in there with his current employer. The 46 year old Dr. Davis accepted that (Georgie –oops - Freudian slip) Bob needed to broaden his horizons. Dr. Davis told Bob he would probably need only a few more sessions to get his issues resolved. A client's looks were no longer a determinant of how many sessions a client would need. Now the focus was on how many visits were allowable by a client's insurance company.

That night Joe slept with the light off. He slept all night. No unwelcome visitations, no flashbacks, just the first good night's sleep he'd had since getting thrown off campus. *If I could add up all those countless hours dwelling on the unchangeable events of the past, how many months…..no, years have I wasted. Where to now? Can I make up for the lost time? Do I have to? Can I go on from here and forget about the wasted time? Can I forgive myself for wasting the time? Has the time all been a waste? Have I done nothing worth remembering? And what about the crazy shit I've done since then because I couldn't accept things as they were so long ago? The suicide attempt, the preying on young women, being a lousy priest. Becoming a priest in the first place!*

His becoming a priest was not prefaced by some grand transformation, a la St. Augustine. Augustine's conversion at midlife (by fourth century standards), when he eschewed sex, came after he had already had a lengthy affair with the unmarried mother of his child. Joe could not really put a finger on, looking back later, what it really was that Brother Martin had wanted to accomplish by taking a vow of celibacy. Was he trying to make a statement? Was he doing it for spite because of losing Georgie? Did he think he "owed" it to God for having saved his life, as if he could not have glorified God as a married man and father?

Or was it simply a way to give his life definition? At twenty-five, and without a steady girlfriend, he was feeling old. His high school friends were (mostly) getting married, not having been delayed by serving in the military. They met girls in college and tied the knot. And his parent's generation, not having been delayed by college after getting out of the service, would have been on their second or third kid by the time they were twenty-five. Attending the seminary took all that off the table and set him on a clear path. Joe never intended for it to be the chaste path of St. Augustine.

As a psychologist, Dr. Davis knew the healthy thing would be to "accept" the past and try to build a healthier future. As a person, he had a hard time letting go of the regret and felt he needed to grieve the loss of all the mental energy he used to expend in reliving (re-dying?) the ordeal of his break up with Georgie. And would he miss the visitations from younger Joe? Has young Joe disappeared for good now that he has figured this whole thing out? Is this how an alcoholic feels after he quits drinking? He doesn't necessarily miss the drinking but misses hanging out with his buddies. Martin felt at once relief and sadness and loneliness.

As each day went by, Joe grew more convinced that Georgie had done what she had to do and that this was just a natural progression of a relationship that, from the start, was not meant to work out. Thinking about the person he had become and the woman he imagined her to now be, he knew it would not have lasted long anyway. At one time he could not think of going on living without her (and he tried to prove it through suicide) and now he could not imagine having gone on living with her. He no longer longed to be with her, but the scars, emotional and physical, would never fully fade.

41

Father Martin was always astounded by how parochial Catholics were; even those who didn't attend parochial school! Even in the same town, if there was more than one Catholic parish, common people had no idea what was going on from one parish to another. Being only 50 miles from Boston, most of his parishioners were originally from the Irish neighborhoods of the city. Once bussing (school desegregation) was imposed in the 70's, many of the Irish families fled to the suburbs. But the Irish, clannish as they are, tended to move in groups. Families from St. Brigid's move to one parish and those from St. Brendan's moved to another, all within a few miles of each other, often in the same town. Families who didn't know each other while living in adjacent parishes in Boston continued to live apart when settling into new parishes next to each other in the suburbs.

This phenomenon provided the kind of cover that helped clergy abuses thrive (fester?). Father Martin benefitted from the fact that no one had ever heard of him when he arrived on the scene as a parish priest at St. Margaret's. He also enjoyed the freedom and anonymity he had when traveling to the surrounding area just outside the parish boundary. Branching out, first as psychologist Dr. Joe Davis, and later as recreational drummer Joe Davis, he felt liberated from his past, present, and future.

Joe had seen the ad for an open audition for "musicians" for the community band in Greenborough, the next town over. Joe had never considered himself a "musician." He was simply a drummer. It had been a while since he had picked up the sticks (the rectory was not an ideal place for playing drums), but, moved by the Spirit, he decided to give it a try. Even with the sweaty palms of a drummer who was well past the point of rusty, Joe survived the audition. He was the only drummer to try out. The community band, he was told, would concentrate on show tunes, jazz, big band standards, and marches. Not the classic rock tunes that were his passion, but a good place to start. Except for how twenty years of neglect can degrade one's skills, he was right back in college. One of the things he fondly remembered about playing drums in the college jazz band was that he was always set up in the back row, just behind the trumpet players. There were two female trumpet players with award winning butts and when they hit the high notes, with both sets of cheeks firmly clenched, WOW, that made it all worth it!

Joe was hoping there might be some similar talent, musical or otherwise, in this community band. His hopes were soon realized when, at the third rehearsal, he spotted a new arrival – a trumpet player named Sheila. She had noticed him too; the drummer in the back wearing a turtleneck even in the July heat.

Determined to make up for lost time, Joe gave himself fully (as fully as one can when leading a double life) to Sheila. Their relationship turned intimate (or at least sexual) almost immediately. He was a psychologist in private practice and they took full advantage of his "flexible work schedule" whenever possible, including both before and after weekly Wednesday night band practices. Sheila was a waitress, cobbling together a living by working a few lunchtimes, a couple nights tending the bar, and every Saturday night and Sunday brunch. *Ironic*, Father Martin thought, *she has the perfect schedule for the wife of a priest….if priests could get married.* She did have the perfect schedule for the lover of a priest who is leading a double life!

Sheila was the first (unmarried) woman Joe had ever been with over the age of 22. She seemed to know what she wanted sexually, and there were none of the power and control issues that were part of the deal in his previous encounters with (young) women. She also didn't approach the relationship from a weak emotional standpoint; truly a new experience with Joe. In short, Sheila was an adult woman.

It dawned on Joe, from a Transactional Analysis perspective, that he had never had an Adult-Adult relationship in his entire life. He was always either in the Parent role (Father Martin counseling coeds or his spiritual children), or the Adult role dealing with Children (Dr. Davis with his clients), or in the role of Child (answering to his Clerical and Administrative superiors). Although leading a double life, as Joe, he felt like this was the closest thing he had ever had to being in a healthy relationship.

Sheila also represented Joe's third toe-dipping into non-priestly waters. As a psychologist, Dr. Davis got a sense that, if necessary, he could make a living in civilian clothes. The community band let him pass for any other single guy involved with non-church related activities. The turtleneck even helped him look the part of a jazz drummer. With Sheila, Joe felt he could carry on a real relationship, if and when he was no longer a priest.

So what was it that kept him in the priesthood? The priesthood has a way of protecting the priest from the realities of life. In one respect, priests are exposed to more grief and emotional pain than any one single individual, with so many funerals and administering to the sick and dying. But in any real sense, the pain and grief they experience on a daily basis is that of others. Much the same way a psychologist can sit and listen to all kinds of aberrant, amoral shit during the day and still go home to a normal life, a priest helps others grieve without having to internalize it himself.

With guaranteed housing, employment, and benefits for life, a priest is immune to most of the stressors afflicting most men. For much of history, the Roman collar has afforded priests with unprecedented, unchallenged, and unencumbered respect and unchecked and undeserved access to the private lives (and private places) of Catholics worldwide. Father Martin had benefitted from this protective shell, but he felt this shell was beginning to crack with his expulsion from the college chaplaincy, and with all the scrutiny the Church was under following the revelations about the priest abuse scandal afflicting the Church. Father Martin realized how difficult it was to keep his vows, having betrayed his oath countless times. He also imagined that it must be exponentially more difficult with marriage vows. With religious vows, only one side had to struggle to be true. With a married couple, both sides have to live up to their end of the deal.

Joe was always curious to know what people did for a living and to find out what they had studied in school. Joe had studied psychology, and later, theology, which made sense for a psychologist and priest. And he was glad to know that nurses studied nursing and architects studied architecture. But there seemed to be many more history majors selling insurance and carpenters who had been English majors. And there were so many law school graduates not working as lawyers, and so many more that were attorneys, but were miserable.

Back at St. Dom's, Joe played in the pit orchestra whenever the drama club put on a musical production. One night after rehearsal, he noticed one of the thespians crying (not an unusual sight, male or female, observed Joe).

"What's up?" Joe offered in a feeble attempt to be comforting.

"I have to change my major."

"That's not unusual. Some kids change their majors more often than they change their underwear."

His attempt at levity fell flat.

"From theater arts to business."

"Really? Don't tell me Theater is too rigorous?" Joe was incredulous.

"My father is making me. He said he would only pay for

college if I majored in business so I could get a job after college."

This sounded perfectly reasonable to Joe, but he knew he needed to come up with a more comforting response. "That's so unfair!" he said, trying very hard not to sound sarcastic. "You should be allowed to follow your passion, whatever it is!" Joe was hoping she might stop crying enough so he could take her out for a beer and moral support.

A look of righteous indignation returned to the aspiring actress…and future business major.

Joe wondered what she was doing now, all these years later. He also wondered what his own passion might be, and why he wasn't following it.

Ever since ninth grade, watching Bob Newhart play a psychologist-straight man on TV, married to Suzanne Pleshette's character, Joe thought he was passionate about being a therapist in private practice. But being a shrink turned out to be a lot less fun than Bob Newhart was having. The clients Dr. Davis saw all seemed deeply flawed; damaged even. Was this just the human condition in the 21st century? Maybe he was just being exposed to a cross section of people on the margins. These were people who, mostly of their own making, were barely keeping their heads above the surface of their quicksand world.

"Dr. Davis, do you ever look at a young girl, maybe ten or eleven years old, and just know that she's gonna turn out hot when she is older?"

"Dr. Davis, is it normal to fantasize about my husband dying in a horrible accident?"

"Sometimes, usually, I imagine my old boyfriend's face when I'm having sex with my husband. Then I go cry in the shower. I feel bad about it, but then I look forward to having sex again so I can fantasize about my ex again. My husband seems happy because he's getting sex. Am I a bad person?"

"Some days I get dressed for work and kiss my wife goodbye and leave in the car. But I don't go to work. I just drive around for a while or sit in my car at the shopping center until I know my wife has gone to work. I'm all out of sick days and we're only half-way through the year. I go home and watch porn all day and jerk off, then take a nap. I make the bed again and get dressed back up in my work clothes before my wife gets home, and she thinks I just got home. She has no idea. I can't stop but I am going to lose my job if I miss any more work. What am I going to do?"

"Dr. Davis, my husband falls asleep watching TV every night. I tell him I'm going to bed and he says he'll be right up. But a lotta times I'll wake up during the night and he'll still be asleep downstairs. He hardly touches me. He gets dressed in the bathroom. Do you think he might be gay?"

"My wife is really mad at me. She said she is going to kick me out if I don't get my act together. I really hate my job and I think I should quit. I've been spending all the time I can playing my guitar and I'm almost ready to make a go of it. But my wife doesn't support me. I just know it is what I was meant to do. I know it is who I am. I need to follow my dream. I am going to be a recording artist. If I don't do it soon, I may never have a chance to do it. But she said I'm crazy and we'll lose the house. That she'll leave me. But I'm losing my soul in that job. It's killing me! I need to get out and follow my dream. And I met this great singer. I know we could be a hit together; she has such a beautiful voice!"

42

Joe Davis had one foot on the dock and one foot in the boat. The outboard was running and the lines had been loosed. He had to decide if he wanted to go for a ride or stay put. His current position could only lead to drowning.

Dr. Davis' practice was building quickly. This was a Good News/Bad News predicament. His goal was to eventually build his practice so he could transition out of the priesthood into self-sufficiency. But the quickened pace brought with it the anxiety that the change was coming, and it was real! He was encouraged to learn that most of his referrals were generated by word-of-mouth since it would have been awkward to advertise in the church bulletin. He expected word-of-mouth referrals from his female clients, but he also received a surprising number from his male clients. As hard as it would be to imagine talking to another veteran about therapy, it was more startling to him that civilian men would ever disclose to another man that he was seeing a psychologist.

So many of his clients initiated therapy reeling from the effects of marital infidelity; either as the aggrieved spouse, or as the exposed cheater. The most interesting case was that of Kris, a forty-something married woman. Kris was actually an undetected unfaithful partner. She blurted out her transgression in the first session, as if she were in a confessional with a priest.

Dr. Davis and Kris spent the next few sessions in a futile search. Dr. Davis was digging to find the real, underlying issue, not satisfied that Kris' presenting problem could be the actual source of her anxiety. That almost never happens. Kris was desperately searching for deficiencies in her marriage to explain (or excuse) her infidelity. Her misguided examination only revealed a relatively happy and loving marriage. Her husband, Aaron, was loving, attentive, and sensitive to her needs. He was an "excellent provider, and even helps out around the house." Her two children were doing well at school and doing all the things kids are supposed to do. Their fourteen year old daughter, the younger of the siblings, was defiant, but Kris attributed that to being "the baby of the family."

Finally, in the sixth session, Dr. Davis started to crack the case.

"Kris, remind me where you are in the birth order of your siblings?"

"I'm the oldest of four; two girls then two boys."

"How were you as a teenager? I mean, what kind of kid were you?"

"Oh, I was a straight A student, you know, honor society and all that. No drinking. No drugs."

"You probably never gave your parents any trouble?"

"No, I was pretty much the perfect child. I helped out at home, babysat my sister and brothers. I even babysat my neighbor's kids. I passed my driver's test on the first try and I never ever got a speeding ticket or banged up the car."

"What's the most outrageous thing you ever did as a teenager?"

"Once I skipped school with my best friend and hung out in a state park all day. Katie drove me back to school just in time to catch the school bus home. That doesn't sound very risqué, I know, but it was a big thing for me…. Oh, and once when my family was staying in a hotel on vacation, I stole a Gideon's Bible."

"Did you go on dates in high school? How were you with boys?"

"Usually we just went to the mall with a group of girls and we'd meet up with a bunch of guys. Nothing ever happened. I went to the movies with boys, but that's about it. Oh yeah, I went to the senior prom with Tommy. Afterwards in his car we kissed…..a lot! But then he touched my breast and I told him to take me home."

"And you didn't have any more sexual experiences as a teenager?"

"Well, not in high school. But I met Aaron freshman year in college and we eventually started having sex. I was nineteen, so technically I was still a teenager."

Now Dr. Davis knew he had solved two cases: the case of Kris and Aaron, and another case he had been struggling with for two decades that he, only recently, thought he had solved. It was clear that Kris had never gone through the normal rebellious stage during adolescence. She never questioned, much less tested, the boundaries set by her parents, teachers, and society. Naturally intelligent, pretty, and eager to please authorities, she had never experienced loss or had to overcome hurdles. Even as she saw her friends rebelling against authority, she consciously decided to walk the narrow path because she saw that it held all the rewards she wanted in life. She just could not relate to "defiance for defiance sake" like her daughter seemed to be going through right now.

Kris had been a one-sided person – only good. She had never seen or experienced her other side. As an adult, with all the things she wanted in life: marriage, children, house, friends, and job, she still lived the one-sided life. But she grew increasingly curious to know what it felt like to not be perfect. She wondered if she were only half a person. She loved her daughter even though the girl clearly had two sides of her personality. Kris wondered if she could still love herself if she lifted the veil, just a little, to see the "bad" side. Maybe it would even make her a better, more complete person in the end? But the idea of cheating disgusted her, and knowing that Aaron might find out made her nauseous. She knew that telling Aaron the affair "has nothing to do with you" would be of no consolation to him.

Simply put, Kris was experiencing a latent rebellion against the authority that was her marriage vows, and the greater mores of society. She came to the therapeutic process feeling a witch's brew of insoluble emotions in her mind's cauldron.

She came to her weekly sessions seeking comfort, release,

validation, clarity, rescue, judgement, and even condemnation. The process of stirring together fear, guilt, exhilaration, remorse, anxiety, worry, love, and shame, ultimately resulted in the realization that she is going through a normal, albeit delayed process, that doesn't necessarily make her a bad person.

For Dr. Davis, the process resulted in the realization that, all those years ago, a girl he thought of as a woman was simply an adolescent who looked, and sometimes acted like a woman. He had finally, after twenty-five years, cracked the case and come to terms with it. With all the introspection he could muster, he concluded this was just a normal phase Georgie was going through at the time. She had had her adolescent crisis of rebellion right when she was supposed to – as an adolescent. He had never had his own adolescent crisis, or had lost his chance as his adolescence was taken from him in Vietnam. He wondered if he could ever expect to be a healthy person having skipped his stage of teenage rebellion.

What he missed, due to an underdeveloped self-examination muscle, was his own responsibility in the demise of the relationship: maybe she was just sick of him making her feel intellectually inferior, and didn't have the tools, or even the awareness to recognize the situation and ask Joe to change. She felt something wasn't right but couldn't put her finger on it. She always felt a little on edge around Joe and couldn't really relax. With Ira she could relax and just be herself; he never challenged her. She thought her best chance of figuring this out would be to do it alone.

43

OH FUCK, Joe thought. *There's that guy from St. Margaret's.* Joe recognized Devon as the bass player in St. Margaret's youth music group. At 24, now out of school for a year, and unable to find a job for which his sociology degree prepared him, Devon was back at his home parish as an "adult leader" of the youth music group.

Joe was certain he would be exposed. Father Martin had even sat in on a couple rehearsals, playing congas on some of the acoustic arrangements. There is no way Devon wouldn't recognize him. Sheila had picked up Joe at his office and driven them both to rehearsal so there was no way he could just disappear.

Don't come over! Don't come over! Don't come over! Devon went over to say hi to Father Martin.

"Father Martin! Hi!"

"Um…Oh…you must have me confused with my brother. Martin's my identical twin."

"Wow, the likeness is uncanny."

"That's what it means to be identical," Joe quipped. "What's your name?"

Devon looked into Joe's eyes. He could swear he saw a brief flash of recognition in those eyes when he first approached him. "My name's Devon. I play in the youth music group at St. Margaret's. That's how I know Father Martin."

"Well nice to meet you…"

"So, you both play the drums?"

"My mother was one of those who thought identical twins should do the same activities and wear the same clothes, all the time. After a while it drove us crazy and we ended up taking different paths. But we both still play the drums. I'm much better though…"

Just then, Mark Bertolo, "Il Maestro" they all called him, was tapping the end of his conductor's baton on his music stand to get everyone to sit down and tune up. Most of the musicians (and the drummers too!) were there as much for the socializing as for the music. There were none of the basket cases he had encountered in the college orchestra; really talented instrumentalists who were strung tighter than their violins, paralyzed with performance anxiety. This group was all fun. It had been fun for Joe too, until just now.

Everyone in place now, the tuning cacophony ensued. Sheila always lined up right in front of Joe, right where he liked her, affording him with the best view of her award-winning butt. By Bertolo's arrangement, the entire band was seated with the exception of the trumpets and the upright bass. As this was the bass player's (Devon) first night in the band he was told to stand toward the back, stage left. Joe looked up from his music from time to time and noticed Devon was looking at him. Or was he looking at Sheila? Hard to tell.

44

"My mom says she went to high school with you but she didn't recall you having a twin brother."

Not him again. This little punk is starting to aggravate me. What are the chances someone else from Valley Park, Connecticut ended up in Thornton, Massachusetts? "Hi there….uh…"

"Devon."

"Yes, hi Devon."

"My mom doesn't remember your brother." His mom had actually told Devon she was sure Joe didn't have a brother named Martin.

Devon, the sociology-degreed, part-time church and community band musician, saw a loose thread and kept tugging on it. It must have been all those identical twin studies he had to read in college that kept him so intrigued by Dr. Joe Davis.

Devon had recently called his mother to compare notes. She knew of the Davis family when she was growing up back in Valley Park, CT. She knew Joe, knew his two sisters, Beth and Sue. She knew Joe had an older brother, but couldn't recall his name. But she had no recollection of a twin brother Martin. She hadn't mistaken the Davis family for any other….there was only one bi-racial family in town.

"Did you know them in high school? Maybe you didn't know Martin if he went to a Catholic high school?" Devon queried.

"Well, that could be Devon. But I seem to remember it was Joe who was studying to be a priest, which always struck me as ironic, given the trouble he got into in high school."

"Do tell, Mother," prompted Devon, showing a flair for the dramatic.

Devon's mother went on to recount the mythological version of how "Joe Davis tried to kill a migrant worker over a stolen bag of Fritos."

"What was your mom's name?" Joe asked.

"She was Karen Longlais."

"Hmmm. It's ringing a bell, but not loudly. Was a long time ago."

"Your brother Martin?" Not letting it go.

"He went to Central Catholic High. I stayed at Valley Park. He knew from an early age he wanted to be a priest."

"Even your voices are identical."

"What can I tell ya? Same genes, same voice, same everything."

45

Alex Smithers came to see Dr. Davis for his Tuesday 11:00 am appointment. This was his third session. Dr. Davis felt he was getting somewhere with Alex. They had had only two sessions and Alex was already opening up about issues with his wife and starting to acknowledge that not all of his problems were of his wife's making. Although his training prepared him to look past the "presenting" problem to the "underlying" problem, Dr. Davis was always determined to home in on the real issue. He believed the key to "cutting to the chase" was his ability to build trust with his client. The client begins to trust the therapist after seeing how the therapist deals with the less significant presenting problem. If the client is not made to feel shame or embarrassment over the initial issue, then maybe, with encouragement and patience, he will share the issue that is really eating at him.

Patience was not Dr. Davis' forte' which is precisely why he wanted to move to second base. But how to get there quickly without skipping first base altogether? Dr. Davis was determined at today's session to try a new approach to build trust: honesty. Unfortunately, honesty was another attribute that was not his forte'.

"Come on in Alex, it is nice to see you again." Dr. Davis' mind was always moving at whip speed. *If only I could focus it on the task at hand!* He thought, *I'm lucky my name isn't Alex Smithers with that lisp I had as a kid. It was tough enough being Joe Davith. Being Alekth Thmitherth would have been a dithathter!*

Sitting forward on his chair, Alex began: "I've had a really good week Doctor, so I was thinking I might not need to keep coming for counseling."

Dr. Davis had seen this curveball before. And he thought the word "counseling" was a telling touch. Some of his more serious and committed clients came for "therapy," or "treatment." Counseling seemed less formal and could be discontinued and restarted on a whim.

"Sounds like everything is resolved, Alex. You're happy with where things are right now?"

"Well…things are manageable and I'm not in crisis anymore."

"Alex, can I be frank with you? When people come here, it's not a casual thing. It is usually only after something really bad has happened, or issues have built up over time to the point that they are having trouble functioning in their daily lives. That's kind of how I see your situation. Things built up to a boiling point before you called me. Am I on the right track?"

"Yes, that's accurate."

"Some people have told me I'm a good counselor, and maybe I am, but I'm not so sure I'm that good that you could already be where you need to be after just two sessions. Would it be

OK if I ask you a few more questions before we decide if today will be our last session together?"

"Sure," Alex replied. He relaxed his shoulders and settled into his chair. Dr. Davis mirrored him.

"The first time you and I met, you told me there were trust issues between you and your wife. She asked for your email password and you refused to give it to her, saying, on principle, there should be some privacy in a marriage. Karen told you there should be openness. And you told her she should…"

"Trust me. There should be trust in a marriage," he proclaimed with indignation.

"I agree there should be trust in a marriage, but I wonder if there has been some reason she's not trusting you right now. Why do you suppose she wanted your email password?"

"I don't know." Silence…. "I don't know how she could suspect me of anything." Dr. Davis made a mental note of Alex's interesting parsing of words: *I don't know how she could suspect me of anything.* This is quite a different thing than saying: *I didn't do anything,* or *I've got nothing to hide,* or *even: she has no reason to doubt me.*

"Suspect you of anything? Like what?" Dr. Davis wanted more but didn't yet want Alex to know he, too, suspected there was a good reason for Karen to not trust him.

"Oh, I don't know. Women always think their husbands are cheating on them."

"There are a lot of reasons she might want to look at your computer, but an affair was the first thing that came to your mind?"

Silence.

"Karen probably knows you better than anyone else in the world. True?"

Alex nodded.

"There might be some little thing you said or did, or just a change in your mannerisms, perceptible only to her, that she picked up on that gave her a tinge of doubt. You told me that this, I think you called it 'paranoia,' …that this paranoia was something new. Maybe she picked up on some little thing recently that makes her uneasy?"

Dr. Davis knew he was doing too much of the talking, but he saw Alex's eyes widen and look up to the left as if he was searching his mind's history tape for a time when he might have let his guard down and Karen picked up on it. Their eyes met again briefly before Alex looked at the floor. His hands fell to his sides in resignation. Dr. Davis knew Alex's next utterance would be the real issue causing his mental pain. And shame.

"I haven't been completely honest with Karen." Silence. "Almost from the start."

"It's OK, Alex. Let's talk about it a little bit."

The sight of a man crying always unnerved Dr. Davis. It was not something he saw much of growing up. His father was a proud black man and not prone to sentimentality. Even at the fall of Saigon men were too much in shock to cry. He still felt shame over the untethered wailing and sobs he himself had

257

displayed when Georgie broke up with him. He knew, from a clinical sense, that crying is a healthy reaction or expression to sadness, but it still made him uneasy when it was coming from a man.

"When we were married for about a year, my old girlfriend, Alicia, tracked me down. We hadn't been in touch since we'd broken up a couple years before. I was still kind of a mess when I met Karen and we got married right away. She really helped me though a lot. Well, it turns out Alicia was pregnant at the time we broke up. So she calls me a couple years later and tells me we have a one year old daughter."

The crying intensified.

"We had broken up because Alicia never wanted to have kids! Then she keeps the baby and doesn't tell me until after I got married. And then she wants me to be in the baby's life. If she had just told me when she found out she was pregnant I would've gone back and we could've been a family and I would've been with my little girl from the beginning."

Alex slumped forward, his elbows on his knees and his eyes soaking the heels of his hands. He took a few deep breaths and continued in a husky voice.

"When I first found out I didn't tell Karen. It would've broken her heart. She can't have children. Now I can't tell her because I should have told her before."

"So, you've never told Karen." Dr. Davis repeated flatly.

"No, she doesn't know any of it. I can't tell her."

"I'm feeling that there's more about this you need to get off your chest."

Alex took another deep breath. "So, at first I figured Alicia just wanted money and I might come over and see Madison; that's her name. I might go see Madison once in a while and drop off the support check. (another sigh) But then it was really great seeing Alicia again, seeing what a great mother she is to Madison, and I'd be there and Madison would go in for a nap, and, well, you know, then things….things just happened."

"Alex, you told me you've been married about five years now? So your affair has been ongoing for about four years? Am I doing the math right?"

"Doc, I wouldn't really call it an affair. Alicia and I got married and I adopted Madison. I know it wasn't actually legal, but we got a justice of the peace to marry us and I shortened my name on the marriage license from Smithers to Smith. I know, real original, right?"

Alex was sitting up now, exhausted but relaxed. Dr. Davis was sitting back, exhausted and shocked, but trying hard to only show the exhausted part of him.

"It sounds like you are living a double life. How much time do you spend with Alicia and Madison, and how do you manage it with Karen?"

"I own real estate all over New England. Karen thinks I need to travel all over and stay in different hotels, which sometimes I do. I just bring Alicia and my daughter with me. Other times she thinks I'm out of state, but I'm just twenty miles away. I spend most of the week with Alicia and the weekends with Karen.

"This must be exhausting, keeping this from Karen?" Dr. Davis thought about how exhausting it is keeping his own dual life from both Sheila and the Church.

"At least I don't have to keep it from Alicia. She knows I need to be home on weekends. But it is killing me. You gotta help me. You gotta help me figure out what to do," he pleaded.

Dr. Davis thought, *I'm the last person he should ask for advice on this. If he figures this out I hope he tells me what to do! Is this the same guy who wanted to end the counseling relationship a few minutes ago? This is going to take some major work to fix!* Exhausted and out of time, Dr. Davis went into his summation.

"Alex, we've covered a lot of ground this morning. I can see you're emotionally spent and will need to process all of this. You did the right thing to tell me this and I know it took a lot of strength to do so. I thank you for trusting me enough to tell it to me. Can I suggest you don't make any drastic changes in your life until we get together again next week? Maybe then we can come up with a good game plan to help you. I do have some homework for you. I want you to imagine having to tell Karen. I want you to come up with what a few possible outcomes would look like if you were to tell Karen about your situation. Then we can talk about it next week. OK?"

Almost immediately, having kept the lunch hour clear, Dr. Davis was alone with his careening mind, bouncing from justification to denial. *At least I never got married under false pretenses, twice*, he thought while denying that his vows to the priesthood were a de facto marriage to the Church. Thinking about how exhausted Alex appeared made him realize how he himself must look trying to juggle his own dual life. He even envied Alex because he believed Alex's dual life would soon be resolved, with Dr. Davis' help, one way or another. While he knew executing the plan would be very painful for all involved, the various options were fairly straightforward:

- Tell Karen you want a divorce
- Tell Karen what's been going on
  - o She'll divorce you
  - o She'll have you arrested for bigamy
  - o She'll accept it – you'll continue on as you are, but in the open
- Tell Karen, but stop the affair/illegal marriage and continue joint custody/child support

Working through the scenarios, Dr. Davis could not think of one viable option that did not include telling Karen. It came to him just then that there was no way out of his own quagmire without telling Sheila the whole truth. Or most of the truth. His potential outcomes were even more straightforward, but equally painful:

- Tell Sheila he is a priest and has been lying to her all along
  - o She'll either accept it or she won't

He had already determined that he must leave the priesthood regardless of what Sheila decides. *If I had any balls,* he thought, *I'd quit now.*

He pledged to himself that, going forward, he would be honest with Sheila, and with his life. *No sense going into all the details of the past. The future is all that matters. Sheila doesn't need to know all the minutiae of the relationship with Kim-Ly, although sharing how she died might garner some sympathy. Sheila won't benefit from knowing how hard I took the Georgie breakup. I don't know how knowing about my suicide attempt would serve anyone. Chances are she'll never meet anyone who knows the whole truth. And most people who did know wouldn't talk about it. I know my family never will. They'll be so scandalized by my leaving the priesthood they probably will disown me anyway. That pain-in-the-ass Devon heard the story about my hanging, but that's just going to remain a crazy rumor someone started because I have a scar on my neck.*

And Sheila doesn't need to know about the trouble I had with the co-eds when I was the chaplain on that little New England campus. It was so long ago I can hardly recall the name of the place. I was a different man then. Those girls were all offered counseling so I'm sure they've turned out fine anyway.

Joe completed the inventory of his memory compartments deciding which parts reflected the new Dr. Joe Davis and could be disclosed, and which parts should just be forgotten. In the course of his lunch hour break between clients Dr. Davis began to feel the outer bands of his approaching relief storm. Now, instead of envying Alex Smithers (or Smith), he pitied him because he knew Alex's solutions would not be so clear cut.

He felt it was perverse, probably unethical, and unavoidable that he was working through his own emotional issues during these sessions that his clients were paying for. Dr. Davis liked to think that it was like a music teacher sitting back and enjoying the music being played by the student during a lesson. But he feared it was more like a bartender being treated to a cocktail by a patron.

The fact was, he was getting long overdue therapy in a quasi-vicarious format. Dr. Davis had long ago given up couching his clinical assessments in Freudian constructs. His therapeutic approach had evolved from sounding the unconscious mind for psychic root causes, to client-centered, phenomenological-existential therapy, to a more behavioral approach. Through this transformation he maintained elements of each perspective and still resorted to Freud's defense mechanisms, when it suited the case. He was clearly in Projection and Counter Transference as he self-counseled in the third person.

That night after community band rehearsal, some of the musicians were heading out for a drink. Joe declined, hoping/thinking that Sheila would do the same. But Sheila had already accepted and thought Joe would come along. They hadn't really talked about their plans for after rehearsal; they always did the same thing, always ending up spending the evening together at her apartment.

At the bar, Sheila, Kathy, Theresa, Angela, and Devon ordered drinks and squeezed around a high top table. Being the only guy didn't bother Devon, having been brought up in a house full of sisters. As the newest member of the group, in only his third week with the band, Devon was the novelty item. They wanted to know all about him: where was he from, what does he do, does he have a girlfriend?

Two of the women were old enough to be Devon's mother. The other two, including Sheila, were about ten years older than him, although the ages of attractive women were hard for Devon to discern, and didn't matter all that much to him anyway.

To make a connection with the group, Devon told them he plays in a music group at a church in the next town. In fact,

Joe's brother is a priest at that church.

"Joe who?" asked Sheila, innocently.

"Joe the drummer. You know? Our drummer. They're identical twins." Devon teased, not convinced Joe really had a twin.

"Really?" asked Sheila, trying to be casual about it.

The others chimed in registering their surprise about Joe's twin as well. Up to this point no one had put two-and-two together about Joe and Sheila, so Sheila's surprise didn't raise any eyebrows.

Joe had never mentioned his priest-brother to Sheila. But then again, he almost never spoke of his family. "It's complicated," he would always say when asked about his family. "Not strained...just complicated."

Sometimes Sheila felt there was more she didn't know about Joe than what she did know, or thought she knew. She didn't even know Joe was a Catholic.

46

Joe and Sheila were spending all of their free time together. They were falling in love. Most of the time it was dinner and "dessert" at Sheila's place. Because she spent her working hours tending bar or waiting on tables, she preferred to cook Joe dinner at her modest apartment.

At 34, and with no immediate marital prospects, Sheila was beginning to feel like an old maid. She'd had a couple failed relationships and even was engaged once. But that was all before she hit 30. Her recent dry spell was partially self-imposed. Her last boyfriend, her "soul mate" Stephen, the one she was going to spend the rest of her life with, turned out to be an IV drug addict. How could I have missed all the warning signs? Am I just a poor judge of character?

Then, while partially resigned to drying up on the vine, she met Joe the drummer. He was charming, OK looking, single, and apparently straight. After Stephen, she was just glad to be in what she thought was an honest and open relationship. "I think my boyfriend Joe is a vampire," she joked with her friends. "He always wears a turtleneck and never takes it off until after dark and the lights are out." But as open as she thought Joe was, she still had questions that needed honest answers. After several "dates" at her apartment, Sheila wondered why they had never, not once, been to his place. Sheila's friends planted the seeds of doubt, reminding Sheila of her track record when it came to judging men.

Maybe he's married and is just here on business during the week? He probably goes home to his wife on the weekend.

Maybe he lives at home with his mother?

Maybe he's a priest?

Maybe he's gay and lives with his lover?

If any of these were true, Sheila hoped it was that Joe was still living with his mother, but at 46, that would be a major red flag!

The next Wednesday, after band practice, as they were headed back to Sheila's apartment, the questions began.

"How could such a great guy like you still be single?"

"I think the timing was just never right for me. I spent my teens in the Marine Corps and my 20s in college. I've spent the last 15 years working on my career and I haven't really concentrated on dating. And besides, I really never met the right woman."

"Joe, why have we never been to your place?"

"It's always just been more convenient to go to your place. I mean, I live in the next town. Everything we do together is here in Greenborough so it's just easier hanging out here."

"Well, I'd like to see your house sometime. It's not that far. Can we drive there tonight?"

Martin had to think fast. He knew this question would be asked at some point but he never bothered to prepare for it. His long term plan was to get an apartment and to move out of the rectory once his therapy practice was better established. After two years, the practice was getting busier, but he still struggled with juggling his priestly responsibilities and building his business. There was a nice apartment building he passed on his way to Greenborough. He was pretty sure he could afford the rent there.

As usual when he got nervous, Joe could feel the lisp coming on. "FUCK" he muttered to himself, "now with everything else, I have to deal with this?!"

"We can drive by my apartment but you can't come in," Joe said, being careful to avoid any words with an "s" or "sh" sound. "My apartment…a total wreck. I didn't think we'd be going there tonight."

"It's OK….How bad could it be? I'd like to see it."

"Really bad. Not tonight. I'll clean it up and have you over nextht time."

"OK, let's just drive by then. I'd like to see your neighborhood at least. You've got all weekend to clean it up. How about you cook me dinner there next week after rehearsal?"

Well, she called his bluff. Martin now had a busy week ahead of him. As they drove by the apartment complex, Joe thought: God I hope one of those units is for rent!

At this point Sheila only had a clear answer to one of her friends' questions: Is he a priest? "No, he's not a priest. He lives in an apartment just over the town line in Thornton. He wouldn't let me go in it so I still don't know if he lives with his mother or is married. I'm pretty sure he's not gay though, just from personal experience."

Martin had never had to buy anything for himself (other than running shoes and turtlenecks). From the time he went into the Marine Corps at seventeen, his food, clothing, furniture, and housing were provided for him. He didn't know the first thing about buying towels, sheets, pillowcases, or even pillows! He looked around his suite in the rectory and compiled a list. Bed, curtains, desk chair, desk, lamp. On the way home from meeting the realtor at the apartment, he stopped at the big box home center. He left the store with towels, a desk chair, and a lamp. He couldn't buy sheets because he didn't know how to answer when the sales lady asked, "Twin, Full, Queen, or King? How big is the space for your desk? Your bed? Your kitchen table?"

Joe had not even thought about a kitchen table and chairs, or even what to put on a table. He had only scanned the visual field inside his suite of rooms at the rectory which did not include a kitchen. Now the list was growing: dishes, silverware, cups, coffee maker. Coffee! Does the refrigerator come with the apartment? What about the washer and dryer? Do I need a laundry basket now? I need pots and pans, serving dishes, condiments. I NEED CONDIMENTS! Martin started to panic. Couldn't I come up with a better lie than 'my place is a mess?' Maybe I'll call Sheila on Wednesday and tell her I'm sick.

Joe called his older sister. "Minnie, I need your help. I need a favor." Joe sometimes called his sister Beth "Minnie;" it was a relic of their childhood. As a young girl, like most Catholic girls in the early '60s, Beth had to wear white cotton gloves to church on Sundays. Joe thought, with the way the white gloves contrasted with her chocolate colored arms, it made her look like Minnie Mouse. Joe had an "I love you because you're my brother/sister" relationship with Beth. Lately they had been in touch more than usual because Beth's oldest son was getting married and he had asked Father Martin to officiate. Father Martin was happy to preside over her son's nuptials as being a priest was one of the few things he did that filled his family with pride. So Joe figured Beth owed him a favor. And he was desperate.

Beth was shocked when she heard of Father Martin's plans to leave the priesthood. "Joe (she never did take to calling him by his religious name) your timing sucks. How is my son going to feel if he gets married by a priest who quits right after the wedding?"

Joe told Beth that the marriage would still be valid, and that he had no immediate plans to leave the priesthood. He just wanted to have a place to stay from time to time for now, and it would be there in case he eventually left for good. He asked her to keep it between them for now. This seemed to placate her but Beth still wondered why there was such a sense of urgency.

"Why do we need to have your apartment all set up by Wednesday?"

"I'm having a friend over for dinner on Wednesday and I just can't do it at the rectory. You're going to love the place," changing the subject. "Maybe we'll have the family Christmas party at my apartment this year."

The two siblings got to work setting up the new apartment.

47

Most everything was in place by Tuesday night. Over the previous few days he started to move some of his very few personal items from the rectory to #3 Lincoln Court. He thought it was a bit pathetic that a 46 year old had accumulated so few possessions in his life, but in a way, it was one of the few ways he had really "followed Christ."

He told Mrs. Schiavone at the rectory he would be staying with friends for a couple days, and he arranged for another priest to say Mass on Wednesday morning. He packed a suitcase with all the non-clerical garb he owned: underwear, jeans, running clothes and turtlenecks. In a small box he packed a framed photograph of his whole family taken about ten years earlier during a backyard picnic when Joe had on civilian clothes. He packed his AM/FM radio that had traveled to Vietnam and back with him. He packed a picture of Eric and him taken on their first day in Saigon. And another photo of him and Eric and Kim-Ly taken on the day before Saigon fell in April, 1975.

How different life would have been for him (and for Kim-Ly) if the road to freedom hadn't been a dead end for her. If he could have just held on and pulled her up as the helicopter climbed, she would have gotten out alive. Did she let go? Did he? How many thousands of times had he replayed the scene, awake and in nightmares, in the almost 30 years since that horrible night.

Would they still be together? Would he have felt responsible for her for bringing her to the States? Would she feel beholden to him for saving her life? Would the love they felt so strongly in Nam be less binding back home where it was less forbidden? Did he really know her other than in the Biblical sense? Was she just using him for a chance to escape Vietnam? Was he just using her for sex because she was young, and pure, and clean? It turned out she was clean, but young and pure….who could tell? But she seemed devoted to him, and he to her.

He had seen others fall or get pushed off the helicopter skids in the chaos to get as many people on board the birds as possible. He never had nightmares about all the others, just Kim-Ly. Maybe it was just that she was one living person whose life was in his grasp. They were touching, they were one, and he was not strong enough to save her.

He placed the photos on top of his bureau and studied them once more. It was always shocking to him that someone who was so deeply etched into his memory could not be readily conjured up without the help of a photograph. Of course, he could still see Kim-Ly's face in his nightmares. It was almost the same with Georgie's image. He had thrown out all the pictures of her, and the two of them together, except for the one taken on their six month "anniversary." He was going to mail all the photos back to her (she liked to save everything and indeed still had all her pictures of her former boyfriend, Alan) but, in a rare act of pettiness, he tossed the stack of photos in the kitchen wastebasket near the telephone. He never regretted throwing them away because he knew seeing these pictures of her (in her bathing suit, curled up with a book on her bed, ice skating) would have been just one more way to drive him crazy. And without the pictures, he could scarcely recall her face.

Joe's sister Beth recognized that, whoever the "friend" was who was coming to dinner at #3 Lincoln Court, they would find it peculiar that the apartment looked like a hotel suite, only more sparsely decorated. She prevailed upon Martin to buy "accent pieces." Martin felt no connection to any of this stuff but he deferred to his sister who had been keeping house for twenty-five years.

He slept there Tuesday night. He wanted to have clean sheets when Sheila visited, but even he realized that, while clean is good, "never-been-slept-in" raises red flags. Sheila had told Martin that he had his own "aroma;" not a bad smell, but distinctly his. He wanted to make sure there was enough of his "aroma" around the place to convince Sheila that this really was his apartment.

One glaring problem remained: Joe had agreed to cook dinner for Sheila, but he had never cooked anything (indoors at least) in his life. In the Corps, in college, in the seminary, and as a priest, Martin never had to cook for himself. His dietary needs were basic and simple: three squares. After eating MREs off and on for three years in the Corps he figured he could eat anything. Dormitory food wasn't much better. Sometimes the old, Italian ladies in the rectory would make something special, and he appreciated it. It just wasn't necessary. In fact, he often felt embarrassed to be waited on by these saintly volunteers. Some of his fellow priests were not so humble. Monsignor Reilly actually told old Mrs. Donatelli that he liked his grapes peeled. Peeled! So Mrs. Donatelli, with her ancient, gnarled, arthritic fingers would take the time and trouble to peel his grapes. All in the name of doing God's work.

So Martin's cooking skills were non-existent. He ventured out to the high end market and purchased pre-cooked items that could be easily transferred to his baking pans. He picked up some wine and beer (Sheila could go either way) and returned "home" to #3 Lincoln Court. Before leaving for band rehearsal, he put the food in the oven on low and set the table.

That night at the table, Sheila knew instantly that he had bought the food. There were two large squares of lasagna cut from some larger missing tray of lasagna. She loved him for the effort and told him so. They shared a good laugh over his "cooking."

Sheila really liked Joe's apartment. She detected a woman's touch in the decorating. Or was it a feminine man's touch? Everything looked brand new. It was brand new. How could EVERYTHING be brand new?!

"Did you just move in here? How come everything, the tables, the chairs, couches, curtains, even the shower curtain still has creases from being in the package…you said your place was a wreck…how could everything be brand new?"

"Well yeah, I bought everything new," now switching into no

"s" mode. "I've only been here a brief time and everything I owned got ruined in a fire at my old apartment. And yeah, I put up the bathroom curtain today. The old one needed to be burned."

"So, you lost everything?"

"Yeah, pretty much wiped me out. But, thingth don't mean anything to me. I'm really OK."

He got his anxiety under control. He was pretty sure Sheila was buying his explanation. He relaxed. "These are the only pictures I was able to salvage from the fire." He motioned to the frames on his bureau.

"Is that you? Where was it taken?"

"Saigon, South Vietnam." He previously hadn't talked too much about his military service with Sheila. He wasn't ashamed of it; far from shame. It was just a left over reluctance to talk about something that elicited negative judgments from people in the past.

"You look like such a baby. How old were you?"

"Seventeen. Right out of high school. I volunteered for the Marines because I thought the war was over and no one was sent to Nam anymore…. I was sorely mistaken!"

"Who's this?"

"That's my buddy Eric. We got sent there together right out of basic training. We became brothers."

"What about this picture? How many years later was this

taken? You look about 30 in it."

"That was only about nine months later, believe it or not. Saigon was a tough town for an American teenager. I grew up fast there. That was taken the day before we evacuated the Embassy."

"Who's the girl?"

"Oh, she's just a local girl. Daughter of one of the embassy housekeepers. Good kid. Just wanted to be in a shot with a couple American Marines."

"Where's Eric now"

"He lives in Missouri where he grew up. We get in touch a couple times a year, but we don't have much to talk about anymore," said Joe, trailing off.

Joe was getting exhausted by all the questions. Having to create truth seemed to be much harder than just telling the truth. But Joe's truth could not be told. Not yet. Not now. He had lost the resolve he had come upon when he was working through Alex Smithers' issues. But with each lie he told, he knew he would have to pay the compounded interest when this truth loan came due. If she knew who he was, he thought, she might still love him. But she would hate him for having deceived her for so long.

Obviously I will have to tell her I was once a priest. But when she finds out I was still a priest while we were dating, it could be over. How do I get to the person I am pretending to be without her finding out who I am now? I've built my house in the sand, but the tide is coming in. How can I move my house without it crumbling apart?

Sheila slept over that night, at peace now that she could check off all the boxes:

Not gay.

Not married.

Not a priest.

Doesn't live with his mother.

In the morning, Sheila woke up a little sore. Joe was proud of his stamina and virility and seemed like he wanted to prove to his younger lover that he was still young down there. After a thirty-year, daily habit of pleasuring himself, he had become somewhat desensitized and so it took him longer to get off; well beyond the point of pleasure (for either partner) and almost to the point of it being irritating and annoying. But, after her previous failed engagement, she was grateful for the closeness and loved having Joe's undivided attention in the bedroom.

She decided to get up and cook him breakfast to save him the embarrassment of fumbling around in the kitchen. *"Wow, he really did have to start over after the fire"* she thought as she was peeling the label off the new frying pan and unwrapping the stick of butter. Fetching the eggs from the immaculate refrigerator she noticed the ketchup, mustard, and mayonnaise jars all still had safety seals on them. *"That must have been some fire! It even ruined everything inside the refrigerator!"*

Although Sheila had been raised a Catholic (survived 12 years of parochial school, she would brag) she somehow seemed unencumbered by typical Irish Catholic guilt. She professed to be a "Cafeteria Catholic" and did so without shame. When she thought about it, which wasn't often, she was determined to bend church rules to fit her lifestyle and morality and still consider herself a Catholic. It was a good way for her to stay engaged with her culture and tradition while she waited for the Church to catch up on women's and social issues. If the Church never did catch up to the times, or she got tired of waiting, she could always opt out then. But for now she would keep her moral head down and remain in the flock.

Up to this point in their relationship, she and Joe had never talked about religion. *Devon said Joe's twin brother is a priest. Is Joe even a practicing Catholic? This morning seems as good a time as any to find out!*

Upon hearing the activity in the kitchen, Joe got out of bed, put on the clothes that had been flung aside so urgently the night before, and walked the eight feet to the kitchen. He stood there silently admiring Sheila's long legs. She was there, facing the stove, apparently lost in thought, wearing just a long tailed oxford shirt. Admiration quickly turned to lust as he imagined taking her again, right here. Right now. Breakfast could wait.

When Sheila turned around from the stove, she saw her "vampire" lover for the first time in the light of day without his trademark turtleneck. Wearing jeans and a tee shirt, his rope burn scar, faded pink against his brown skin, was clearly visible and could not be ignored.

"Good morning!" she offered.

Her beautiful bright smile melted him. *Wow*, he thought, *this was the first time (well, first time since college) he had ever slept all night with a woman. (That sort of thing is frowned upon at the rectory!)* And to have someone say "Good morning" was precious. Of course, people wished Father Martin "good morning" all the time, but it was always "Good morning Father." To have a woman wish him good morning; just good morning, made him feel "normal" for the first time in, well, maybe for the first time in his adult life.

"Good morning Sheila. Thanks for staying last night. I had a wonderful evening and it's great to have you here to wake up next to."

Sheila melted too. Maybe breakfast could wait?

For Sheila, there had been many mornings she woke up next to a man. It had become routine. She and Stephen, her then fiancé, weren't exactly living together, but most mornings they woke up next to each other, either at her place (usually), or his apartment (sometimes). They kept clothes, toothbrushes, razors, and phone chargers at each other's apartments, and often talked about moving in together. But there was something about Stephen's personal habits that seemed a little off. And his moods were unpredictable. He seemed to spend more time in the bathroom than usual for a man. He always locked the door. *What is he doing in there? Sitting on the pot? Grooming himself? He's not taking a shower; I would surely hear the water. I bet he's in there masturbating! That's it, he's jerking off. That's explains why, after his extended bathroom sessions we don't have sex for a couple days. How could he do that when I'm home, right here on the other side of the door?*

For months Sheila kept running down this wrong fork in the road, until one day at his apartment, she heard a sickening thud from inside the bathroom. "Stephen? Everything all right in there? Stephen, you OK? Stephen?"

She took a kabob skewer from the cutlery drawer and, sticking it in the hole in the doorknob, unlocked the door and found Stephen slumped on the bathroom floor. His "kit" was resting on the edge of the tub. She saw the spoon, lighter, syringes, small bags of white powder. She saw the thin rubber hose tied around his bicep, a syringe still sticking out of the inside of his forearm. In an instant her world came crashing down.

"Stephen! Stephen! Are you OK? Can you hear me?"

Did he OD? Did he bump his head? He was breathing rapidly. Her first-aid training suggested the rapid breathing was more likely to be related to a drug overdose. But he also had a burgeoning red bulb on his forehead. She called 9-1-1. She gathered her belongings, left the apartment, and sat in her car across the street and watched, as first the ambulance, and then the police arrived.

When they first met, Stephen had hurt his back at work and was given OxyContin by his doctor. He seemed to be taking a lot of pills when he was going through physical therapy treatments, but she hadn't seen a pill bottle around for a long time. She figured he no longer needed pain meds once his back had healed and he had returned to work. Sheila had no idea Stephen had switched to heroin as a cheaper alternative to pills once his doctor cut him off.

It took fifteen minutes for the EMTs to emerge, pushing, pulling, and carrying Stephen's stretcher down the six front steps of his apartment house. By then a small crowd had assembled, but through the crowd Sheila could see Stephen's head. It wasn't covered by a sheet; only an oxygen mask. *You don't give oxygen to a dead man,* she thought. Stephen wasn't dead….just dead to her.

The smell of burning butter brought her back to the moment. She removed the frying pan from the burner.

"So, is that scar on your neck why you always wear a turtleneck?"

"Yes."

"You know, it's not that visible."

"You noticed it right away."

"What I mean is, it's not that bad….that came out wrong. I mean, it kind of gives you character."

Joe figured this would not be such a good time to tell Sheila one of the reasons he became a priest was because the roman collar would hide his scar.

"Well, I don't like the way it looks," Joe answered honestly.

"How did you get it?"

Relatively few people, at least in his post-college life, had ever seen Joe's scar. When he returned to campus after his suicide attempt, when the abrasion from the ligature was still fresh, there was really no way to hide his neck from his dorm mates. Communal showers in his all male dorm made sure of that.

There was no sense trying to hide it anyway; word of his meltdown had already spread through St. Dom's campus before he even returned from his two week "rest," as his mother called it. He wondered if he should transfer. He had considered it before when he was hoping to be closer to Georgie. He was now considering a transfer to another school to be away from his past.

Joe had first worried that he would have to explain how he acquired his "injury" but the reality was, everyone already knew, so for the next two and a half years at St. Domenic's no one ever asked him about it. It always astounded Joe that the rumor mill was so pervasive that even the subsequent incoming freshmen he encountered in his last two years, even they never asked him about it. *Was my story written about in their orientation materials?* So Joe, marked with the scarlet ring around his neck, made no attempt to hide what could not be hidden, and never talked about something that was only spoken of behind his back.

The turtleneck was a creation of Brother Martin the seminarian. Martin recalled encountering two St. Domenic's priests at a non-college off campus event. In the days before it was shameful to be a priest, Martin (then Joe) wondered why these two priests were dressed in civvies, one in a jacket and tie, the other in a turtleneck. Were they out on the town as a gay couple? Were they each testing the waters of a life after priesthood? Did they just want a night out without being spotted by well meaning, pious women or self-righteous men asking for special prayers for their "wayward niece" or "nephew who's having trouble finding his way?"

In any case, Martin remembered thinking that Father Necktie looked like an imposter, but Father Turtleneck successfully bridged the cleric-layman gap. And a turtleneck provided much better scar coverage!

Sheila was really the first person in his adult life to get a real close look at Joe's neck scar. All of his previous "encounters" with young women had been in the dark, or he had kept his shirt on. So when Sheila asked how he had acquired his "character mark" he was only semi-prepared with his seldom needed explanation.

"I got it in the Corps during a ropes training exercise."

Sheila knew Joe didn't like to talk about his time in the Marines so she thought she should just let it drop. But she couldn't help thinking about something Devon had told her one night as she finished up her shift at the restaurant: Joe Davis had attempted suicide as a college student.

"Joe, have you ever attempted suicide?"

"I just told you, the rope burns came from a training exercise in the marines." Joe said, a little sharply.

"No, I'm not talking about the scar on your neck. I'm looking at the scars on your wrist."

Until that morning she had never seen his neck or his arms uncovered and in the daylight. She thought of his long sleeved turtleneck as uncomfortable, given the summer heat, but not otherwise strange, just a little eccentric. Her former boyfriend, Stephen, had worn long sleeve flannel shirts year round. Of course, she would later learn, he was hiding needle tracks. Other than the scars on his wrist, Joe's arms were pristine, much to Sheila's relief. His arms were still surprisingly muscular. "Once a marine, always a marine," Joe would say.

Joe didn't seem like the kind of person who would shoot heroin. But neither did Stephen. Sheila didn't know what "kind of person" uses heroin. Even when she was with Stephen she was unaware of his drug use, until he overdosed. Only looking back did she see some of the signs she might have recognized contemporaneously if only she knew what to look for. Based on new sensitivity to those signs she determined Joe was not a drug user, but it was still a relief to see his clean arms, except of course for the suicide-like scars on his wrist.

"Oh, that." Joe was partially relieved as he actually had an honest answer that could explain these scars. "Remember the picture I showed you last night? The one taken in Saigon with Eric and the local girl? She wasn't just a local girl. I tried to save her during the evacuation. I was hanging onto the grab bar on the helicopter with one hand and I was hanging onto Kim-Ly, that was her name, with the other hand. I couldn't hang on. As I was losing my grip on her (his voice husky now) she dug her nails into my arm. I watched her die after she fell to the roof of the embassy as we were lifting off. She's why I don't like to talk about my time in the Corps."

"I'm so sorry," Sheila said softly, "I shouldn't have pried."

After a brief silence, she just couldn't hold back and she continued her line of questioning:

"Why have you never mentioned you have a twin brother? And that he's a priest?"

"You've been talking to that kid, Devon, haven't you?"

"He says his mother knew your family growing up."

"My brother and I are not very close."

284

"You have to be the only identical twins I ever heard of who are 'not close.'"

"We've just taken different paths in life. Other than genes we don't have much in common. You'll probably never see the two of us in the same place at the same time." For once, Joe made an accurate statement, albeit only inadvertently honest. His mission to tell Sheila the truth was off to a bad start.

48

Karl Strikeland had been referred to Dr. Davis by a psychologist a couple towns over. Karl needed treatment of a "sensitive" issue, according to Dr. Katz, and it was best that he seek help somewhere outside the small town of Maplewood.

"I'm sorry Mr. Strikeland. Were you waiting long?" Dr. Davis was still sweating, even after showering, from his late afternoon run. The turtle neck didn't help.

"No, you're not late Dr. Davis. I just got here early 'cause I didn't know how long it would take, you know, with traffic 'n all."

"Well, make yourself comfortable. I'm not sure how much counseling you might or might not have had, but I want to make sure we make the best use of our time, seeing you came some distance, and I thought we'd start with some questions. Is that OK? Good. Had you been seeing Dr. Katz for a while or was it just to get a referral?"

"I saw him a couple times, but he didn't think he could help me, plus, he said sometimes people with problems like mine, well, he says, sometimes it is better to get a little space between the person and the problem."

Dr. Davis had no idea what that meant but he was intrigued enough to pay attention.

"So, you're dealing with a very sensitive issue?"

"I had an affair. I was unfaithful to my wife."

Dr. Davis wondered what was so extraordinary about this affair that Dr. Katz didn't feel comfortable seeing Karl. But he also knew that the presenting problem is seldom (never) the real problem. He probed deeper.

"Sounds like the affair is in the past tense. How long ago did it end?"

"Eleven years ago. It really wasn't an affair. More like a fling."

"Have you had any counseling in the meantime or has it just become a problem lately?"

"My wife and I saw a marriage counselor for a couple visits right after my daughter was born but that's it. I had my fling when she was pregnant."

"So the issue has now become more of a problem…all of a sudden? Can you tell me a little more about that?"

"The problems started with the fling, but other stuff has come up….lately."

"Something of a more sensitive nature? Something so sensitive you can't talk with anyone in your own town?"

Karl searched for words in the brown and gold carpet. The

long period (sixty seconds) of silence bore a hole in his forehead as he sanded down the knees of his jeans with his rough hands. Now he was sweating.

"It's OK, Karl. You can tell me anything," Dr. Davis offered in his most empathetic voice.

"My daughter is disabled."

"Um hum," encouraged Dr. Davis, convinced that having a disabled daughter was not a good enough reason to seek counseling in another town.

"She has syphilis," whispered Karl, sinking further into the upholstered chair.

Dr. Davis hoped Karl was referring to another daughter; not the one born after the "fling" eleven years ago.

"She got it coming through the birth canal," he continued, dashing Dr. Davis' hopes for a happy ending to this therapeutic relationship.

"And you were the one who transmitted the disease to your wife while she was pregnant? You contracted syphilis through your affair?" Dr. Davis' voice was markedly less empathetic now.

"Yes."

"And you didn't tell her in time so she could have had a C-section and avoid spreading it to your daughter?" Dr. Davis thought this was a good enough reason to *move* out of town; not just go for counseling thirty miles away.

"I didn't know I had it until the baby was born and the doctor put it all together later. My girl has one eye that isn't quite right, and the doctors say she might not be able to have children."

Dr. Davis was momentarily sidetracked by this repulsive revelation. It certainly would explain why Karl's wife had pushed him into counseling (men almost never came voluntarily). But it didn't explain why he was coming now, eleven years after negligently disfiguring his daughter. He decided to dig some more.

Dr. Davis searched for the correct words, but all the right words were too judgmental. "Karl, you just told me some things that are very sensitive, and I thank you for trusting me enough to tell me them. I'm still just a little confused. What happened that made you come for counseling now….after all this time?"

"My wife said I had to come," Karl offered flatly. In the ensuing silence Karl realized his concrete answer was not going to cut it with Dr. Davis. "I've been removed from the home by Social Services. There was an incident."

Dr. Davis remained silent.

"There was some touching," Karl stated flatly, as if he was describing how a pencil sharpener works.

"Some inappropriate touching?"

"Yes."

"You inappropriately touched your daughter….on multiple occasions?" Dr. Davis suspected Karl would not have been removed from the house after a single alleged "incident" of inappropriate touching.

"I didn't say multiple occasions," Karl said defensively.

"But that's what happened, right?"

Dr. Davis was trained to pick up on certain words when spoken by addicts or abusers. "An incident" never meant "an" incident: there were always several incidents, the same way "I stopped by the bar for a drink" always meant multiple drinks. The abusers' litany of defense mechanisms were: denial, minimizing, blaming, intentionality (I did it to teach her a lesson, or, it was for her own good), or claims of loss-of-control. Dr. Davis considered Karl's failure to disclose the Social Services order at first as "denial." "There was an incident" was minimizing. He knew the next thing out of Karl's mouth would be some form of blaming.

"We have a special relationship, my daughter and I, you know, because of her condition. We have a closeness and we were cuddling, and my hand just went there." Karl made a downward motion with his offending right hand while narrating, as if to demonstrate. "She didn't seem to mind and she squirmed and giggled. In a way, I think just by the way she was sitting on my lap, she was kind of hoping I would touch her there. I told her this was our special time and not to tell her mom because she would get jealous of our special hugging and might make me leave the house."

Dr. Davis, now well outside of his comfort zone, wished he could end the session right then and refer Karl to another therapist, or even to the police, and get away from this monster. He wanted to vomit. *It wasn't bad enough that he gave his daughter syphilis; he had to fuck up her head as well?* It was obvious from the way Karl described "the incident," totally devoid of compunction, that on some level he still believed sexually assaulting a child is acceptable, if you have a "special relationship." This wasn't a phobia or a compulsion, when patients rationally know they should believe or behave in a certain way but can't seem to stop themselves. Karl only came for help after he was taken away from his child, and because he was forced to by his wife. Very little therapeutic benefit is derived when a client enters counseling under duress....especially when the therapist is repulsed by the client. The merciful clock indicated it was time to wrap up. Karl felt better that some of the tension was relieved just by sharing his (side of the) story. Dr. Davis hated that Karl should be feeling any relief right now while he had to transition back to his personal life saddled with Karl's deplorable baggage.

Dr. Davis finished up his evening appointment and reluctantly scheduled another for Karl. He hurried over to the restaurant, hoping to bump into Sheila as she was finishing up her shift. He would sometimes sit at the bar and nurse a drink while he waited for her. Although he didn't think of himself as a "drinker," at least not a drinker by Vietnam Vet standards, after the counseling session he had just finished, Joe wanted a drink and he wasn't going to just "nurse it" tonight. Opening the door, his mood immediately went from bad to worse. Upon entering the bar area he spotted Devon sitting on a stool chatting up Sheila. *Jesus! He's like a virus the way he keeps popping up everywhere.* Pasting on the manufactured smile he usually reserved for counseling sessions and family gatherings, he approached the bar.

"Hello," he called out.

"Oh hi J-Joe!" She stammered at his unplanned arrival.

"Hey. What are you doing here?" asked Devon, still unaware of Joe and Sheila's relationship.

"Just stopped by for a drink. How 'bout you?"

"I just came by to say hi to Sheila."

"Really?" Joe asked incredulously, not looking at Devon, but rather up at Sheila.

Her eyes grew wide as her smile devolved into a grimace, indicating Devon's visit was unexpected and maybe even unwelcomed.

Joe clenched his teeth to match her as she moved away down the bar to attend to another patron.

"She's too old for you," Joe said aggressively.

"She's too young for you," Devon returned volley.

"This woman's a major leaguer. I can handle major league pitching. You're more suited to Little League."

"My mom said you tried to kill yourself."

So there it was. In the half lifetime since he hanged himself, not one person (besides Sheila seeing the shirtless Joe) had ever mentioned it. Ever. *And now this punk drops this on my head?*

Joe had never killed anyone in Vietnam. Never even fired his weapon. In his life the closest he ever came to killing a man (not including himself) was when he "pranked" the migrant worker on the tobacco farm. They both paid dearly for that incident. He wasn't morally opposed to killing someone, if it was justified. *Wow, I really am a terrible priest.* He had reconciled in his adult mind that it was not justified to kill a man for stealing a sandwich. *But stealing a girlfriend? I'd like to kill Devon, ...and his mother right now!* He left the restaurant without ordering a drink.

49

Devon just couldn't let it go. He had other reasons to doubt Joe Davis' story. There was that first night of community band rehearsal, where, upon meeting Joe, Devon was sure he saw a glimpse of recognition in his eyes. But maybe that was just a reflection of Devon's mistaken recognition. Then there was the time a year prior when Father Martin sat in with the church youth music group and played the conga drums. Devon had complimented Father Martin on his playing and asked if musical talent had run in his family. Father Martin had replied that he was the only kid in his family to show an interest or talent in music, even though his mother had once been a pianist. Now, finding out that both twin brothers played the drums, the original story just didn't fit.

In spite of knowing (or maybe because of knowing) Joe had an interest in Sheila, but not realizing they were already a couple, Devon started showing up regularly at the restaurant just as Sheila was finishing up her shift. Sheila was always amazed that men could find her attractive while she was sweaty and exhausted from being on her feet all evening. *Maybe they just like a woman in uniform? Or a woman waiting on them?* she wondered.

On one such "I happened to be driving by" visits, Devon

shared his sleuthing notes with Sheila. Sheila even shared that she had asked Joe about his estrangement from his twin brother, Martin, and that Joe said they had taken different paths in life. That's all.

Devon told Sheila how his mother didn't recall there being a brother named Martin, and that it was Joe who had entered a seminary after attempting suicide.

"And how is it that two identical twin brothers, who were supposedly estranged, both live in the same town a hundred miles from where they grew up?" asked an incredulous Devon.

"That is a bit odd," admitted Sheila. Sheila felt only a tinge of guilt over these covert intelligence gathering meetings. Having learned a hard lesson from former beau, Stephen, on the pitfalls of not really knowing one's lover, she was determined to learn as much about Joe as she could, from all available sources. Yahoo and Google had not yet become the go-to sources to verify your lover's relationship resume. Compounding her guilt was the feeling that, after having lived through Stephen's duplicity, she was so happy to have found someone "honest" like Dr. Joe Davis. But she wanted to be sure she wasn't being naïve.

To Devon, these late evening rendezvous were a way to poison the well for Joe and worm his own way into Sheila's heart. To Sheila, ten years Devon's senior, the attention was flattering. But she had no interest in Devon as a mate. Joe was right: Devon was not ready to hit in the big leagues.

Since I have nothing to hide, (this is just a platonic friendship with another bandmate who just happened to be a guy, for whom I have no romantic interest) there is no reason for not telling Joe about our (increasingly frequent) visits, right?

"You've got to be fucking kidding me!" was Joe's response. Immediately Joe's mind shot back to the spring of 1979 when Georgie disclosed the kiss from Ira Benjamin Shapiro that quaked Joe's foundation. "Thith hath to end, and it hath to end now!" Joe shouted, losing his grip.

Sheila had never seen Joe like this before. Never heard him shout; never had seen such anger in his eyes. Never heard him slur his speech. He hadn't struck her as the jealous type. *And there is nothing for him to be jealous about! What could explain such a fierce over-reaction?*

"No more. I don't want him there. He can't drop by at your work anymore" Joe lapsed unconsciously into no-lisp mode. "You have to end it. Now! You might not be into him, but to him, you're a girlfriend, not only a friend. Don't put you and me through it. If you don't end it now, it will end badly later. Believe me."

"I can't have friends who are guys?"

Here we go again! Thought Joe.

"Not a guy wanting to be your boyfriend."

"He doesn't want that!"

"Really?"

"Well, how do you know he wants to go out with me?"

"I've been around the block a time or two. Would he be dropping by after work to meet up with a guy friend? No way."

Good point, thought Sheila.

"And anyway, Devon told me he wanted you. He didn't know we're together. I didn't fill him in either. Maybe it would have been better if I did tell him we're a couple."

This was the first time Joe had actually used the word "couple."

At this point in her life, Sheila knew, at least in her heart, that Joe was right. She hated the "unfairness" of it all, not being able to have guy friends while she was in a relationship. Then she thought about her married girl friends. None of them seemed to have single guy friends (the only one who insisted to her husband that she should be able to make and keep male friendships was, coincidentally, no longer married.) The only (straight) guy friends that are permitted are those that come joined at the hip with their spouse. Sheila's single girl friends have some guy friends, but they are all single guys, and are viewed as much as prospective spouses or bed mates, as they are true friends.

What finally cemented the self-convincing exercise for Sheila was when she tried to imagine how she would feel to suddenly learn that Joe was stopping by to see another woman "friend" after work.

Yes, Joe is right. These visits with Devon have to stop. But it would take a while longer for her to process Joe's near-violent reaction to the whole Devon affair.

50

Frank Jankos was one of Dr. Davis' regulars. Forty-seven, balding, paunchy, married father of two young girls. After three months of counseling, Dr. Davis still couldn't quite figure out why Frank was coming to see him. To this point, Frank had never mentioned or admitted to abuse of any kind, not as a victim or a perpetrator. He wasn't a drinker or a druggie. His presenting problem was a mild and generalized anxiety. His narrative changed somewhat over the three months and Dr. Davis noted the fluidity of Frank's version of the facts. Joe knew there was more to the story; there always is. Usually, if it took this long to uncover, the real problem was a doozey. This time was no different. Frank Jankos had put off marriage until thirty-nine, late by most standards for a first marriage. He had been in what he thought at the time was a casual relationship with a co-worker. Her name was Brittany. She had a steady boyfriend at the time, but this didn't deter the relationship with Frank. It just made them more careful. Frank was aware of Brittany's "serious" relationship and it didn't bother him, so he said. On the contrary, he seemed to prefer it that way. There was no commitment from either side.

"We planned to break it off when she got married. We had sex one last time the night before she got married, right before she had to go to the rehearsal dinner. We were fine with that. I wasn't going to get in the way of the sanctity of marriage," Frank's catharsis began, apparently oblivious to the hypocrisy regarding the "sanctity" of his own marriage.

As a psychologist, Dr. Davis was supposed to treat his clients without becoming judgmental or emotionally involved. He didn't like where this session was headed. Ever since his experience in college, when he and Georgie told the interloper Ira Benjamin Shapiro to back off, that they were "serious" and were planning to get married someday, Joe had a hard time respecting any man who continued pursuing a woman who professed to being in a "serious" relationship.

Frank continued: "Since Brittany and I were still working together, we had a hard time not seeing each other. We could no longer go over her house because her husband might be there so we ended up at my place, you know, just to talk. But it always went further."

"So, you're telling me you continued to have an affair with a married woman?" Joe interjected, not even trying to stifle his judgmental tone. "How long did this go on for?"

Frank looked down at his feet. "It's never stopped. Well, it has pretty much stopped. About three months ago."

"About the time you started coming to see me?" Joe often would set up an appointment at intake with the spouse of any client he was going to treat individually. Sometimes, if he did not suspect ongoing abuse that would put either partner at risk of physical harm, he would schedule a joint appointment followed by appointments with each partner individually to get a baseline. This time Joe wished he had had the initial appointment with Frank's wife, Kristi. She would have told him precisely what prompted Frank to seek counseling.

"So, when you say, 'it's pretty much stopped,' what does that mean?"

"No, it has stopped."

"When was the last time you had sex with Brittany?"

"Last Wednesday."

"So, less than a week ago? And the time before that?"

"It had been a few weeks."

"So, you stopped a few months ago, except for a few times since then, including just last week?"

No response

"So you've stopped……until the next time." It wasn't a question.

"I can't promise you it won't happen again, if that's what you're looking for."

"It's not me you need to make a promise to. The only thing I'm looking for is honesty…to yourself. I guess I'm not sure why you came to see me. I assume it has something to do with your affair with Brittany?"

"My wife found out about the affair. She made me come here or she was going to leave me. She wants to know what kind of sick bastard cheats on his wife with a married woman."

"Frank, you have been coming here for three months. I am wondering why it took so long for you to tell me about Brittany. It makes me wonder if you are only trying to placate Kristi by going to counseling but you really don't want to end things with Brittany."

Dr. Davis did his best Carl Rogers, staying silent for the next forty-five seconds. Finally, the pressure getting too much, Frank started to cry.

"I love my wife, but I love Brittany too. Even if I leave my wife, Brittany can't leave her husband...not now. She's pregnant."

There was more silence. This time it was a stunned silence; not an engineered silence (he imagined even Carl Rogers gasping to himself!). Joe marveled at all the ways people fucked up their lives. It was as if the human condition compelled otherwise happy people to erect obstacles to their happiness, and then complain about being trapped in their despair. All people want what they don't have. People without things want more stuff. The haves yearn for simplicity. Lonely people want love. People with love want conflict. Dr. Davis broke the silence.

"You are looking for someone to make a decision for you....so you won't have to be responsible for what happens next." The inflection of his statements always rising at the end. "What have you told Kristi about your "progress" here?"

"I told her it is going well. That it is good to have someone to talk to. That I'm getting better."

"Does she believe that?"

"I don't know."

"Do you believe that?"

"Not really......I'm not sure what better is. I mean, it is good to have someone to talk to, but I don't know if I can live without either of them. I was in counseling before, you know, when I was younger. I had five years of counseling and I left there still messed up."

"I don't think you're 'messed up' but I do think you are confused and are lacking some insights into your feelings. And instead of having five years of counseling, some people have one year of counseling five times. Have you told Brittany you are seeing a counselor? Does she know that Kristi knows about the affair?"

"No, not yet."

"Because if you tell her she will end the relationship? "

"She'll be pissed that Kristi knows and she'll be afraid Kristi will tell Brittany's husband."

"Kristi has known for three months. You are OK with Brittany's husband finding out from your wife even before you tell Brittany that your wife knows what's going on?" No response from Frank. "So, we're back at the point where you are hoping this whole thing blows up, forcing your hand, and you won't have to make a decision. Have you given any thought about how that will impact the four adults and the three children involved?"

"Not really."

"If you do nothing and just let this run its course, can you see any possible way this story will have a happy ending…..for any of you?"

"Probably not."

"I'm sorry to say, Frank, that we are out of time for today. Do you want to come back and talk some more next week?"

Frank nodded, disappointed and relieved that the session was over. Dr. Davis glanced out the window. Billy Paul's 1972 hit, *Me and Mrs. Jones*, started to play in his mind. Dr. Davis forced his attention back in Frank's direction.

"Your homework for next week is to write down your predictions of what will happen if Kristi gets in touch with Brittany's husband before you tell Brittany she knows about you two. And, be thinking about what your options will be if Kristi finds out you haven't ended it with Brittany."

Dr. Davis wanted to go right back to the rectory and take a shower. Usually he could wall off his emotions from his professional work. It was getting harder to compartmentalize as he began to see more of himself in some of his counseling clients. Although he was not ruining anyone else's marriage, he did admit his life was in conflict with his vows. He wondered if Frank actually hated Kristi and Brittany, rather than loving them as he professed. How could Frank care so little about the disaster that was about to befall his own, and Brittany's family, that he would passively let his faithless acts play out?

Dr. Davis viewed psychotherapy as a process of peeling the psychic onion. Although he was academically qualified to provide therapy, he wondered if he had the temperament or the psychological stability to be analyzing other people. *Plenty of emotionally damaged people provide counseling,* he thought. *Plenty of spiritually bankrupt men are working as priests.* Joe wondered if his own charade of being a priest was a manifestation of his hatred of God. Was his contempt for his priestly vows just a way of getting back at a God who, years ago, had deprived him of the happiness he felt he was entitled to, and destined to enjoy?

51

On clear nights Father Martin sometimes ventured up to the roof of the now mostly abandoned convent, diagonally across the asphalt playground/parking lot/courtyard from the rectory. Looking out at the night sky reminded him of the calm, pre-evacuation nights spent on guard duty atop the Embassy in Saigon. The two scenes were really very little alike. The night sky over St. Margaret's convent lacked the blue-green iridescence of the clammy South Vietnamese atmosphere. About the only similarity was the sense of solitude and insignificance such an infinite vista engendered in the soul.

His evening star-gazing brought him back even further, to the times when he and his little sister, Sue (Q), used to lay in the backyard grass on partly sunny afternoons imagining the clouds as various animate objects. Only now, seeking mental and spiritual clarity on cloudless nights, Father Martin would stare at seemingly random bunches of stars, trying in vain to connect the dots of his disjointed, duplicitous life.

Father Martin was getting increasingly desperate to build up Dr. Davis' private psychotherapy practice to the point where it could be self-sustaining and he could finally, officially leave the priesthood. He had largely left, at least mentally and emotionally, when he began dating Sheila. He suspected he had never been truly spiritually engaged with his vocation. If he ever had been, it was long gone now.

Since his neck scarring incident in college, he could not afford any "bouts of depression." But Father Martin knew his bouts of *desperation* were just pit stops on the depression highway.

By any standard, young Joe Davis had experienced desperate episodes: he had, after all, watched his young Vietnamese lover recede from his grasp as his helicopter ascended away from the Embassy's makeshift rooftop helipad. Living through the actual trauma of seeing Kim-Ly plummet to the rooftop, Joe felt that he too had fallen to the nadir of his existence. He was yet to realize the true psychic depths of human suffering.

But only once before had he succumbed to a "bout" of lingering desperation. As a sophomore in college, when things between Georgie and Joe were coming undone, but before he recognized the speed and extent of the unraveling, Joe was desperate for the end of the school year. *If I can just hold it together with Georgie until we get home for the summer, we can repair the damage and move on together. I just need to get her home, away from all those sniping guys; safe back in my arms,* he thought.

He was, he thought, in a race against time. Then, as now, he had an unfounded and overdeveloped sense of confidence in his ability to make everything right, if given just a little more time. Then, as now, he didn't recognize that the race wasn't only against time, but also against truth.

One Tuesday morning Father Martin was making hospital rounds when he was startled to recognize an old friend in intensive care. Father Sullivan, a would-be mentor for young Brother Martin, was now dying. Father Martin spoke softly, reassuringly, and sympathetically to his former running buddy and personal philosopher. Seeing Father Sullivan rekindled the guilt and shame Father Martin had felt periodically throughout his priesthood for not following Father Sullivan's pious example. As he was saying goodbye for the last time, Father Martin said, "I'm so glad we were able to see each other again as I don't know how much time you might have left."

Father Sullivan reminded Father Martin, "None of us knows how much time we have left."

Joe's new race was with Sheila. Sheila, at thirty-four, was not going to wait much longer to take their relationship to the next level of commitment. She had "wasted" four years with her "junkie" boyfriend, Stephen. In Joe, Sheila had found her new "soul mate," a mate not without some quirks. From his tendency to be a loner, to his estrangement from his identical twin priest-brother, to his fashion sense (turtlenecks in summer!) to his parsimoniously disclosed mysterious background, Joe Davis was indeed a bit odd.

But Sheila loved him. Deeply. Fervently. The Catholic part of her wanted to legitimize their union (did they even have a union?). Joe had never mentioned marriage although he did say he wanted to "leave everything else behind and just be together forever." That meant marriage, right? (Joe never had a problem making commitments; only keeping them.) And they had never discussed kids. Family was important to Sheila and she struggled with the notion of a couple being a family if there were no children.

Sheila had to keep resetting her family implementation timeline. She had been ready seven or eight years ago with Stephen, but she serendipitously sensed something in Stephen was not quite ready. *If Joe were to propose to me this month, and it takes a year to plan and pull off a wedding, and then I immediately go off the pill, and we get pregnant right away, we're looking at two years from now, at the very earliest, before I become a mother.* She did the math: if she was going to be a mother by age 37 (the age she had set as her limit) she only had six more months to elicit a marriage proposal and set the process in motion!

Her fallback position, which she hated to consider since she had wasted so much time with Stephen, and since she had invested (not yet wasted, she hoped) a year with Joe, was to start all over again with a new, yet-to-be-identified, father of her children. *That would set me back at least another year! What if I stopped taking the pill now? Sometimes guys need a little push to move them in the right direction.* Sheila, experiencing her own "bout of desperation," thought about her friend Caroline who had become pregnant while on the pill. Her doctor had blamed it on the antibiotics she was taking that rendered the pill ineffective.

And didn't Sheila feel a slight cold coming on? Maybe if the cold were called an "upper respiratory infection" she could get some antibiotics? *And if I was still on the pill when I got pregnant, it wouldn't really be my fault.* That could be her cover story.

She hated being deceitful, but the worst part of deceit was getting caught. And the beautiful end would certainly justify the dishonest means, even if she never came clean with Joe about the true genesis of their personal Creation Story.

Joe was oblivious to all of Sheila's gestational computations. He was focused on concealing his priestly identity from Sheila, at least until such time as he could make a clean break from the collar. Hiding his double life was getting increasingly difficult. To hide even a hobby from a partner (were they even partners?) would be hard enough. But to conceal a vocation that really was, or should have been, an all-consuming lifestyle, required constant vigilance.

Once he did break free he would have to decide whether he comes clean about having been a priest, or continue running with the story of his fictitious twin brother Martin. *Maybe I could kill off this Father Martin? After all, hadn't I once tried to eradicate Joe Davis by suicide? Does Sheila really believe my twin brother story? How much had our community band mate, Devon, told Sheila over drinks about Joe Davis' real past? Did Devon believe the identical twin story?* To "kill off" someone Sheila doesn't even believe exists would just dig himself deeper into the pit of obfuscation. *Maybe I could kill off Devon!*

Joe had inadvertently come close to exposing his clerical past (present!) to Sheila a couple times during arguments. "I'm just as Catholic as you," Sheila would argue when Joe tried to clear her up on misconceptions about Church teachings or history. "How did you become such a know-it-all on all things Catholic? Maybe you're closer to your brother Martin than you let on?"

Joe attributed his intimate Church knowledge to his studies at St. Domenic's. "Anyone who showed up for class in their first two years at St. Dom's learned the same things I did." But even he acknowledged (to himself) that he knew far more than the average Catholic undergrad. Their first fight had actually been about the Virgin Mary! Sheila, like so many Catholics, believed that Jesus' birth to His virgin mother was the result of the Immaculate Conception. Joe's insistence that the Immaculate Conception had to do with Mary's birth, not Jesus', was met with disbelief and scorn. The lack of resolution of this argument led to their next fight: the supposed universal infallibility of the pope.

What had been engaging theological discussion fodder during his seminary days, became a source of friction between Joe and the lay-educated Sheila. As in the past, Joe had a hard time recognizing that sometimes it was better to agree than to be right, especially when being right in ecclesiastical matters might expose a level of religious training unavailable to the common layperson.

52

Father Martin woke up early one Wednesday morning. Wednesdays were always quiet in the rectory. There were no marriages, baptisms, or confirmations. Technically he had to be available any day before morning mass to hear confessions but only the old, Italian ladies bothered to confess anymore. And most of them were either in nursing homes, or dead. Their sins were mostly contrived and "reconciliation" was just a ritual practice and a chance for an old lady to have a few minutes of a priest's undivided attention. Old ladies had unremarkable sins. Occasionally one with dementia would show up for confession. She might not remember what she had for breakfast that morning, but she would have vivid memories of juicy offenses committed decades ago.

Wednesday was also the slowest day for wakes and funerals. Monday was the day for holdover funerals for anyone who died late in the previous week and couldn't have a funeral on Saturday (reserved for weddings) or Sunday (regular mass schedule). People who died Saturday through Tuesday were usually laid to rest on Thursday or Friday.

But this early morning at the rectory was especially quiet. Father Martin looked at the green glow of his Timex Ironman runner's watch. 4:21 AM. "Huh, a prime number!" On long nights of guard duty on the roof of the embassy in Saigon, MSG Joe Davis had memorized all the prime numbers to 500; well actually to 503. Since he usually woke to his O-six hundred alarm, waking to a prime number was a rare treat.

Father Martin looked out his window facing the parking lot and church. The pastor had better views from any of his three rooms, but associate priests were relegated to second-class accommodations. Yesterday's fine early spring weather had given way to a raw, gloomy thirty-eight degree morning. Now that he was up, there was no getting back to sleep. If the weather had been better, Father Martin would have donned his turtleneck and gone for a run, even in the pre-dawn darkness. Gone were the days when he would run in any weather. *I'll run after mass,* he thought to himself, *if it clears up*.

He showered, shaved, and dressed in his clerical garb. Since Mrs. Rinaldi wouldn't have breakfast ready until 6:30, he stayed upstairs and prepped for the 8:00 mass. Preparation for mass had become an increasingly rare effort for Father Martin. The ritual nature of the Catholic mass did not change from day to day, and only slightly between liturgical seasons. *Maybe I'll think of something cheerful to stick in there on this shitty day,* he mused. Since he had the time he decided to craft a short sermon rather than just dusting off one of the "ol' standbys." He had been thinking of the Jews in Exodus, with their wavering faith in G-d and Moses. *Yet even as they knew not where they were going, nor what kind of life they would find there, still they walked on in faith. Their former lives had become unsustainable.* Father Martin could relate their plight to his own life, at least on some level. He knew his days as a priest were numbered and he faced an uncertain fate as "former priest, Dr. Davis, boyfriend of Sheila."

His mind wandered away from the flock of Israelites. *What do I really know about Sheila? She's pretty, mid-thirties, funny, comes from a big Irish family, works as a waitress, is a willing and participatory sex partner. But do I really know her? I know she had been engaged to Stephen, but she was so naïve, or out-to-lunch that she didn't even know he was a heroin addict until he OD'd. Is she as superficial as I am? How has she not figured out by now that I'm a priest! Maybe it's willful ignorance? Maybe she won't be shocked when I finally come clean?*

The whistle of the teapot down in the kitchen brought him back to the homily. *I guess I better make this sermon relatable to the morning mass-o-chists instead of me. I'm not so sure they'd be ready to learn I've been living a double life.*

Having had his gastric juices stimulated by the whistling teapot and the clanging of the frying pan on the cast-iron grate, Father Martin got to work scribbling down a "quickie sermon" suitable for a weekday mass.

"My brothers and sisters in Christ, I've been thinking lately about the journey of Moses and the Jews through the desert. The Jews as a people had a choice to make. They could either stay where they were in Egypt and be subjected to continued servitude, at best, or slaughter at worst, or follow Moses into the desert to a better place. The only thing they brought with them toward their uncertain future was their faith. Faith in God, in Moses, and faith in each other. Their faith was tested many times along the way. The Book of Exodus tells us many strayed from their faith, if only temporarily, when the going got rough, and they desperately turned to idols and false deities. But God was on their side, even when they didn't recognize Him working through his mortal servant, Moses. In faith they persevered and made it to their new land.

"In our own lives, how many times have we embarked on a new life-journey and lost faith along the way? Has the faith and support of someone else; a friend, a family member, a priest, ever buttressed our own faltering faith to help us along the way?

"Fast forward four thousand years to the story of today's Gospel. Jesus went into the desert for forty days with no supplies. Now, Jesus knew where He was headed….He's Jesus. But His journey was also a spiritual journey and He must have had some of the same doubts we all have. Since He was physically alone, He had to rely solely on God to sustain Him while He prayed and persevered through His spiritual journey.

"The point my brothers and sisters is this: the human condition requires us to take journeys, be they physical, emotional, or spiritual. You probably will find strength from others along the way, but no matter what, you will always have God to help navigate the way. Even if you turn away from Him, He is still patiently guiding you back to the ultimate destination, Salvation. Let us pray."

The aroma of bacon and eggs had made its way upstairs and down the oak and fir hallway and under the closed door of the associate priest's room, washing away the morning's gloom.

53

On his afternoon run along Court Street in the downtown area of his parish, Father Martin ran along the sidewalk until he came to a cordoned-off section of fresh concrete. Running in the street past the setting-up expanse, he noticed two sets of footprints which were about to become a permanent record of either carelessness or vandalism. One pair of prints belonged to a human, probably a teenage boy. The other set of impressions belonged to some breed of bird. Father Martin wondered if the boy and the bird were both "bird-brains" for having walked in wet cement.

Then he thought about the impressions made by the feet landing at just the right time in the not-quite-dry concrete. If the feet had arrived earlier there would have been a mess, for sure, but the sludge would soon have found its own level, leaving no permanent record of the insult. If the feet had landed later on dry concrete, although the impact might have been harsh, there would be no visible sign of injury to the hard surface as it was no longer impressionable. *Impressionable.*

So many things had happened to young Joe Davis before his

own emotional cement had fully cured. Returning from Vietnam he was sure he was no longer an impressionable kid. But the hard outer cortex was just a thin façade which could not protect his gel-like psyche from the slings and arrows and shod feet of his interrupted adolescence.

It took a lot of years but he now came to realize why the premier events of life, some tragic, some glorious, had become indelible stains in the seat fabric of his memory bus. Every man was once impressionable and remembers his first kiss, his first lover, his first bicycle, his first wake, his first fist-fight, his first baseball glove, his first car accident, his first job, his first break-up, the first time seeing his father cry...

54

"Come on in Ms. Uh, uh, Gerbronsyscz."

"Just call me Joy."

"OK, Joy, but how did I do with the name?"

"Not bad!"

"Thanks. I grew up in a half Polish, half Irish neighborhood so I'm pretty good with a lot of consonants."

"Well, it's not an easy name. I sometimes wish I had taken my husband's last name, Gioia, but I didn't want to be 'Joy Gioia.'"

"Have a seat over there. What brings you in to see me today?" Dr. Davis liked to get right to the point.

"I've just been feeling down lately. A lot of shit….I'm sorry."

"That's OK. You can say 'shit' in here. I've said a lot worse myself."

"Well, a lot has been going on in my life but it just seems the whole world has gone dark lately."

"OK, how long have you been feeling like this, Joy?"

"It's just been a couple months, you know, work, family. I mean society in general seems really messed up."

Dr. Davis gave Joy an understanding nod of the head, something he did not have to manufacture.

"All of the lightness has drained out of my life." Joy exhaled as if it were her life's last breath. Dr. Davis couldn't help thinking that his client's name was a misnomer.

"We will have to talk about your feelings and why you're feeling like that, but would it be OK if we backed up and did a short intake interview first?" Dr. Davis learned the hard way not to skip the intake process. Seemingly innocuous statements uttered upfront can become valuable clues later on in therapy. It took discipline to stop a client in their tracks to ask seemingly mundane questions (age, marital status, age of children, profession, birth order, accident/illness history) especially when it is tempting to delve into a readily expressed, juicy presenting problem. But as a trained therapist, Dr. Davis believed in the importance of examining the basement before assessing the flaws in the upper floors.

It took a few sessions to determine if Joy's "down" feelings were clinical depression that needed a pharmacological consult, or if they could be treated by talk therapy alone. During the fourth session, Joy Gerbron (the name she used professionally) trusted Dr. Davis enough to reveal the likely source of her angst. Joy worked as a pharmaceutical rep for Pinnacle Pharma, a large and successful family run drug company. All the material wealth she and her family enjoyed was the result of her fabulous success selling the company's flagship product,

OxyMortix. She had been trained and taught to truly believe that the pills were a non-habit-forming godsend to alleviate the pain and suffering of millions. Pain, the "fifth vital sign," could now be conquered. She learned which doctors would accept gifts and which doctors still refused to see the light. She continued to "return to the well," visiting doctors whose prescribing patterns and volume were just short of unbelievable.

But then the rumors started churning, both in the press and internally with colleagues. *Maybe these pills aren't so safe? Maybe the company owners weren't just the altruistic philanthropists we've been taught to believe?*

One of Joy's co-worker friends had done the math on one of their star performer clinic customers. Based on the number of drugs prescribed by the three licensed doctors at the clinic, an opioid prescription was written, by each doctor, on average every four minutes, twelve hours a day, seven days a week. This didn't factor in any bathroom, lunch, or golf breaks. Anyone could see there was something very wrong going on here.

And yet Joy, and most of her colleagues, "returned to the well" and continued to reap the financial and material rewards. Some patients were helped. Some died. Countless others became addicted.

"Doc, this is not who I am. It's not who I think I am; who I want to be. I've set up a lifestyle for me and my family that I could never replicate. It just wouldn't be fair to my family if I were to quit and find something else."

Recognizing the obvious cognitive dissonance, Dr. Davis could only offer the most vapid of responses: "It seems like you've got yourself quite the moral dilemma on your hands."

Joe Davis had learned to endure a Spartan existence. His childhood in Valley Park, Connecticut, his stints in Vietnam and the seminary, and his life as chaplain and parish priest all reinforced the notion that one could survive (if not be happy) with very few material possessions. Of course, Dr. Davis was just beginning to provide for himself and he had no real clue what it was to have to, or even desire to, provide for a family. He could not relate to Joy or her lifestyle. Dr. Davis understood Joy's concern that it would be a major adjustment to her family to have to live without, or at least live without as much as they had become accustomed to. Dr. Davis felt a moral superiority to Joy, a feeling he was not usually in a position to experience.

"When you say, 'this isn't who I am,' you mean you don't see yourself as the kind of person who would grow wealthy selling a product that ruins others' lives?"

"Right. I don't want to be that kind of person but I think maybe I've become that person."

"What kind of person does your family see you as?"

"Well, I hope they see..."

Dr. Davis cut her off. "We all hope others see us in the best light possible. How do they really see you?"

"I don't know." Joy looked down in silence. Dr. Davis waited silently, lowering his gaze from Joy's eyes, looking vaguely in her direction but not focusing hard.

Joy continued, "I guess my husband sees me as a good provider. I'm the higher earner in the family. I don't know how the kids see me. I'm not sure they even think about it. They have their own lives and, I think, they just take everything for granted."

"We all play several roles in life. You're a wife, mother, daughter, sister, breadwinner. You seem to be focusing only on one role in particular. You seem to be defining your identity, your value as a person, just by that one role as breadwinner. You see that role negatively, and if that role defines you, then you must be a bad person. You don't want to be a bad person so you want to change your identity. If your family only sees you as a breadwinner, and you make a change in that role, you're afraid, in the absence of other feelings for you, that they will no longer value you as a person. The material shock to their lifestyle will drive a wedge between you and them. Does this sound about right to you?"

"I know being a pharmaceutical rep is only one role in my life. But I'm having a terrible impact on society. What kind of person would let herself play that role? I mean, I didn't always feel this way. I used to think I was a force for good. I was curing people's pain, letting them resume their normal lives. But now that I know the truth, as long as I keep pushing this poison, I can't be a good person."

"Have you ever been driving to an appointment to a new doctor's office and taken a wrong turn?"

"Sure, many times."

"Did you know right away you had taken a wrong turn?"

"Sometimes I'd know it right away and would have to turn around."

"What about the times you didn't see your mistake right away? What happened then?"

"Well, I'd get lost and have to backtrack to find another way around."

"But you'd never just park your car where you got lost; turn off the ignition and just give up? That's where you are right now. You found out you've been driving down the wrong road and maybe it's a dead end even. You're scared because you don't know any other roads to take and they all look bumpy and treacherous compared to the road you've been on. And up until this point, you really enjoyed the ride!"

Joy and Dr. Davis each separately marveled at how this seemingly complex issue could be distilled down into such a simple notion. She had taken a wrong turn down a dead end street. Dr. Davis suspected that maybe it was too simplistic. But it seemed to refocus Joy's perspective, and anyway, it was getting close to the end of the hour.

"Joy, it feels like we made progress today. I do have some homework for you if you'd like to come back for another session." He never assumed they would just keep coming back. "I want you to write down all the different roles you play in life. List a few things you have to do for each role, and how you feel about them. OK? Then write down how you think your husband and kids see you in each of these roles. Will you do that for next time?"

When Joy was gone, Dr. Davis reflected on the session. He

congratulated himself for not letting his value judgements contaminate his sterile therapeutic theater. He consciously held back from expressing his disgust at Joy's husband's tacit complicity in all this (he had been so close to quoting Scripture: 'for the love of money is the root of all evil'). This ironically named woman just spent fifty minutes talking about herself and her family relationships and not once uttered the word 'love.' He felt this did not portend well for her. Dr. Davis wondered if her homework assignment would yield any helpful fruit.

It was a lovely May afternoon so Dr. Davis decided to go for a run to clear his mind. He thought about Joy and the lack of real joy in his own life. Springtime in New England, with all its natural green, rejuvenating beauty, should lift the spirits of almost anyone. But Joe always felt gloomy this time of year. Something in the spring air annually triggered his malaise and reminded him that most of the bad and unresolved shit that happened to him in his life occurred in springtime. He had witnessed the death of Kim-Ly during the fall of Saigon in a long-ago April. He lost Georgie in May. And the end of each academic year as a student brought the return of his depression when he had to go back to socially barren Valley Park, Connecticut for the summer. He even felt the loss every spring as a college chaplain when his "flock" disappeared at the end of the semester.

Failing to flush out his head during his run, Joe committed to taking a vacation just as soon as he could arrange it.

55

Vacations had to be approved by the bishop. More accurately, the "bishop's administrative liaison." Father Bevilacqua, the "BAL," had his favorites out there in the parishes, and Father Martin was decidedly not one of them. It didn't help that Father Martin referred to Father Bevilacqua as "the bishop's secretary." And that was to his face! Out of earshot he referred to Father Bevilacqua as "Father Water Boy," a loose mistranslation of his Italian surname. It was damned near impossible to get a vacation approved, at least when you wanted it, unless you were one of Father Water Boy's favorites.

Father Martin needed a vacation but settled for a few days respite with only the pastor's approval. He knew he would soon be getting "away" permanently. He just needed a few days to get his head together to plan out how and when he would resign his post; what to say, how to say it. Then, how to transition to civilian life. It was a lot to work through in just a few days.

He would take Amtrak to visit his seminary friend, Pete Quinn, now Father Thomas Aquinas Quinn. Joe had always chided Pete for going overboard with his pick of a religious name. "Thomas Aquinas? Really? Why not just pick Father Jesus?"

At first Pete felt ridiculous having picked such a lofty name. *Why not just keep Peter? He is the father of the Catholic church after all,* he thought. Too late. Even worse than being pretentious was being indecisive. That last year in seminary, Brother Martin took to calling Pete "Brother T.A." which everyone else thought was short for Thomas Aquinas. Martin and Pete knew that T.A. was for Tits and Ass, a fitting nickname for a guy who shared Brother Martin's interest in the opposite sex.

Father T.A. Quinn had been at St. Albert's parish in New Rochelle, New York for six years, an eternity for a priest who had begun to feel, like Father Martin, that ascendency to pastor was not in God's plan. "Who'd you piss off to get sent here?" Father Martin kidded. "Even the child molesters get to stay in their own diocese."

"They needed someone who speaks Spanish," Father Quinn answered glumly. "Who knew minoring in Spanish would come back to bite me in the cajones!"

As he waited in Boston's South Station terminal, Father Martin looked up at the board as the litany was announced. "Now approaching on track 6, Amtrak's Northeast Metroliner service to New York Penn Station with stops in Westwood,

Providence, South Kingstown, Westerly, New London, New Haven, Stamford, New Rochelle, and New York City."

"Someday, if Pete's still down there, I should just take the express to New York and have him meet me there instead of killing half a day on this local train!"

The biggest decision this morning had been about which persona he would abide while traveling. It was a crapshoot really, depending on whom fate chose to seat next to him on the train. If he wore his non-clerical attire, some chatty Cathy would pester him. "What do you do? Where are you from, where are you going, why are you going there, why are you traveling alone, etc." The few black friends Father Martin had all wore their best suits while traveling. This, they believed, cut down on the condescending looks all black men receive when they are out and about. Father Martin didn't own a conventional business suit. He didn't know if his usual black turtleneck and black (priest) blazer made him look like a jazz man, as he had once been told, or if it made him look intimidating, as he had sensed by the averted glances and evasive maneuvers of strangers in his path.

Dressed as a priest, he might be accosted by some self-righteous, or genuinely righteous Catholic seeking special prayers or remembrances for themselves or someone in their family. On one trip he even had a poor fellow ask him to hear his confession, right there on the train!

Worse were people of any faith who thought it was OK, ever since the emergence of the burgeoning clergy sex abuse scandal, to openly condemn all priests, painting them with the wide brush of scorn for the horrific sins of the few. Joe hoped it was "the few" anyway.

There was a time when he was the one initiating conversations with fellow train travelers. Pre-Sheila Joe, dressed as a civilian, had found himself sitting next to a lovely young woman on a southbound Metroliner.

"That's a pretty big rock," Joe had said, pointing to her diamond ring.

"I guess it is," came the cold response.

"So, you're in a relationship then?"

"Well, I'm either engaged, or I'm wearing a diamond ring on my ring finger to make people think I'm engaged. Either way, it should be a signal to guys like you that I'm not interested."

"Or, you could be wearing it to attract guys who are not interested in a long-term relationship, knowing that you're already engaged. Maybe you're just looking for a fling?"

"Maybe you should just mind your own fucking business," was her final salvo as she collected her bags and moved to an open seat at the other end of the coach.

Today he decided to try his luck with the roman collar. He just didn't have the energy for a four hour trip and coming up with a new back story of who he was and what he was doing there. He also didn't want to have any of Father Quinn's parishioners questioning his sexual orientation. Two priests hanging out together didn't raise any eyebrows. A priest and a single male friend together in public usually elicited a few chuckles and got the church ladies talking.

He made his way to the platform on track 6. He instinctively stood a few yards back from the yellow strip with the raised rubber knobs and took up a defensive posture. From his vantage point against the stanchion, Father Martin could see all the other passengers lining up for the approaching train. His Marine Corps mantra echoed in his brain: "Never allow anyone to get in your *six* except a brother marine." He wasn't preparing for any specific threat. Nothing came to mind. But that wasn't the point. It was being unprepared for the unexpected threat that would get you killed.

By the time he realized his hyper-vigilance might cost him his choice of seat, it nearly had. There was still one set of seats on the left side at the end of the car near the toilet. Taking the window seat and plopping his overnight bag down on the aisle seat, he fished out his ticket to New Rochelle. Father Martin liked the left window seat when heading south toward New York. He looked forward to the coastal vistas from New London to Stamford in his native Connecticut.

On family trips to Rocky Neck State Park as budding juvenile delinquents, he and his brother would perch themselves on the stone foot bridge above the tracks and drop (or throw) little rocks onto the passing Amtrak trains below. Now, on train trips Father Martin always listened for the sounds of rocks, thrown by a new generation of vandals, hitting the metal roof as his train passed under pedestrian bridges.

The train pulled out of South Station and Father Martin pulled out a legal pad and pen and decided to write his homily for his nephew's wedding. *At the very least I'll look busy and no one will bother me.* After several minutes staring at the blank yellow paper, he glanced out the window. The train was picking up speed as it left Boston city limits. Father Martin watched the back yards of homes, warehouses, and vacant lots whiz by. He couldn't help thinking with curiosity and disgust, that rail travel is the ugliest form of transportation. *How is it that people just throw all kinds of shit out by the tracks? For $53 I get a window seat in a moving tour of New England's finest trash heaps. For a few more bucks I could have been on the express train and we'd be going so fast this crap would be just a blur.*

Father Martin fondly recalled his train rides through the German countryside after his Saigon evacuation. His future was wide open then; uncharted and unknown. Sometimes the unknown at nineteen is better than the known as a grown man. At least better than Father Martin's known. The unknown didn't have any memories of Georgie, any suicide attempt, and the nightmares and ghostly visitations hadn't started yet. And there was no toggling back and forth between turtlenecks and roman collars. The unknown also had no Sheila, although Sheila is still largely unknown, even now.

I'll never get that homily written at this rate!

The train slowed as it approached the first stop. At the Westwood stop the doors opened. A few passengers got off. Many more got on. *Don't make eye contact. Don't make eye contact*, he repeated to himself as he stared down at his legal pad.

"This seat taken?"

"Uh….no."

The intruder gazed down at the bag on the seat but said nothing and held his ground. Father Martin grabbed the bag without looking up. The train lurched ahead as the doors closed with a hiss. The loud speaker crackled: "Next stop Providence, Rhode Island in twenty-five minutes."

After several minutes the seated newcomer broke the silence. Father Martin expected the first question to be, "You're a priest?" as if no one in Massachusetts could yet believe there are black priests. Or even a single black priest!

"So, how are you?"

Father Martin turned to look the inquiring interloper squarely in the face.

"Oh Jesus! It's you!"

"It's been a long time, Martin."

"Yeah, so long that I thought you were gone for good. What are you doing here?"

"What are *you* doing here? So, you're a priest today, or are you going to a costume party? Just last night you were having sex with Sheila one last time before heading off to a 'psychology conference.'" He repeated: "What are you doing here?"

"I'm done with you."

"I thought I was through with you too, but I'm beginning to think this may never be over. Last time I visited you, you were so sure which way you had to go. You had a plan. You were ready. You had a target in your sights but you couldn't pull the trigger. Some marine you are!"

"Providence, five minutes" the conductor announced on his way through the car, snatching up seat markers as he passed. "Make sure to collect all your belongings." Father Martin sat in silence and looked out the window. The train slowed, then stopped. More on and off.

Shaken by his encounter, and slowly realizing the deeper meaning of the question "Why are you here?" Father Martin sunk deeper into his seat and into himself, trying to will his inquisitor away.

"This seat taken?" a woman's voice asked. Startled, Father Martin turned to see that the aisle seat still had his bag on it.

"This seat taken?" she repeated.

"Uh, no. It's all yours." Father Martin offered.

How long have I been asleep? Was I even sleeping? Father Martin wondered. It had been a while since he had been "visited." He always hoped these were just sleeping dreams. He feared they were hallucinations.

"Oh! You're a priest!" she said.

"Oh for Chrissake" Father Martin said to himself. *"Here we go…."*

"I mean, I don't think I've ever seen a… a…." she stammered.

"A black priest?" Father Martin offered. He threw a lifeline to the young woman clad in the Boston Bruins jersey. "We're about as rare as a black hockey player."

The ice broken, she jumped right in: "Are you assigned to a parish? Which one? Where are you headed? Do you get to travel a lot? Have you met the pope? What do you think of the new cardinal?"

He did his best to answer all her probes; some responses factual, some fabricated. Father Martin cut her off before she could start the Level II questions (how do you feel about interfaith marriage, same-sex marriage, mercy killing, abortion, divorce?) While he had ready answers to all these questions, he didn't care to engage with this stranger on a train. He also didn't want to encourage her for fear she would ask the Level III question: "So, why'd you become a priest?" This is a question he had internally grappled with for as long as he was a priest. Other than Eric Sklar and Father T.A. Quinn, few people in his life had ever asked him that question. Most probably believed he had had a conversion following his "miraculous" recovery from the hanging. Others assumed his vows were inspired by the wonderful example of the priests at St. Domenic's. Father Martin knew the answer was not so simple, and he sensed neither of these explanations played a significant or pivotal role in his "vocation" to the priesthood.

As "hockey mom" droned on, Father Martin was transported back to that Saturday in 1979.

"Maybe I should just become a priest…" Joe blurted out desperately during the breakup.

"You'd be a great priest!" Georgie offered supportively, hopefully.

"Don't say that!" Joe had only said it as a cheap, hollow threat. A half-baked idea that maybe by saying something so outrageously desperate that Georgie would magically see that the only way Joe could ever be happy was for her to change her mind and save him from his threatened life of celibacy.

At the time he said it, the idea of becoming a priest was foreign to him. He once complimented a college priest on his homily, inadvertently inducing the priest to ask Joe if he felt a "calling."

Joe was horrified and physically recoiled at this question, then immediately felt ashamed for humiliating Father Foley who himself must have heard the calling as a young college student.

When a young man is fully consumed in, and consumed by a love affair with a young woman, he would never, ever seriously consider becoming a priest. Joe's decision to take the holy vows involved several constructs. Each piece was complicated and some pieces were mutually contradictory. After many years of occasional, and often opaque, introspection, Father Martin settled on a theory: after his nearly fatal broken heart (compliments of Georgie), he would never again put himself in that position; so empty, so vulnerable, alone, and hopeless. He would shield himself, hidden amongst the other "religious," so many of whom were also surely hiding from the perils of intimacy-gone-south. He was reminded of St. Paul's words: *Better to have loved and lost than to have never loved. What bullshit! St. Paul had never been in love with a woman.*

Father Martin extended his hand. "By the way, I'm Father Jackson."

He tried to use the most "black" sounding name he could think of. "If you're ever in Holbrook make sure you stop by St. Mary's to say hello."

He picked a town in the diocese he had never heard anyone say they were from, and he wasn't even sure there was a Catholic church there, never mind a "St. Mary's." "I hate to be rude but I've got to get my homily written for a funeral mass I am celebrating tomorrow." Father Martin was always uncomfortable with the idea of "celebrating" a funeral mass. Usually, funeral goers were not in a celebratory mood. But he wasn't really going to a funeral. Someday the truth would set him free. Just not today.

Tiffany, who had not officially introduced herself and remained nameless to "Father Jackson," apologized for being so "nosey" and a "pest." Had Father Martin bothered to find out her name he certainly would have thought "Tiffany" an oddly girlish name for a woman wearing a hockey jersey.

56

It was a little strange to be sitting in the rear of the church while another priest said mass. Father T.A. gave Father Martin the option that morning to concelebrate mass but seeing as it was all in Spanish, Father Martin passed. It had been too many years since he learned rudimentary Spanish in high school. Celebrating mass in Spanish would have required a lot more proficiency than conversing with migrant workers on the tobacco farms around Valley Park, Connecticut. Father Martin could have just stayed in bed or gone for a run, but he was curious for a perspective he hadn't had in decades; that of a congregant. *Will Sheila and I attend mass together after I leave the priesthood?*

He took this trip to New Rochelle seeking validation. Reassurance that being a priest sucks. That most priests, like him, had joined for the wrong reasons. That chastity and celibacy were not realistic in today's Church and society. That it was OK to walk away, and that there was no shame associated with quitting, especially if it was because of falling in love. *Am I falling in love?*

I can serve God in other ways, he told himself unconvincingly. *Who am I kidding? I've never served God. God may have been served, but only as an accidental by-product of some action I took for some other motive.*

Father T.A. was also seeking validation in the visit. Martin Davis' life was a cautionary tale for the few who knew him well. Behind the façade, he was a failed priest. Yes, even a failed man. He led a dual life, but neither half could stand alone as a whole person. He made promises with no intention of fulfilling them. They were the promises to keep in touch made by children on the last day of summer camp. He had been through life's agitator and spin cycles a few times, but never came out clean. As much as he wished his friend well, Father Martin couldn't help trying to bring T.A. down so they could be on the same level, just like they used to be.

After mass, they walked over to a café on the corner of Depot and Commercial Streets where they knew they would eat for free. There was no sign saying "priests and cops eat for free" but it was understood.

"Do you ever think about that girl you were seeing when we were in seminary?" Father Martin tried picking a scab that had long since healed over, leaving nary a scar.

"You mean Sharon?" Father T.A. offered, knowing Father Martin didn't mean good girl Sharon.

"No, not Sharon. Why would you be thinking about her? Guys don't remember girls like her. I mean, that other girl. You know…the one with all the daylight down there?"

"You know, Martin, they don't call it 'daylight' anymore. It's called thigh gap. Her name was Kitty and no, I don't ever

337

think of her anymore. Haven't in years."

"Ever wonder what she looks like now? She's pushing 50. I'll bet the 'gap' has filled in."

"Why have you been thinking about my old girlfriends?"

"I've been thinking about a lot of things lately," Martin confessed. "Remember how we used to rate girls in one of three categories? Girls you want to date, girls you want to marry, and girls you should stay the hell away from?"

T.A. laughed, "Yeah, you were always going after the ones I said we should stay the hell away from!"

"That's just because I knew I was going to be a priest and would never have to marry them. Still, I've been thinking about that girl Angela. Remember her? She was a good kid. I guess she was in the category of girls you want to marry. I never really gave her a chance. She adored me and she knew I was 'in school' but didn't know it was the seminary. She might have made a good wife. Who knows? She hardly let me touch her so I broke it off with her. I mean, I was going to be a priest; I couldn't really be getting into a relationship, could I?"

"Did you ever think you should've broken it off with the seminary instead?"

"I think about that all the time," Martin admitted quietly. He thought at the time he entered the seminary he was being courageous. He was ready to make a lifelong commitment and needed to take a leap of faith to get there. He wondered now if joining religious life was courageous or cowardly; a way to avoid the real challenges of adult relationships. For the last twenty-five years he struggled internally to figure out if attempting suicide was a courageous or cowardly act. Was the fact that it was only 'attempted suicide' really a failure? Did he intend to fail? Did Joe have to overcome physical obstacles to try to kill himself? Or was the greater battle one of overcoming psychological obstacles? Did the fact that he never again attempted suicide mean he could never again muster the requisite courage? Or just the opposite…. had he never again been that cowardly? Even his curious actions with Georgie, when the relationship was unraveling, still made him wonder if he had been courageous or a coward. Was he just a coward to stay with her during the period when she was "just not sure anymore?" Maybe the courageous thing would have been to just walk away. Obvious things are not obvious to those in love.

Over the last five years, Father Quinn had gradually, but tenaciously, put in the hard personal work of reforming his life, ultimately recommitting himself to his life as a priest. He had never formally renewed his vows. To do so would be to publicly acknowledge the life he had been living, and he figured it wouldn't do anyone any good to expose his transgressions to the flock. Catholics' faith is fragile and they have certain ideals for clergy they need to believe in. Having put in the hard transformative work, and knowing Father Martin had not, it was validating for Father T.A. to see his old friend's life as the mess it was. (Even reformed priests can still harbor terribly uncharitable and un-Christian thoughts to prove their own righteousness.)

Father Martin attributed Father T.A.'s transformation to "growing old, growing up, and giving up." But he was jealous that his friend's life seemed settled, and indeed happy. His sarcastic parting words to his old friend were: "Just when you think your cup runneth over is when you spill the mingled water and blood."

I'm getting older too. Maybe I should grow up and give up. Give up the collar, that is. He had already come to this decision. Several times. There really wasn't any back-and-forth. It was all forth. This is what he needed to do and he knew it (he would never be free from young Joe Davis' visits until he did.) He had promised himself to come clean after his nephew's wedding. But when after? A month? A year? When?

Pete asked Martin, "Have you ever atoned for the things you did when you were a young priest?"

"You mean the hugging incidents during the counseling sessions?" Martin still had a hard time calling sexual assault by its name when he had been the perpetrator. "I've moved on and am trying to be a better person now. I might not be a better priest, but I'm trying to be a better person......when I can."

Father Martin had no sense as a young man that the things he did at the time, that he knew, or suspected were wrong, would cause him such lingering shame and regret so many years later.

Pete let it drop. He didn't care if his lack of rebuttal was taken as tacit approval of Martin's qualified answer; he was just satisfied with himself that he had planted the seed of atonement.

The Eagles song "What Do I Do With My Heart" came through the diner's speakers. It brought Joe back to 1979 even though the song wasn't released until a few years later. *Wow, that's fucked up! Time to leave.*

Alone at last, seated this time on the right side of the third car on the northbound Amtrak Metroliner, Joe had time to think. Sometimes when he allowed himself to go there, he imagined what his life would now be like if his suicide attempt had been successful. Beyond the obvious, that once you kill yourself, there is no life, at least not in this world, thinking about it filled Joe with both regret and peace.

Joe Davis believed in Heaven. The afterlife. But the afterlife existence he now imagined was momentary and fleeting. In his last few moments of consciousness hanging there by the lawnmower cord back in 1979, as life was leaving his body, time became compressed. Joe observed at the time, with a detachment that seemed unnatural, that years passed in seconds without feeling rushed. He had never before, or since, achieved such mental clarity. He assumed, looking back, that this momentary mental sharpness must be what prompts many suicide attempters to abruptly change course and fight back against their own mortal attempts. For those who felt regret or remorse in that instant of clarity, they would throw open the car door to release the carbon monoxide into the garage while fresh air flowed in to the rescue. Or they might jump out of the warm bathtub, and with blood spurting from their wrists, they would run, slipping on the floor with wet feet, to the kitchen, pick up the receiver and dial the operator, screaming for an ambulance. Or drag themselves from their bed, jam their fingers down their throats, vomiting any undigested pills into the wastebasket on top of the used tissues, wet from final crying episodes, hoping it wasn't too late, that the pills hadn't yet taken effect. Choosing hanging, Joe hadn't left himself any options, even if he had had a change of heart during his moment of clarity, which he didn't.

When he emerged from the coma, no one was as surprised as Joe that he had survived. And he was alone in his disappointment. But he always remembered and cherished those few transient seconds of complete sobriety when the answers to life's questions seemed knowable. Joe longed for that feeling of knowledge but realized it would only come again at the moment of death. Joe Davis had never regretted his suicide attempt. Had it been successful it would have spared him from many years of intrusive thoughts, nights filled with nocturnal terrors, and visitations from his former self. It had been a sincere, not half-hearted attempt and reflected who he was at that very moment in his life. Although unable to live in the present, nothing could stop him from dying in the present.

What a relief it would be not to be a priest, not to live a dual life, not to have Vietnam flashbacks, not to have to earn a living on his own, never again to have intrusive thoughts of Georgie. Freedom from all those troubles would come with a price: his life. But then he could, he hoped, ascend to the afterlife. It was comforting and tempting to imagine cleaning his life of all this baggage, to immediately achieve that clear, transcendent truth through one final, mortal act. *It's ironic,* he thought, *how little thinking or planning I did before actually trying to kill myself, and now I'm spending all this mental energy on something I would never try again.*

So much of the relief he yearned for, he knew, could eventually be achieved in this life, but only after going through hell on earth. The major stressors in his life that were within his control (being a priest while being in a relationship) could be eliminated. He wondered if his recent increase in stress from everything coming to a head was causing the resurgence of late of the intrusive Georgie memories and Vietnam nightmares, the "visitations," and the occasional lisp. He needed to come clean. He needed to do it soon.

At the bottom of the yellow legal pad that contained what he knew would be his final sermon, he wrote: *I promise myself I will resign my position as associate pastor this Sunday, June 21, and fax a letter to the bishop that afternoon leaving religious life. I will tell Sheila everything at dinner Sunday night. —Joseph Martin Davis*

On the train that Friday afternoon, Father Martin read through the rail-inspired homily one more time and made a few edits. It wasn't his best work, but it was general enough that he could use it both for his nephew's wedding and for his farewell mass the following day. And if a last minute funeral comes up, he could make it fit that "celebration" too.

"My brothers and sisters in Christ, from the moment we are born we are at the point of no return. We each were sprung from the womb never to return. We learn to crawl, to walk, to ride a bike…all in the forward direction. We live our lives and envision our progress, making strides ahead of us. We are on rails, going forward. Sometimes we look back to see how far we've come to motivate ourselves to continue on. We look back but we can't go back. We are each riding in our own personal train car, heading to the ultimate destination. In times of turmoil we sometimes try to go back. Try to fix things. Try to right a wrong. We want a "do-over." But we can't really go back to the way things were. If we were to go back, the way things *were* will have changed and it is only the way things *are* at the present time. Every experience and emotion that you've had since you left the-way-things-were, have altered the reality, so without a time machine, things the way they were can never really be the same again.

"When Jesus visited the apostles following His resurrection, His friends wanted Him to be as He once had been, in human form. But He was changed; transfigured really. There is no going back. No turning the train around.

"When you are born, you are on a track connected to other train cars: your mom, dad, siblings, grandparents, other family members. Over time, more train cars will hook up to yours, and some will drop off at various stops along your journey. Some cars will travel with yours for the whole trip. Others will take sidetracks that will intersect yours from time to time. No one knows the length of their track. Only God knows. There's an old Hebrew saying: "People plan; God laughs."

"There is no real way to stop your train car before you reach your ultimate destination. You may try to speed it up or slow it down, but it never stops completely until you reach your final destination. You may get sidetracked too, maybe just for a little while until you get back "on track." Maybe what you thought was a sidetrack will become your new main line.

"As you travel on your way you will pass some beautiful scenery, as well as see the back lots and trash heaps of life. You will pass stops along the way where you could switch tracks, and you wrestle with yourself afterwards for not having changed, or for having taken some new route that no longer seems like the right way to go. You can't actually be on two tracks at the same time any more than you can go forward and backwards at the same time. But often we spend part of our lives physically on one track, but with our minds, our hopes, our desires, on another track, riding along, not actually being anywhere.

"We waste the journey fixated on where we think we're headed, not appreciating where we are right now. Sometimes we travel so fast everything we see outside the window is just a blur. The beauty is still there. We just can't focus on it. Sometimes we are asleep, or drunk, or stoned, or angry, or distracted, or so preoccupied that we miss the scenery altogether.

"We might find that we are chugging along with other train cars that are holding us back or pulling us off in the wrong direction, trying to derail us. It may take years to realize this is happening. Some are cars we invited to tag along so we could give them a boost. We thought it would be just for a while but now they won't do anything to help propel the rest of the train along. Sometimes we are tired and we are the car that needs to tag along for a while. Have you ever ridden along with another car and later realized the train was headed in a direction you knew was wrong?

"The only real beauty and satisfaction in life comes from the other train cars you travel with along your journey. We are tempted to look for shiny, new, sleek train cars, but then find it makes us feel all the more dull and broken down next to them. Do we feel better when we find other cars that are functional, but might be dented, scratched, or a little rusty? You know these cars have had a rough ride, yet they keep rolling along, sometimes with just a little loving push from us.

"Do we know where we are going? We hope so. Do we know

how to get there? The answers are in our prayers. We don't know who will get there with us. We don't know when we'll get there, so we need to have our eyes open and be ready when it's our stop. But the most important questions on this journey of life are:

Are we awake and aware of where we are right now?

And, **Why are we here**?

Let us Pray."

That night, after his nephew's rehearsal and dinner, alone (at last) in his room at the rectory, Father Martin laid out his clothes for the morning wedding. In a couple days he would be shedding the roman collar for good. *Now that Sheila has seen me without my shirt, maybe it is time to ditch the turtlenecks too. No, baby steps*, he thought. He undressed and took a shower in the adjoining bathroom. He let the steamy water wash away his weariness. He emerged refreshed, and quickly realized he was no longer alone. The visitor sat on the end of Father Martin's bed, not saying a word.

Father Martin was long past the point when such an intrusion would shock him, but it was still unsettling to be confronted, yet again, by this unexpected and unwelcome guest.

"You should just leave. You have no power over me anymore."

"Do you believe in God?"

"I don't believe in you."

"Do you believe in God?"

"I don't know," Joe responded honestly.

"You either do or you don't."

"I don't know if it's that simple. But if you want a yes or no, then I don't."

"I don't believe you."

"Fine, go fuck yourself then."

"You should believe in God, and you should believe in me. I am God and I am you. You tried killing us back in '79, and you might have succeeded, except for me. I saved us….really I saved you. I was never in danger of dying. I'm God. I am in everyone. I thought you would have figured this out by now without my telling you. I couldn't wait forever for you to recognize me. I'm immortal, but your time on this earth is limited. I cut you a break when you were twenty-one because you were just a foolish, love-struck kid. The next time you do something stupid I won't bail you out."

"You're a hallucination. If someone heard me talking to you they'd think I'm crazy."

"Maybe you are crazy."

"I'm in a good place now so why don't you just disappear and I'll see you at the pearly gates," Joe said sarcastically, not quite convinced his visitor was not really God.

"You think you can just make a clear break from all this? No consequences? No atonement? Everyone is just going to forgive you and move on even if you never fully come clean? Either your fantasy life is way out of whack or you really are crazy!"

Joe walked past his apparition as if it wasn't even there. He headed to the bathroom where he found a little yellow pill, and cupping his hands under the faucet, gulped down the only thing he had found that could make his visitor recede from his waking consciousness. He glanced in the mirror, over his shoulder: no one there. He glanced in the mirror into his own eyes: no one there.

Joe eased into bed. He drifted off to sleep more determined than ever to leave the priesthood, set things right with Sheila, and to stop believing in God just as soon as he could.

57

The guests were starting to arrive at St. Paul's Catholic Church for the wedding of Jason and Kaley. Father Martin was in the vestibule, but not yet wearing his celebrant vestments. He liked to greet early arriving wedding guests while still in his black priest garb as he thought it put people more at ease. He liked to be seen as just another member of the flock, albeit the only one wearing a roman collar. Today was a special day since Jason, the groom, was his nephew. Father Martin would know most of the guests, at least the ones seated on the groom's side of the aisle. Standing out here would give him a chance to meet some of Kaley's family.

"Good morning. Welcome to St. Paul's." Father Martin only felt mildly out of place as a visiting priest at St. Paul's. As a priest he knew he would be universally accepted at any Catholic church. Some neighborhoods might be less welcoming than others, but never had anyone dared comment on his relative uniqueness. The black uniform mostly overrode his black skin. The guests on Kaley's side would have long been over their shock of seeing a black priest since they had gotten to know Jason. Jason, like Father Martin and the rest of his family, did not seem like "typical" black people. They had grown up, almost exclusively, around white people and had "assimilated nicely." Father Martin, by this point in his development, felt he could read the thoughts of new acquaintances just from their facial expressions. He was usually correct.

"Good morning Father. Shame about the rain."

"Yes, it's too bad. But maybe if we all pray really hard, it will dry up before picture time," he joked.

He greeted several more guests headed for both sides of the church. Now the groom's side of the family arrived, including some of the more senior members. Father Martin greeted his nephews, the groom and best man, and directed them to the front of the church where they must camp out until the start of the ceremony.

As the crowd of family members thinned a bit, Father Martin spotted the small frame of his elderly father. He greeted the tired old man warmly. While a seminarian, Brother Martin had realized that he and his father didn't have what could be called an adult-to-adult relationship. He had pledged to make it a priority. Now, more than twenty years later, they were still in the same spot. Although he lived only a few towns away, they didn't see each other much these days. Father Martin cited his busy schedule as the main reason, but if he were honest with himself, he would have known it had more to do with not being able to look such a good Catholic in the eye, when he himself was such a lousy priest.

His father, as proud family patriarch, insisted on a prominent role in the procession of his grandson's wedding. He would lead the procession, followed by the groom's parents, then by the bride's mother, and finally the flower girl. Bringing up the rear, as it were, would be the bride and her dad. Father Martin wistfully remembered when the whole "procession" consisted of a bride and her father, with maybe a flower girl and a ring bearer. He felt the rest of the entourage should be seated in advance and stand on signal like everyone else.

Father Martin knew that this was the last wedding he would ever officiate as he longed to leave the priesthood and begin his new life, maybe even with Sheila. He decided to keep his feelings about a simpler wedding procession to himself as he needed to get through this ceremony without pissing off his sister, the groom's mother, so she would keep his secret about his impending departure from clerical life.

He daydreamed what his own wedding would be like if he ever got married. *Probably not a Church wedding! Maybe my family would be too scandalized to show up?*

A crack of thunder outside brought him back to reality. He spoke to his father. "Well Dad, it's getting to be about that time. I need to go get my robes on. I'll be back in a few minutes to get this show on the road."

A few last minute stragglers were ascending the church steps as Father Martin turned to go. As they stepped toward each other for a quick greeting, they instantly recognized each other.

"Oh my God, Joe!"

"Sheila? Oh no! What are you doing here?"

"You're a priest? Oh my God! Oh Jesus!"

She ran down the slippery steps, losing a heel as she crossed the sidewalk. She ran across the road. To where? Anywhere.

Away from this unbelievable nightmare.

Father Martin followed after her calling out, "Sheila, wait! Come back Sheila!" He ran down the steps and across the sidewalk, gaining on her.

The driver never saw Joe, dressed as he was all in black, on this dreary, rainy day. Joe was lifted up a few feet and landed hard on the windshield before rolling off the side and hitting his head on the curb. The cranial thud and screech of tires and brakes caught the attention of the vestibule gathering and they watched in disbelief the tragic scene unfolding in slow motion before them.

By the time the family members reached him, Sheila was kneeling by his side, watching his blood mingle with the rainwater as it coursed its way to the sewer grate. Slowly, with trepidation, Joe's father approached his, once again, lifeless son. Then he sat some feet away on the wet curb, the bitter rain falling freely on his bald head, and he wept.

THE END

ACKNOWLEDGMENTS

This book is a work of fiction. References to real people, events, or locales are used fictitiously. All incidents and dialogue are the product of the author's imagination and should not be considered real.

To my wife, Cecily Hassett-Salley:
Thank you for providing patient, constructive criticism, and nearly forty years of encouragement.

I would like to acknowledge Bob Drury and Tom Clavin for their descriptions of Marine Security Guard life in their excellent book, <u>Last Men Out, The True Story of America's Heroic Final Hours in Vietnam,</u> (Free Press, a division of Simon & Schuster, 2011).

Warm Ways Words and Music by Christine McVie, Copyright © 1975 by Universal Music - Careers Copyright Renewed, International Copyright Secured. All Rights Reserved. Reprinted by Permission of Hal Leonard LLC.

Two Love Birds Words and Music by Tim Hassett-Salley, All Rights Reserved.

Cover illustration and design by Brigid Griffin.

THS 5/13/2019

ABOUT THE AUTHOR

Tim Hassett-Salley was born in 1960 in rural northeastern Connecticut. He received his B.A. in Psychology and Music from Providence College and earned his graduate degrees in Counseling from Bridgewater State University. For many years, he maintained a private psychotherapy practice counseling violent and abusive men.

He is married and has three adult children. He resides in Massachusetts and plays the drums in his spare time.

Made in the USA
Middletown, DE
29 January 2021